PURSUING A DUKE

Widows of Mayfair, Book 2

Christine Donovan

ARE YOU SIGNED UP FOR DRAGONBLADE'S BLOG?

You'll get the latest news and information on exclusive giveaways, exclusive excerpts, coming releases, sales, free books, cover reveals and more.

Check out our complete list of authors, too!

No spam, no junk. That's a promise!

Sign Up Here

www.dragonbladepublishing.com

Dearest Reader;

Thank you for your support of a small press. At Dragonblade Publishing, we strive to bring you the highest quality Historical Romance from some of the best authors in the business. Without your support, there is no 'us', so we sincerely hope you adore these stories and find some new favorite authors along the way.

Happy Reading!

CEO, Dragonblade Publishing

**Additional Dragonblade books by
Author Christine Donovan**

Widows of Mayfair Series
Loving an Earl (Book 1)
Pursuing a Duke (Book 2)

Dedication

This book is dedicated to my mother, Alberta May Murray. Thank you for your unwavering love, support, and encouragement. Because of you, I have become a strong, independent, and creative woman. I love you with all my heart!

CHAPTER ONE

London, 1805

"PLEASE, MAMA, MAY I wear the ice-blue evening gown trimmed with lace and seed pearls and the matching pelisse? It will bring out the color of my eyes. It's so close to white that no one will notice the difference." Miss Emmeline Connolly, the only child of Baron and Baroness Connolly, was making her come out at the Duke and Duchess of Westport's ball—the first event of the Season.

Baroness Vivian Connolly was foraging through the wardrobe, discarding one gown after another. "I cannot find the white gown with the gold trim. Emmeline, did not Madam Serena deliver it yesterday with the rest of your wardrobe?"

Emmeline and her maid, Clark, whom she preferred to call Amanda, locked eyes in the mirror over the dressing table with secretive smiles. "I don't recall seeing it." It was a lie. She hated that gown and knew it would be her mother's choice for her first ball. All her other gowns were perfect except for the snow-white one with its high neckline and long sleeves. It was so far out of fashion that she would be gossiped about and find herself a wallflower. Once a wallflower, always a wallflower. And she refused to become one—she had dreamed about her first Season for years.

To be honest, at times they were less dreams and more nightmares.

The thought of attending soirees, Almack's, and house parties excited and terrified her simultaneously. But she had not waited all these years to become an unfashionable debutante no young gentleman would want to court. So, with Amanda's help, they'd hidden the gown in the bottom of a trunk in the attic, where it would never be found. It could wither away and mold for all she cared.

"I will send a letter to Madam Serena demanding credit for a beautiful gown she never delivered." The baroness sighed and brought the ice-blue gown to Amanda. "I suppose this will have to do."

"It will be perfect," Emmeline said with a smile to her mother. The dress made her look mature and alluring for eighteen. She had heard from her close friend, Lady Catherine Featherstone's older sister, who had married a handsome and wealthy marquess after her first Season, that standing out during the first ball was essential. All the eligible bachelors looking for wives would discreetly inspect each debutante and come up with a mental list of ladies to pursue based on looks, dowries, family lineage, and how merging the two families would benefit them. Emmeline wanted to be on all the gentlemen's lists. Even the Debrett's guide listed her family as prominent. She could not allow her mother to spoil her chances of making a good marriage.

"I admit," Mother said, "you look lovely in this gown. The white one was matronly if I'm being honest. The paleness of this blue brings out the color of your eyes, and with your contrasting dark hair piled high on your head with white pearl pins, you are stunning, my dear."

"Thank you, Mama." Truthfully, Emmeline's insides trembled with nerves, but her mother's words helped her swallow her panic. She may appear put together on the outside, but inside, she was a quivering mess. Crowds and loud noises bothered her—not loud noises as in screams or gunshots, but it was deafening when hundreds of people gathered together in one place and talked amongst themselves. A vibration surrounded her, making it difficult to understand what anyone was saying, making her anxious and panicky, making her want to run away to the sanctity of a private, soothing place.

As a child, she had snuck into their ballroom and hid beneath a cloth-draped table during a ball her parents had hosted. Even at eight, she was angry that her parents had not let her attend. Sneaking peeks beneath the cloth and watching the beautiful ladies and handsome gentlemen dance and socialize in gorgeous clothing was exciting, but after a time, she had curled up and fallen asleep to the cadence of loud voices, orchestra music, and laughter. Until she woke up suddenly, her hands covering her ears, wishing the sounds would end. But there was no way she could leave her hiding spot without being seen. She was stuck until the wee hours of the morning with her hands over her ears and tears streaming down her face. The beautiful people of earlier turned into ugly monsters as the hour grew later and later. Because of her anxiousness and having drunk a full glass of milk at dinner, she had wet herself and had to stay sitting in it until the last of the horrible people had left her home.

The next day, she had wished she would never have to grow up or attend a ball. She confided in her governess what she had done, and the kind woman had kept her secret.

Fortunately for Emmeline, she'd recovered from the ordeal of that night—well, almost. She still hated crowds and noise and sometimes saw monsters when her eyes were tired. Tonight would be a test of her maturity. She had worked hard fighting down her demons and believed she was ready for the night ahead. She would use the breathing exercises her governess had taught her if an attack of nerves started to overtake her. And if that didn't work, she had a list of things to picture in her mind to distract her. Hopefully, all would go well, and she would have no phobias tonight.

THEIR CARRIAGE STOPPED in front of the Duke and Duchess of Westport's prominent London mansion. Lanterns illuminated the home, making it glow in the dark eerily. Wide-eyed, Emmeline stared out the coach window, her trembling, white-gloved hands gripping her reticule.

"Are you excited, my dear?" her papa asked in a deep, gravelly voice.

Papa was a true gentleman. He was older than her mother and tired easily these days as his health declined, which worried Emmeline. Losing her dear papa would crush her. She loved him with all her heart, as did her mother. No kinder, gentler, more patient man existed as far as she was concerned. As his health had waned this past month, she feared her parents were keeping secrets from her. On occasion, she witnessed her mother staring vacantly into the family drawing room with tears in her eyes. Hoping she was wrong about her papa's health, she would try to enjoy the ball and confront her parents on her fears soon.

"Yes, Papa," she replied. "I am excited but terrified I'll trip when introduced and land at the duke's feet."

His large, bony hand covered hers. "Nonsense. You have the grace of a butterfly." *Butterfly*. Her papa's nickname for her.

His words soothed her as her heartbeat slowed to almost normal. Once she entered the ballroom and found Catherine, all would be well. Her dance card would fill up, and she would fly across the floor with butterfly wings on. Every handsome young man would want to dance with her. She would become a diamond of the Season. Bouquets would arrive in the dozens tomorrow, and their drawing room would have standing room only with all the possible suitors vying for her attention.

Emmeline would reflect later that wishes and dreams were good to hope for, but reality was entirely different.

CHAPTER TWO

ONVERGING ON THE outskirts of the ballroom, Andrew Hampton, the Earl of Quincy and heir to a dukedom, along with his three friends, watched and discussed the debutantes as they were announced into the elaborate ballroom one after the other, along with their mothers or chaperones.

None of the gentlemen in question were looking for a wife. At nineteen years of age, they attended university. Standing with Andrew was Mr. Edmund Weston, heir to the Earl of Langford, Mr. James Caldwell, the second son of a baron, and Mr. Aiden Fitzpatrick, the son of a wealthy, prominent member of the *ton*. Their purpose in studying the debutantes and their mamas was to learn who to avoid at all costs.

Andrew, sipping a glass of champagne, studied the young ladies, most dressed in virginal white, forced smiles on their lips as they floated into the room, no doubt on legs wobbly from nerves. His twin older sisters had made their come out several years ago, and they had prattled on relentlessly to him about the goings-on at these events and how nervous they were at being introduced at their very first ball. He had thought they were exaggerating, but by the petrified looks on most of the debutantes' faces, he believed them now. Thank Christ, gentlemen were not subject to the same scrutiny.

"Are we expected to dance tonight . . . with . . . these debutantes?" Aiden Fitzpatrick asked, his body visibly shaking. "Because I, for one, don't want to find myself with a ball and chain at my age. I haven't had time to sow my oats or have a mistress."

"I'm with him," James Caldwell added. "My brother needs an heir, not me. I want to bed as many widows and actresses as I can before I have to marry."

"What about you, Weston?" Andrew asked. "You will need an heir someday. Are you ready to settle down?"

His friend took that exact moment to sip his champagne, which caused him to choke. Andrew smacked him on the back, hoping he wouldn't draw unwanted attention to the four of them. They needed to finish university and make their mark in the world before drawing the focus of young ladies with hearts in their eyes and marriage on their minds.

"Thanks for nearly killing me. The damn bubbles went up my nose." Weston cleared his throat. "When I finish university, I plan on starting an import and export business with Caldwell—and both of you if you are so inclined. We are already looking to buy a ship. So, no to marriage and an heir anytime soon. My uncle is in perfect health. When I inherit, I will consider it then."

"So, why are we here?" Andrew questioned as his eyes followed a beautiful debutante as she took a turn around the ballroom, her arm linked with a tall, willowy friend with auburn hair. His eyes were riveted on her unguarded, smiling face, with perfect features surrounded by glorious, dark-as-night, hair. Her figure was voluptuous and displayed nicely in her pale-blue gown. Before he realized it, his heart was pounding inside his chest, and he felt lightheaded. It was not a good start to the Season if he was already attracted to a young lady.

"What has piqued your interest? Or should I say *who*?" Fitzpatrick queried.

"What?" Andrew shook his head and turned his eyes away from the lady, who was almost upon them. "The young lady with dark hair coming this way with the tall redhead. I may have to beg an introduction. She intrigues me." He could not believe he had admitted that.

All three of his friends laughed.

His brows drew together. "What is so funny?"

Fitzpatrick's eyes followed the lady in question. "She *is* stunning, and her eyes light up her face. How do I get an introduction?"

"Wait." Andrew put his hand out in front of Fitzpatrick. "I saw her first. You can't think to usurp me by getting an introduction before me." Any young man would need a formal introduction before he could ask for a dance and sign her dance card. Lucky for him, the Master of Ceremonies, Lord Garvey, the Duke of Westport's brother, was nearby, and Andrew signaled to him.

As the two ladies approached, and before they strolled right by, Andrew, with his heart thumping wildly inside his chest, heard Lord Garvey say, "Ladies, I wish to present these fine young gentlemen to you. Lady Catherine Featherstone, Miss Emmeline Connolly, may I present Lord Quincy. Lord Quincy, Lady Catherine and Miss Connolly."

Andrew bowed over Lady Catherine's hand as she curtsied. He struggled to keep his attention on her and not Miss Connolly. He then turned and bowed to Miss Connolly, taking her hand in his hand as she curtsied.

"It is an honor to make your acquaintance, Lord Quincy."

"The pleasure is all mine, Miss Connolly." He would dream later of this moment when her light-blue eyes looked into his and her lips curved up into a smile, taking his breath away. The thought of letting her hand go bothered him, and he didn't look too deeply at why.

After Lord Garvey had completed all the introductions, Andrew asked, "Miss Connolly, may I request a dance?" He nodded to her dance card, which was tied to her wrist by a white ribbon.

She removed a pencil from her reticule, and Andrew scribbled his name on the first line.

Fitzpatrick moved beside him, actually nudging him out of the way. "May I request a dance as well, Miss Connolly?" Fitzpatrick smiled at her but smirked at Andrew, challenging him to intercede. Like bloody hell would he challenge him and cause a scene. Nor did he object to his friend's interest in the beautiful Miss Emmeline Connolly since Andrew wasn't looking for a wife. Only a young lady to dance with, exchange pleasantries, and perhaps steal a kiss or two.

As the first strings of a country reel played, Andrew offered his arm to Miss Connolly. "Shall we?"

She placed her hand on his forearm and replied shyly, "We shall." A becoming shade of pink stained her cheeks, and Andrew swallowed down the sudden desire humming throughout his body. If that little contact with Miss Connolly had his member stirring, it was time to visit a bordello.

By the time the dance ended and they were winded, Andrew knew he would never be the same, nor would his heart. Miss Connolly was the most stunning creature he'd ever seen, and he hated returning her to her friend. He was afraid some other, more worthy gentleman would steal her away from him. In a matter of half an hour, he'd become besotted. He was far too young for that to happen. And when he looked at Fitzpatrick, his eyes wide with jealousy, he knew it was not a good sign.

AFTER CRAWLING INTO bed and snuggling beneath her counterpane, Emmeline stared up at the ceiling, reliving the Westport ball and how she had never felt anxious from the sounds and crush of people.

When she arrived home, she'd soaked her feet in warm water and lavender oil because they were sore and blistered from dancing the entire night. After dancing with the Earl of Quincy and Mr. Fitzpatrick, her dance card filled up quickly, as had Lady

Catherine's. She danced with and was introduced to so many gentlemen, their faces and names blurred together except for Lord Quincy and Mr. Fitzpatrick. They were etched into her brain for all time.

Never had she had such a fun and amusing time with men before. Catherine had also enjoyed herself and attracted the attention of the Viscount Appleton. He was nearly thirty but very handsome and charming and seemed quite taken with Catherine and she with him. Perhaps she'd met her future husband on the first night of her first Season.

The Earl of Quincy and Mr. Fitzpatrick were only nineteen, and Emmeline's heart fell to her toes because she knew they were too young to be considering marriage. However, if single gentlemen attended a private ball, wasn't it presumed they were actively seeking a bride? Somehow, she didn't believe they were. Sighing deeply, she rolled onto her side, drew her knees up, and told herself not to fall for either of them. It would only cause her fragile heart to shatter.

Finally, her heart slowed, her breathing evened out, and she fell asleep, dreaming of two very handsome friends.

"Good morning, miss," Amanda said the next morning as she entered the room and pushed open the curtains, letting in the warm sunshine. "Wait until you see all the hothouse flowers delivered bright and early this morning."

Sitting up, Emmeline rubbed her eyes and squinted from the sunlight filtering inside the room. "Really?"

"Yes. Six if I counted right."

Climbing off the bed, Emmeline sat at her dressing table. "Let's hurry and do my hair and dress so I can see them." She clasped her hands together. "I'm so excited. My very first ball last night and my first flowers which did not come from Papa this morning." Her hands flew to her stomach, which hosted a family of butterflies. "Oh my, it probably means I'll have callers today." Her heart skipped. Would Lord Quincy and Mr. Fitzpatrick come to pay a morning call? Indeed, if one came, would the other? She was dizzy from the excitement of the possibility of seeing both of them. She said with a wistful sigh, "I'll wear the yellow muslin day dress this morning and change into the pretty blue one for my callers."

When she entered the large entry hall downstairs, her pulse jumped at seeing the bouquets in all different colors on the long hall table. She stopped at each bouquet, inhaled the aromas, admired the blossoms, and opened the card accompanying each. The Earl of Quincy had sent beautiful red roses, and Mr. Fitzpatrick had sent yellow ones. The other bouquets, beautiful roses intermingled with colorful wildflowers, had come from the Marquess of Littleton, Baron Fieldstone, Mr. Percy Thompson, and Mr. George Tyler. Emmeline had danced with each of them, but her excitement came from the roses' senders. She couldn't help if her heart yearned for Quincy and Mr. Fitzpatrick. But which one did she yearn for more? The Earl of Quincy had to be six feet tall, had light brown hair, deep green eyes, and a handsome face with chiseled features. Mr. Fitzpatrick, also tall but slightly shorter than Quincy, had chestnut brown hair and brown eyes with a hint of amber. He was the most handsome man she had ever seen. Both men were fit with broad shoulders and narrow waists. Though perhaps she was being silly, attracted so to the first two men she'd met and danced with.

The hours dragged on as Emmeline sat in the family drawing room with her mother embroidering a delicate lace handkerchief for her dear friend Catherine's birthday. The clock on the wall drew her eyes every few minutes, making the time go by at a snail's pace.

"Our drawing room will be full to bursting if all the gentlemen who sent flowers call on you today," Mother said as she worked on a needlepoint pillow cover.

"Will they all come?" Emmeline wasn't interested in all of them, only two. Would she truly have to entertain them all?

"I do hope so." Mother tied off her thread and snipped it with her small scissors. "Your father and I discussed the gentlemen who sent flowers, and we both agreed that the Marquess of Littleton is an excellent prospect. He is older than the others, nearly thirty, so he will be serious about taking a wife. He is rather handsome, wealthy, and comes from a well-respected family. The other potential suitors are younger; two are very young and merely filling their time, I believe. The Earl of Quincy will become a duke one day, but I can't believe he is serious about taking a wife now. Goodness, he is only a year older than you. And the same goes for Mr. Fitzpatrick. They both still attend university."

Sadness filled Emmeline's heart at hearing her mother's words—true words. Everything she said, Emmeline had thought herself. Perhaps friendship was all Lord Quincy and Mr. Fitzpatrick sought. Friendship, would that be so bad? It would be if she lost her heart to one of them.

As for the Marquess of Littleton, he was not exactly handsome but not all that unpleasant to look at if you ignored his close-set brown eyes, which made his nose appear more prominent. He was relatively short but still taller than her. He seemed affable enough and had good manners. He said all the proper things. He didn't leer at her with his eyes as their host did. The Duke of Westport had said shocking things to her, and she couldn't get away from him fast enough when the dance they shared ended. He'd said things she didn't understand, but she knew they were scandalous.

"Have you taken a liking to any of them?" Hearing her mother's voice pulled her from her musings.

"Honestly, I mostly enjoyed my time with the Earl of Quincy and Mr. Fitzpatrick. They are good friends, and when I wasn't on the dance floor, I spent time with them, Catherine, and their other two friends, Mr. James Caldwell and Mr. Edmund Weston—you remember, Cousin Henry's heir."

"I see."

"Do you?" Once she said the words, she wanted to take them back. They were admitting how interested in them she was.

"I understand you like the earl and Mr. Fitzpatrick, as they are closer to your age than the other gentlemen. But I truly believe you will have nothing more than a passing acquaintance with them. Neither is in a position to marry now. Entitled gentlemen like them leave university and spend several years making their mark on Society. They become rakehells, take mistresses, gamble, and fuel the gossip rags. They are most often either forced into marriage because of a scandal, or they take a wife around the age of thirty. Gentlemen do not have strict rules governing them as young ladies do."

"I know. How unfair."

"You must go prepare for your callers."

SITTING ON A deep burgundy settee with her mother awaiting callers, Emmeline's hands trembled, and her entire being vibrated from nerves, excitement, or a combination of both. Would the butler ever enter the room and introduce someone . . . anyone? The suspense was killing her.

When Ward finally appeared, he did so with six gentlemen in tow. She was so shocked that she truly missed him announcing their names, which was unfortunate. Last night had been such a whirlwind that she needed a refresher of which name went with which gentleman. Lord Quincy and Mr. Fitzpatrick managed to take the two chairs directly opposite the settee, leaving the other four gentlemen to sit farther away. All held their hats in their hands while the marquess, whom she did remember specifically from last night, also had a fashionable walking stick.

Mother offered tea and biscuits while Emmeline's eyes fluttered between her two closest visitors. According to her mother, she should give her attention to the marquess since he was actively seeking a bride, but her heart wouldn't let her.

"Did you enjoy your first ball last evening?" Mr. Fitzpatrick asked. Today, he was dressed in brown and tan riding clothes and brown boots, almost the same shade as his hair. His brown eyes were bright, and his smile caused her heart to flutter.

"I did. I was worried I would be affixed to the wall with all the wallflowers, but to my astonishment, I wasn't."

His brows drew together. "I cannot imagine that ever happening."

Her cheeks warmed. "You are too kind."

"That is our Fitzpatrick," Lord Quincy interjected. "Always being kind to the ladies."

The friends shared a look that rattled her teacup in her hand. She didn't know them well, but she recognized the signs of jealousy well enough to know they were each interested in her and warning the other to stay away. But she refused to come between the two friends. So, how did she prevent that from happening? She knew she couldn't choose which she liked better just yet; she was hardly acquainted with them. Perhaps she should look to the marquess after all, except that would be futile since he didn't appeal to her in the least.

After all the callers finally bid farewell, her mother turned to her, looking upset, and said, "I wish you had engaged the marquess in a deeper conversation. I fear he looked bored and disappointed you paid such little attention to him. I'm not worried about the other three who stood off to the side, but you knew how I felt about Littleton."

Her mother was right, of course. She had been rather rude to the marquess. If he called upon her again, she would be more attentive. "I'm sorry, Mama. Lord Quincy and Mr. Fitzpatrick kept my attention and were quite entertaining."

"Yes. Well, they were. I even found myself hiding laughter a time or two. But will giving all your interest to them get you engaged?"

Engaged. Yes, she wanted to find a husband, but she didn't want to be betrothed this early in the Season. She wanted to enjoy the festivities and get to know someone before she became betrothed. She wanted to flirt with handsome gentlemen like Lord Quincy and Mr. Fitzpatrick. She wanted to dance until the wee hours of the morning. She wanted to stroll in a garden on the arm of a suitor. She wanted to drop her fan purposely and have an admirer to pick it up for her. She wanted to experience so many things before an engagement and marriage tied her down. And most importantly, she wanted to marry for love.

Once she became betrothed, the fun would end. The planning of her wedding would take precedence over anything else. The modiste's fittings for her trousseau would occupy her days, and the evenings would be spent with her betrothed. No more flirting, laughing, and enjoying herself.

No, she refused to listen to her mother. There was no reason Emmeline needed to find a husband this Season. Her entire life she had been preparing for her debut; why should it have to end so quickly?

"YOU DO REALIZE," Andrew said as they mounted their horses and made their way toward Brooks's on St. James's Street, "we cannot both pursue Miss Connolly."

"Why not?" Fitzpatrick said. "If we promise not to let her come between our friendship. She will eventually choose one of us, and the loser will bow out gracefully. That is what friends do for each other."

Had he lost his bloody mind? If, say, a month went by, and both he and Fitzpatrick fell in love with Emmeline, and she chose the other, how would that not come between them? Andrew's head hurt thinking about what might happen. Perhaps he should bow out now before his heart was invested one hundred percent? Unfortunately, he didn't think he could, because what if she chose him? Of course, all this worrying could be for nothing. Tomorrow, she could announce she was engaged to the Marquess of

Littleton. Women were fickle creatures that Andrew could never figure out.

LORD QUINCY AND Mr. Fitzpatrick, now called Andrew and Aiden in private, doted on Emmeline for the next two months, lavishing her with attention. Even though her mother swore neither of them would offer for her and all her other potential suitors had bowed out, she allowed the courting. With her mother as chaperone and her father home because of his declining health, one or the other, and sometimes both of them, took her to the theater, the opera, soirees, and private dinner parties. There was also Almack's on Wednesday evenings and ear-splitting musicales on occasion.

The more time she spent with them, the more her heart became entangled. Even though she had the most wonderful time each night, she cried herself to sleep. The thought of choosing one over the other made her heart break into tiny pieces. She had no idea you could love two men simultaneously. Why had no one warned her? When she spent time alone with Andrew, she was convinced he was the one for her. She loved him and couldn't live without him. Then, the next day, she would take a stroll in the park with Aiden, and her heart would flutter for him, and she couldn't see herself with anyone but him.

Something was seriously wrong with her. She hated herself for her indecisiveness. The longer three people remained in this courtship, the more complex the decision would be for her, for she didn't want to hurt either Andrew or Aiden. Nor did she want to cause friction between them. No matter that they joked about nothing tearing their friendship apart, she didn't believe them. When the time came for her to choose one or the other, she was sure the gentleman pushed aside would resent the other. How could he not? Perhaps she should break off both courtships. It would nearly kill her and eviscerate her heart to do so, but it would be the kind thing to do.

She never had the chance to call anything off, nor did she believe she would truly have been capable of doing so. And three days later, sitting in the family drawing room, her mother consoled her over the turn of events. "There, there," her mother said as she hugged her daughter. "All is well. You were fortunate enough to have two marriage proposals. And now you will marry Mr. Fitzpatrick. You love him, don't you?"

"Yes." Emmeline sobbed into her mother's bosom. "I do love him. But . . . but . . . I love Andrew, too." She hiccupped several times. Her lungs ached from crying, and her heart had nearly ceased to exist. "I was going to choose him, in truth, but he withdrew his offer. I don't understand. He seemed so sincere in his offer of marriage. And then today I receive his note with two sentences. All it said was, 'I regret my offer of marriage and need to rescind it. Please forgive me. Andrew.'" She breathed in her mother's subtle flowery scent, trying to calm down. "I love them both. How will I ever survive this?"

"Oh, my dear daughter," her mother said with such patience Emmeline didn't know where she found it. "You will have a wonderful life with Aiden. You said so yourself, you love him. In time you will forget the love you had for Lord Quincy and wonder how you could ever have thought you loved anyone but Aiden. Now dry your tears. We have a guest arriving for dinner."

Aiden was dining with them that evening, and she didn't want to have puffy eyes, making him think she was unhappy with their betrothal. She loved Aiden. She did. She wanted to be his wife.

Until Andrew's face flashed in her mind, and then she loved him.

All of this was too much for her. Never in her life had she expected to be heartbroken when she was engaged. She should be rejoicing.

AFTER TAKING A nap, using cold compresses on her eyes and then cucumber slices, Emmeline looked refreshed enough to face Aiden at dinner. Papa wasn't feeling well, so besides them, it would only be Mother. Mother sat at her usual end of the table, with Emmeline on one side of her and Aiden on the other. Her eyes kept straying to him as she nibbled on one course after the other. He looked relaxed, happy, and very handsome, dressed in navy blue with a cream linen shirt and cravat.

Every time their eyes connected, heat radiating from his creamy brown eyes had her insides aflutter. They had never done more than kiss, but sitting opposite him now, her body reacted to his heated look. When they retired to the drawing room after dinner, her mother gave them time alone with the door ajar.

"I thought we would never be alone," Aiden said as he drew her close. One arm circled her waist, and the other cupped her cheek. "You are so beautiful. I can't wait to spend the rest of our lives together. I have a surprise for you."

"You do?" she asked, more than a little intrigued.

"I purchased a townhouse on Hyde Park Street for us. I can't wait to show it to you. I think you're going to love it, and you can decorate it however you wish. All I care about is living there as husband and wife. And after we are married I'm going to spend time each week preparing to oversee Fitzpatrick Industries. Although I can't imagine my father ever giving up the reins completely to me."

"What about finishing university?"

"There is no need. My future is set. My family is wealthy and respected among the *ton*, even if my father runs a company. We shall never want for anything."

"I understand, but I thought . . ."

"Don't think," he whispered right before he kissed her with all the desire she'd witnessed in his eyes during dinner, causing them both to gasp and breathe heavily. His hands roamed her body up the sides of her waist until his thumbs caressed the outside of her breasts, and she moaned into his mouth as the sensations made her dizzy. He broke the kiss and placed barely-there kisses down her neck and across the tops of her breasts. "I can't wait until our wedding night." More kisses. "Until I can make love to you properly." He took her mouth, devouring her as one hand cupped her behind, pulling her tight to him. She gasped at the hard bulge in his breeches. Her hips moved of their own accord, grinding into him, shocking her with her wanton behavior even if she didn't know what she sought. Her insides coiled up tight, and she felt the wetness between her thighs and a pleasant tingling sensation there as well. She may not understand what she needed, but her body did.

"Easy there, my love," he murmured. "I'm almost at my limit."

Moving them to the corner of the room behind the slightly ajar door, Aiden leaned her against the wall. With his intense eyes on her, she couldn't look away as he lifted the front of her skirts, his hand finding the opening in her pantaloons, and he touched her. A gasp escaped her lips, and he covered her mouth with his, silencing her. His fingers opened her folds and touched her most sensitive spot. She would have collapsed to the floor if Aiden had not tightened his grip on her with his free hand.

"Easy, my love. Just close your eyes and let your body relax. Enjoy my touch."

And so she did, and moments later, she clutched his shoulders; her body trembled and exploded, sending her into some euphoria she didn't know existed. When her body calmed, and Aiden righted her skirts, he grinned at her and said, "I love you."

"I love you." And at that moment, she loved him with all her heart and would forever.

IT WAS AIDEN'S and Emmeline's wedding day. Andrew's insides were tied up in knots because he didn't know if he could make it through the ceremony and wedding breakfast afterward. He'd already emptied the contents of his stomach into the chamber pot. It was better to be sick now than during the ceremony.

He owed it to one of his closest friends to attend. If he didn't, gossip would spread, and he couldn't allow that to happen. He wanted their marriage to be perfect and not tainted with the whispers of another man. Even if it had been true once, it would never be true again. He had come to terms with the fact that he'd lost Emmeline four weeks ago when the first banns were posted. *Liar.*

His valet, Clayton, cleared his throat. "My lord, you must leave now. Mr. Weston and Mr. Caldwell are waiting in the carriage."

"Yes." Functioning in a fog, Andrew exited his parents' townhouse and climbed inside Weston's carriage, facing backward beside Caldwell. He hoped neither of them would ask how he was.

But, of course, no such luck.

"Are you going to make it through the ceremony?" Weston asked, concern etched on his face.

Taking a deep breath and noticing, yes, his heart still hurt like a bloody bugger, he replied, "Shit, I hope so."

Weston added, "For what it's worth, you did the right thing. Aiden loves her."

What about me? I love her. "I know." When he woke up every morning alone from this day forth, he would tell himself that he had done the right thing for the rest of his life because his love for her would never die. He would have vowed never to marry if he hadn't had to do his duty to the dukedom someday and produce an heir. But with twin older sisters and then him, and no younger brothers to inherit, he had to do his duty and marry . . . eventually. He already pitied the woman he took for a wife. She deserved so much better than him—a man with a jaded, broken heart.

"We are here," Caldwell said as the coach stopped. The driver opened the door and flipped down the stairs.

Andrew exited the coach and stared up at St. George's, Hanover Square, knowing right then and there that he would never step foot in that church again as long as he lived. He would join St. James's Church the first chance he had.

If his heart hadn't shriveled and died weeks ago, he would have thought it was a beautiful ceremony. The bride took his breath away. The groom looked happier than Andrew had ever seen him. Meanwhile, his throat burned from unshed tears he fought to keep from escaping. He would not cause anything to ruin this perfect day for the bride and groom, even if he wanted to bellow out the words for all to hear, "Emmeline is mine. I love her. She belongs with me." Instead, he pretended to be calm and happy for the loving couple.

Once the church ceremony ended, they proceeded to the Connolly residence for the wedding breakfast. Andrew found his place card at the opposite end of the table from the new Mr. and Mrs. Aiden Fitzpatrick. Thank Christ, he thought, as he toyed with the food on his plate as the courses came and went. He knew he would cast up his accounts right there in front of everyone if he ate anything. He didn't care about embarrassing himself, but he wouldn't do that to Aiden and Emmeline. Even if his jealousy was making him crazy, there was enough of the gentleman in him to keep from causing a scene. At least he kept telling himself that. He loved them both too much to spoil their happiness even as he sank to the lowest depths of despair imaginable. Never to be whole ever again as long as he lived.

The only thing that soothed him was the unending wine poured by the footmen. He was drunk when the happy couple left. Thank bloody hell the torturous wedding breakfast was over, and he could go home and break out the whisky and get foxed, really foxed. Because, as much as he tried not to picture Aiden making love to Emmeline and taking her innocence, he couldn't. It was all he could see in his mind. He needed to drink himself to oblivion. It would be the only thing saving him from his tormented visions.

Back inside Weston's carriage, Andrew collapsed against the squabs, sloshing wine onto his clothes as he'd taken his glass with him, and said, "To Mr. and Mrs. Fitzpatrick. May Aiden fuck her well and good."

He overlooked his friends' winces as he dropped his glass and succumbed to his drunken stupor, his life never to be the same.

CHAPTER THREE

Four Years Later

"WE HAVE ARRIVED." Aiden nudged Emmeline when the carriage came to a halt. Another carriage stopped behind them, carrying Aiden's valet, Emmeline's maid, and their trunks.

"Did I fall asleep?" Emmeline asked as she straightened her hat.

Aiden chuckled. "Yes. But fear not. You missed nothing on the ride but the greenery of the countryside, cows, and sheep." He kissed her cheek. "How are you feeling?"

"Better." Emmeline was still recovering from a miscarriage she'd had the previous week. They both were. They had been hoping for a baby for the past four years, yet it seemed it wasn't meant to be. When they'd found out she was with child, they were so overjoyed. Until they weren't.

Emmeline wouldn't lie; their marriage for the past four years hadn't come without problems. The worst of them revolved around their friend, Andrew Hampton. Aiden was uncomfortable with the feelings she'd once had for him, feelings she insisted didn't exist anymore. She had done all she could to convince him his fears were unfounded, but he had put distance between himself and Andrew and she blamed herself for the loss of their close friendship. Her marriage to Aiden was never supposed to come between the close friends.

As for what Aiden referred to as being uncomfortable and she called being jealous, he had nothing to worry about. She loved Aiden—with most of her heart. Not that she would let him know that. To herself she could confess that a small piece still belonged to Andrew, but it would cause a disaster if Aiden ever suspected. Already, he sometimes made remarks about not being worthy of her. Which he was in every way possible. He adored her. He loved her. He was patient and kind with her.

Emmeline did everything she could to ease Aiden's burdens and treat Andrew as a friend—not too good a friend, but be friendly toward him. Thankfully, they did not see him often.

Unfortunately, he was attending this hunting party at the Marquess and Marchioness of Sutton's country estate. It was their first time seeing each other in over six months. Not long enough and yet too long. She tried never to think of Andrew; she did succeed most days, but other times, his handsome face and memorable voice snuck up on her when she least expected it. She immersed herself in being the most loving and perfect wife to Aiden, never giving him any reason to regret their marriage or doubt her love. She certainly never regretted marrying him. Even if she thought about Andrew occasionally, she couldn't imagine not being married to Aiden. Even if she could go back in time, she wouldn't change a thing.

"You know he will be here?" Before the carriage door opened, Aiden placed his index finger beneath her chin, forcing her to look into his worried eyes.

"I know." She smiled, trying to ease the fears that plagued him whenever Andrew was around. "You need not worry." She leaned in and kissed him. "I love you. I chose you. Please, let it rest."

He pulled her into a life-squeezing hug. "It's odd because whenever we are with him, I'm so overjoyed to be with my closest friend. But then in my mind, I see you with him and wish he weren't with us. I'm trying to stop that."

"I know." Emmeline prayed that this would be one of those

times Aiden buried his discomfort, and they had an enjoyable time together again with all of Aiden's friends. It wasn't just Andrew attending—Weston and Caldwell were as well.

The door swung open to reveal the men themselves: Andrew, Weston, and Caldwell.

"Finally, you have arrived," Weston said as he held out his hand to Emmeline. Before she knew it, she was outside and engulfed in Weston's arms. "It is so good to see you." He released her and slapped Aiden on the back. "Good to see you, my friend. It's been much too long."

Aiden laughed, "I'm not the one traveling the world, sailing the seas in search of riches like you and Caldwell."

Caldwell's eyes widened. "You should see the places Weston and I have been. You won't believe the stories we could tell."

"You two are doing well," Andrew said, insinuating himself into the conversation. "While the rest of us aristocrats live a mundane life in London, drinking, gambling, and socializing to our hearts' content."

Andrew's words and how he said them bothered Emmeline. Gambling and drinking to excess weren't things he'd been known to do in days past. Although people did change. And they hadn't exactly stayed in touch much over the past four years. Any correspondence they received was addressed to Aiden, and Andrew apparently only ever inquired about her good health. She understood Andrew's reluctance to send her a letter and why he never really asked about her. He, of all people, knew Aiden. Probably better in some ways than she did. Most likely, he knew about Aiden's unease when they were around him, and took care not to cause him any worry in that regard. Emmeline should commend Andrew for his stand-offish behavior where she was concerned, but it hurt.

"Yes," Aiden said, wrapping her arm through his. "You two have created a gold mine. We are going to greet our hosts and freshen up. We will see you soon."

Aiden started walking, giving her no choice but to leave their friends staring at their backs. "Please slow down, Aiden. I can't walk as fast as you, and I'm famished, lightheaded, and still experiencing mild cramps."

"Forgive me."

He eased his stride, and she could see and feel the tension coiling up his body. She didn't have to ask why his mood had changed suddenly—it had to do with two things. The first was that Aiden had been asked to join Weston's and Caldwell's business venture years ago but had declined because they were getting married, and he wouldn't risk losing money they would later need. Not that they needed the money, as it turned out. Aiden's father's business was solvent. But she believed his pride was injured because he hadn't invested with them, and now the business was very successful. The other, of course, was seeing Andrew. Not that Andrew had even acknowledged her existence. No greeting . . . nothing but a sideways glance in her direction, his features guarded.

Their hosts, the Marquess and Marchioness of Sutton, greeted them in the drawing room.

"Marquess, Marchioness," Aiden said with a bow. "Mrs. Fitzpatrick and I are honored to be your guests."

"Indeed." Emmeline curtsied. "Thank you for inviting us. We look forward to spending time with you both while here."

The marchioness took both of Emmeline's hands in hers. "It is wonderful to see you again after such a long time. I hope you and I can catch up and reminisce about our times as young girls."

"I would like that." The marchioness was the older sister of her childhood friend, Catherine, now the Viscountess of Appleton.

The housekeeper escorted them to their guest room. "Your trunks will be delivered shortly," she said. "Oh my goodness, here they are now. I'll leave you to get situated, and if you need anything, please send word to me personally."

Beckett and Amanda followed the trunks into the room. Without being told, they began to unpack silently. Emmeline looked around the lovely room which faced the back gardens and boasted plenty of light filtering in through the windows. "This is a charming room. Bright and cheery." Standing at a large window, Emmeline pointed. "Come see—the gardens below are colorful and full to bursting with guests. Do you wish to rest, or would you like to join the festivities? There are tables set up with food and drinks." Just then, her stomach grumbled, reminding her she was hungry.

Aiden chuckled when he heard her gurgling stomach. "Let us go to the gardens and partake of some food. I can't have my wife perishing from hunger."

"We need to change out of our traveling clothes and freshen up first." Emmeline went behind a screen with Amanda following, her arms full of a seafoam-green muslin day dress with matching spencer. When they emerged several moments later, Aiden was changed and waiting. "I need another minute while Amanda fixes my hair."

Aiden and Emmeline, refreshed and stylishly dressed, made their way down two flights of stairs and followed the chatter coming from the back gardens. Exiting the double doors on the far wall of what looked like a music room, Emmeline sighed. It was a relief to be out of the confines of the carriage and move her sore body. Aiden, ever the gentleman, fixed a plate for her and sat her at an unoccupied bench while he returned to fix himself one.

Emmeline's eyes traveled around the garden, taking notice of those in attendance. She had hoped her friend Lady Catherine would attend since they had not seen each other in over a year, but she'd recently given birth to her second child. She was beyond happy for Catherine and her husband, but that couldn't stop the pain lancing Emmeline's heart or the tears threatening to escape. She dabbed her eyes with the napkin Aiden had given her with her plate. She was being overly emotional. Many women had miscarriages. She would find herself increasing again soon. At twenty-two, she had many more years to have children before she was considered past her prime.

Tell that to her broken heart. It refused to listen to reason, and she blinked back tears.

"Sorry it took me so long," Aiden said as he sat with a plate of food and two glasses of lemonade. He handed her one. "I didn't spill a drop."

"Thank you." She sipped the cool drink, which eased her parched throat. "I'm surprised at the number of people here. There must be thirty guests."

"At least. Some are inside. I'd say closer to forty."

"How many are attending the hunt tomorrow?"

"I haven't seen the attendees list, but I'd imagine most of the men and some ladies will ride along." He took a sip of his drink. "Do you want to accompany me?"

"No." Her body was still healing, and the jostling of riding and sitting on a saddle would be uncomfortable.

He patted her hand. "I didn't think so. I want you to take it easy and not overdo it. Do you want to go up to the room and rest before dinner? I believe it is a formal affair with dancing afterward."

"No. I'm a little tired, but I'll be fine. Sitting here in the sun is restoring my energy."

"Do you mind if I go to the stables and look over the mounts for tomorrow?"

"No. Don't worry about me."

"I always do, though . . . ever since—" his voice cracked. He squeezed her hand and kissed her cheek. "Truly, don't be a warrior. Rest if you need to."

Once Aiden left, taking the empty plates and cups, she adjusted her skirts and watched the servants clear the food and tables away. She found herself alone and enjoyed the peace, quiet, and privacy. A light breeze brought a mixed scent of the nearby blossoms her way, and she inhaled the fragrances. Bees buzzed from flower to flower, pollinating the plants. Her eyes fluttered closed, and her muscles eased as the heat from the sun penetrated through the fabric of her clothes, melting the tension away.

"May I join you?"

Her heart fluttered at the sound of the familiar voice and all the air whooshed from her lungs. She opened her eyes, looking up at Andrew's handsome and guarded face.

"You may." She scooted over on the bench as far as she could, which wasn't much before the armrest jabbed into her side.

After he sat down, he looked at her with uncertainty and something else. A great sadness, she thought. "How are you?"

She lowered her gaze to her hands folded together on her lap. She could not tell him the truth so she only said, "I am well. And you?"

His chuckle warmed her heart. "I am well. Thank you." He paused. "I have written Aiden several times, and he has never replied. Is he upset with me?"

She glanced his way and immediately wished she hadn't. The devastation in his eyes had her swallowing back tears. "He received your letters. I assumed he wrote you back. I'm sorry he hasn't and worried you. He is fine. We are both fine. He is busy helping his father with his business. He works almost every day in some capacity. We are staying in London for the most part and keeping to ourselves. We hardly socialize. Aiden doesn't enjoy large gatherings. And to tell the truth, neither do I."

Rising, he nodded his head, his gaze elsewhere. "That is all I wanted to know. I hope you are both happy."

Before she could answer, "We are," he was gone, leaving her wondering why Aiden hadn't responded to Andrew's letters. But that conversation was for another day when they were home in London with no distractions. Being rude to Andrew would not solve whatever problem Aiden might still have with him. Did he perhaps have other issues with Andrew besides the obvious? Could they have had a falling out because of something else? In truth, it would ease Emmeline's heart if their distance had nothing to do with her. The guilt that plagued her was a heavy burden to carry around day in and day out. It would be a long life if something didn't change. Not that there was anything for Aiden to be envious of when it came to her brief courtship with Andrew. They had never even kissed.

Thank goodness Aiden had no way of knowing her thoughts and dreams regarding Andrew, though. She suffered enough remorse over that for the both of them.

Emmeline rose from the bench and decided to rest before dinner, after all. Her husband had not returned, and she was bored from sitting alone. She didn't want to rehash the same thoughts in her head she always did when having a melancholy moment. She would not waste another moment trying to fix what was wrong with her husband's friendship. Nor would she reminisce about the past between Andrew and her. It never solved anything and only made her more unsettled, anxious, and sad. Aiden needed his friends now more than ever. If only he wouldn't push them away.

Upon entering their away-from-home bedchamber, she rang for Amanda. When she arrived, she helped her undress down to her chemise. "That will be all, Amanda. Thank you."

"Yes, ma'am."

Pulling the covers down, Emmeline climbed beneath the cool sheets, turned on her side, and closed her eyes. The strains of traveling and seeing Andrew proved too much for her, and her mind and body craved sleep.

DINNER AND DANCING began pleasantly enough that evening, but by the end Emmeline couldn't wait to return to her room for the night. The strain of the day, and worrying about Aiden and how much he was overindulging in port, only added to her worries. Little by little, since their wedding, his alcohol consumption had increased. He rarely got fall-down drunk, but she agonized over it nonetheless. When she brought it up, he convinced her he was fine. But he wasn't. She wanted him to see the family physician, but he refused. She had finally given up recommending it because the conversation never solved anything. When sober, Aiden was a loving and attentive husband. But when overindulging in spirits, he became overly quiet and brooding.

She needed Weston's and Caldwell's assistance getting him to their room. It took all her strength to keep her eyes averted from them so they would not see the tears in her eyes and the frustration in her soul. It would be a miracle if he were well enough to attend the morning's hunt.

ANDREW GROANED WHEN Clayton entered his room and opened the curtains. "Good morning, my lord. The hunt begins promptly in one hour. I brought you a breakfast tray. Shall I return to help you dress?"

"No, I can manage." Climbing out of bed, he stretched as he went to the window. "Cloudy, not windy. It will do for a hunt," he said to himself. After taking care of his morning ablutions, he perused the tray. Eggs, sausage, toast, and marmalade, along with coffee. Clayton knew he needed his morning coffee to function and pretend to be human and interested in the day.

To his father's dismay, the past four years had found Andrew floundering. He had very little to occupy his time until he inherited his father's estates and titles, which he was in no hurry to do. As a privileged and leisurely member of the *ton*, he was expected to socialize, dance with the debutantes seeking husbands, and attend house parties like this one. He also found plenty of time to visit his clubs and gambling dens.

The latter caused friction with his father. He had recently acquired debts beyond his monthly allowance and needed his father's help to pay. He hadn't needed to witness the disappointment in his father's eyes to know a change in the trajectory of his life was needed. He desperately sought to acquire purpose in his life. Turning into a wastrel was not what Andrew had foreseen for his future. And the reality of being a wastrel wasn't something he was proud of. Quite the opposite—he despised himself for it. But somehow, he wasn't capable of changing his path. His heart and soul were damaged, making him care less about what happened to him or his future. He was a bloody mess being held together by his cravat.

Dressed in hunting attire, he made his way to the stables, where the participants in the event were meeting. Andrew had brought his horse, Merlin, with him. He always preferred his mount to one being supplied by the host. Hunting was not one of his favorite pastimes, but just as today, he would participate because it was expected of him. Not only that, he hoped to have a private word with Aiden. They'd promised each other four years ago that Emmeline would never come between their friendship, yet that was precisely what had happened.

Before long, the four friends had ridden off together, separating from the other hunters and the hounds. None of them had it in them to hunt today. To Andrew's surprise, Aiden had brought several flasks filled with whisky, and he passed them out.

"Can't ride with my closest friends without libation." He held up his flask. "To friends!"

"To friends!" Weston, Caldwell, and Andrew toasted in unison.

Andrew held up his flask again, "To the best friends a gentleman could ever wish to have!"

"Here, here!" three voices called out.

After an hour, the four stopped at a stream to water their horses and partake in bread, cheese, and fruit their host supplied to each participant. Not that they were actively participating. None of the friends were avid hunters. This time together was more about friends getting reacquainted after many years apart— at least, Andrew hoped it was.

Quite some time went by before they left the stream and

made their way to an open field, and Andrew said, "Who wants to race?"

The moment the words left his mouth, he knew he shouldn't have said them. None of them were in any condition to race—they were all deep into their cups. But he rarely cared about the consequences of his actions lately, and the words had slipped out almost of their own accord.

"Yes!" Aiden said, nearly sliding off his mount in his enthusiasm fueled by whisky.

"I'm too into my cups," Weston said as he slithered off his mount and landed on his arse.

"I'm with Weston," Caldwell said with a laugh as he dismounted. "You two go on. Weston and I will sit here, watch, and try not to fall asleep."

"Andrew's a better rider than me, so I think I should get Merlin to compensate for it."

"Merlin needs strong guidance and delicate handling. I don't think it's a wise idea for you to ride him. I'll give you a head start." As impaired as he was, Andrew still knew it wasn't a good idea to have Aiden ride Merlin. Merlin was a beast and didn't tolerate others riding him. And not to be judgmental, but Aiden wasn't the best horseman.

"What the hell?" Aiden bellowed, looking enraged, as he staggered down from the saddle. "Wise, my arse. I can handle your damn horse just as well as you can."

The last thing Andrew wanted to do was cause more of a rift between them, so against his better wisdom, he relented. "He is yours. I'm going to ride Weston's mount." He dismounted, landing on wobbly legs and handing over the reins to Merlin who immediately tossed his head up and down and side to side in protest.

"Okay, gentlemen." Weston teetered to his feet. "The first rider to . . ." he paused and put his hand over his eyes to shield them from the sun, "to ride to that huge oak at the end of the clearing and back is the winner and shall hold the title of the fastest racer ever to live!"

All four of them burst out laughing. "If you say so," Aiden remarked as he mounted Merlin. There was no need to adjust anything since Andrew and Aiden were close enough in height.

Andrew adjusted Weston's stirrups as Weston was slightly shorter than he. When comfortable on Weston's horse, he moved beside Aiden and nodded. "May the best man win."

Aiden snickered, "You bet your arse I will."

Caldwell stood off to the side, swaying on his feet. "Is this a good idea? You two are foxed and don't know the terrain."

"To hell with the terrain." Aiden took another swig from his never-ending flask, almost unseating himself. "We are invincible."

"Hell, yes," Andrew drawled, "invinca . . . something."

"Ready?" Weston stood between the riders. "On three. One. Two. Three!"

Andrew urged his horse on, surprised his mount was a good match for Merlin. Andrew could barely hold on as he felt the effects of the whisky sloshing around in his stomach, wanting to come back up. The wind took his hat off, and his hair blew in his eyes, making it difficult to see anything but Merlin and Aiden to his left.

To stop the world from spinning and give him something to concentrate on besides leaning over the saddle and throwing up, he focused on Merlin becoming more agitated as Aiden used a crop on him. Merlin never tolerated such treatment and he should've warned Aiden not to use one.

Andrew urged his horse to go faster and he came right beside Aiden who appeared to struggle with the reins. Panicking at what he saw, Andrew yelled, "Whoa, Merlin, whoa."

Several things happened then that Andrew could never again unsee or forgive himself for. Merlin came to a sudden and violent stop that sent Aiden flying over his head. Aiden tumbled to the ground in a broken heap as Merlin went up on his hind legs. When he came down he stomped on Aiden with his full weight.

At the same time Andrew's eyes witnessed the vicious actions, a scream split the air, and then silence. Andrew's heart lodged in his throat as he jumped out of the saddle and dropped down beside his friend's fractured body. He didn't need to see his sightless eyes looking up into the sky to know he was dead. Aiden's face was twisted up in silent agony. His mouth open as if he were still screaming.

Andrew staggered to his feet and vomited the contents of his stomach just as Weston and Caldwell arrived.

"What the fuck?" Weston yelled as he dropped to his knees, tears streaming down his face.

Caldwell was vomiting.

Suddenly sober, and wishing he weren't, Andrew placed his hand on Weston's back. For support or his own comfort, he didn't know, nor did it matter. All that mattered was that his best friend in the entire world was dead, and it was his fault.

CHAPTER FOUR

IT TOOK SOME time before the friends could process the grim situation. Then they draped Aiden's body face down on his mount. Andrew climbed on Merlin, even though it was the last place he wanted to be, and grabbed the reins of Aiden's horse, and led the way back to the Sutton Estate. Not a word was said amongst them. Andrew's heart burned inside his chest. His throat was scraped raw, and his eyes stung from the copious amount of tears he couldn't seem to stop from flowing down his face. Even though he had witnessed it, he couldn't comprehend that Aiden was gone. This sort of tragic thing happened to other people, not to them. The four of them had been the closest friends since their first day at Eton. Four friends were now three.

"Christ," he mumbled as he fought the bile rising up his throat. How could this be happening? His entire being was numb and encased in fog. Nothing appeared real. It all seemed dreamlike and incomprehensible. Andrew felt as though he was living somewhere in between death and reality. It was an awful place to be. And knowing he was responsible for Aiden's death only heightened everything happening around him. He was the one who had suggested racing. He was the one who had allowed Aiden to ride Merlin against his own better wisdom. There was already another strain on their friendship, and he hadn't wanted to create more by refusing to let Aiden ride his horse. And because of that, his friend was dead.

As they rode slowly, Andrew's mind kept screaming, "Make it right!"

Instead of going to the stables, which was another decision he would come to regret, Andrew led them to the front of the estate, forcing his mind to focus on what must be done. He prayed Emmeline was nowhere close by. He didn't want to see her, nor did he want her to see Aiden's body like this. What would he tell her? How could he tell her Aiden was dead because of him? He had to remind himself that this wasn't about him. It was about Aiden and Emmeline. Emmeline became a widow at the age of twenty-two.

"Bloody hell," he swore as they stopped before the double front doors. A footman hurried forward, his eyes wide. "Please get the marquess and hurry," Andrew said. The footman rushed off while the three friends dismounted and handed their horses to a stable boy who suddenly stood beside them. It wasn't long before Lord Sutton hurried down the front stairs. His eyes went to Aiden's body draped across his horse.

"Someone, please tell me what happened," the marquess groaned. "And please tell me that is not the dead body of Mr. Fitzpatrick!"

Lady Sutton gasped and covered her mouth as she hurried down the stairs with a crowd of ladies following closely behind, no doubt coming from the drawing room, wanting to see what the commotion was about.

"Please don't let Emmeline be among them. Please don't let Emmeline be among them," Andrew mumbled.

Sutton held up his hand. "My dear, take the ladies back inside the drawing room now."

"Is that . . .?"

It was too late. He heard her voice. Before he could move, thank Christ, Weston rushed forward, grabbed Emmeline by the arm, and hurried her back inside the house and to the currently vacant library. He and Caldwell were on their heels. Caldwell quietly shut the door, giving them privacy.

Weston led Emmeline to a chair. Andrew nudged his way in front of her and fell on his knees, taking her hands in his trembling ones. Hers were shaking as well, and her face had lost all color.

"What happened?" she whispered.

"We were being stupid," Caldwell interjected.

"We were all drunk," Weston added.

Andrew swallowed down the lump in his throat, and before he could say anything else, Weston blurted out, "We raced. Aiden fell off his horse. It happened so fast. I'm so sorry." He dropped his head into his hands, his body shaking as he sobbed. Caldwell stood off to the side now, silent in his grief.

"He raced while drunk?" Emmeline questioned, her eyes wide with shock. "But Aiden is a terrible horseman. I can't believe he would do such a thing. And how could Lord Sutton have given Aiden anything but a docile mount knowing how badly he rides?"

Andrew looked at his two friends and shook his head ever so slightly hoping they understood that he would explain the rest.

"He rode my horse, Merlin. Though he is as tame as they come." The lie about Merlin being tame came easy to his lips, but his insides churned with the untruth.

"How badly is he hurt? Did someone call for a physician? I want to see him." Emmeline tried to pull her hands from his and stand, but Andrew didn't let her go, forcing her to stay seated.

"I'm sorry, Emmeline. Aiden is . . . is . . . dead," Andrew choked out through the tears clogging his throat.

Her eyes widened, and she shook her head. "No. No. No. He can't be dead. Not my Aiden. Not Aiden. Noooo!" she screamed as she pulled her hands from his and shoved Andrew away so forcefully he ended up on his arse on the carpet. She ran to the door, but Caldwell blocked her from exiting. "Noooo!" she screamed again. Andrew scrambled to his feet, hurried to her, and tried to console her. But she was inconsolable as she started smacking him in the chest repeatedly and yelling over and over again, "No! No! No!" The hitting didn't cease, and he didn't stop her. As far as he was concerned, he deserved her anger and much more.

When she finally tired and gripped his upper arms for support, he clutched her to him, one of his hands rubbing her back. "I'm so sorry. I'm so sorry," he murmured. Time was suspended indefinitely as they sobbed into each other's arms.

⟫⟩⟨⟪

EMMELINE BECAME AWARE of several things at once. She was sobbing uncontrollably in Andrew's arms. His body shook against hers as he cried, too. She couldn't see Weston or Caldwell, but she knew they were there. Was she having a nightmare and still lying in bed?

No. The pain in her chest was all too real and excruciating.

The lump in her throat was real; she felt it every time she swallowed.

Her tears, which she thought would never dry up, continued to slide down her face and soak the front of her dress and Andrew's shirt.

Life as she knew it ended when Andrew said, *Aiden is dead.* How was that possible? Why did he have to be the one to die? She wanted her mother, and she needed to go home. She hadn't felt this broken since her father had passed two years ago.

Two hours later, Emmeline was sitting with her maid in her carriage for the four-hour trek to London. Behind them, Andrew, Weston, and Caldwell rode on horseback while Aiden's body was strapped to the top of Andrew's carriage inside a wooden box. Behind them was Beckett with her and Aiden's trunks. Rolling behind them all were Weston's coach, their valets, and trunks.

Sitting beside Emmeline, Amanda held her hand. Not a word was said during the carriage ride, and they never made a stop. She couldn't speak as she was shrouded in sorrow so acute she didn't know if she would ever come out the other side. Ever be whole again. Ever feel anything else but this sadness overwhelming her soul. As she sat, holding Amanda's hand, Emmeline stared out the window, seeing only a blur of green and brown.

Eventually, the countryside was replaced with the sights and sounds of London. Emmeline tugged her hand from Amanda's and covered her ears. She felt suddenly eight years old again, a little girl hiding beneath a table during a ball. Her senses were hyper-aware, and she wanted to scream, run, and hide away where no one could find her. The sounds bombarding her were the worst. They surrounded her, paralyzing her in her seat and making her gasp for air. The noises cocooned her body and refused to let her free.

When the carriage door opened, her eyes widened, and her gasps for air increased which made her dizzy. Swirls of blackness spun in her eyes until nothing.

ANDREW SWEPT EMMELINE into his arms as her mother rushed down the front stairs. "What has happened?" the dowager baroness asked, pale with worry.

"She has fainted."

"Come this way." The baroness led Andrew into the house and up the stairs and had him place Emmeline on the drawing room settee. "Why did my daughter faint? And where is her husband?"

Weston and Caldwell followed them into the drawing room, looking as if they wanted to be anywhere but there. Weston replied before Andrew could. "There was a riding accident. I'm so sorry. Aiden is dead. His body is being brought in."

"No," the baroness cried as she sat on the edge of the settee, stroking her daughter's hair. "My poor, poor girl."

"Mama," Emmeline murmured as her eyes fluttered open,

and Andrew's entire body froze as he glimpsed the silent agony from deep within her eyes.

Her mother continued stroking Emmeline's hair. "Gentlemen, thank you for returning my daughter and Aiden's body, but we would prefer to be alone with our grief."

Andrew, Weston, and Caldwell left with their heads down and hearts heavy. At least Andrew's heart was, and he had no doubt his friends' were as well.

THE NEXT FOUR days were the worst of Emmeline's life. Aiden's body was laid out in the public drawing room. People came by and paid their respects. Her mind and body refused to comprehend it all. It was better that way really. She didn't cry, nor did she feel much of anything. She was just numb. Her body moved, and she heard herself say all the proper things to the visiting mourners, yet somehow, she didn't exist. A fog blanketed her, protecting her from her pain and allowing her to go on.

When Aiden's body entered the earth in the graveyard on Mount Street for the parish members of St. George's, Hanover Square, she walked away knowing half of her had gone into the ground with him.

TWO AND A half long years after Aiden's death, Emmeline was shocked when Andrew showed up at her door late one night, drunk. She'd barely seen him since the day she'd buried Aiden. She'd become a recluse, barely leaving the house and not socializing except for the Ladies' Society of Mayfair she belonged to. The members and her charity work kept her busy enough and saved her sanity. She did not need the London social scene. Life as she had known it was over for her.

"What are you doing here?" she asked, pulling him inside. "Get in here before someone sees you." Once inside, she tugged him up the stairs and into the drawing room, forcing him to sit in a chair. Before settling on the settee, she checked the ties to her robe, hoping she was sufficiently covered.

Sitting, her hands trembling on her lap, she studied Andrew. Gone was the impeccably groomed and put-together young man, and her heart ached. Before her sat a man she didn't recognize; his hair was overlong and disheveled. His clothing was askew, and his cravat was untied and bore wine stains. His scuffed boots looked like his valet hadn't polished them in weeks. But what shocked her the most was how much weight he'd lost. His cheeks were hollowed out, and his eyes sunken, bloodshot, and rimmed with dark circles. His overall pallor was gray-tinged. If she didn't know any better, she would think he was on death's door. Tears sprang in her eyes, and she fought them back along with the lump in her throat. It went without saying that her heart had pounded inside her chest from the moment she opened the door.

"Can I get you anything? Something to drink or eat?"

His hands tugged at his hair, and he made an unintelligible sound. "Something to eat would be nice."

"Excuse me while I see what I can find in the kitchen." She hurried down the stairs to the kitchen, where the cook always left food for such an occasion as visitors in the middle of the night or someone needing a snack. Mostly, she left it for Harrison, her butler, as he spent many wakeful nights in the kitchen. Emmeline fixed a plate of cold turkey, bread, and cheese with a glass of lemonade and hurried back to Andrew, surprised to see him still awake. She had been almost positive he would fall asleep while she was in the kitchen. She handed him the plate and placed the glass of lemonade on a side table.

He ate in silence, his attention focused solely on his food. When only crumbs remained on his plate, he put it on the side table, picked up the lemonade, and downed the glass.

"Thank you," he mumbled.

She barely heard him. She cleared her throat. "What brings you to my door at this hour?" She would be lying to herself if she hadn't been waiting for him to come to her door once her mourning for Aiden had ended. But the more time passed—and he still hadn't come—the more she sank into despair that he would never come. Perhaps he had never loved her. Now finally he came, one and a half years out of mourning, and he looked to be at death's door. She fought back the tears—her intuition warned her he wasn't here for her.

His shoulders rose and fell as he inhaled and exhaled. "My father threw me out. Threatened to disown me. I've been staying at Mayfair Imports and Exports. Weston and Caldwell have a sofa in their office."

Emmeline's mouth opened in shock as she tried to find the words to speak. "He threw you out?"

"I think I made that clear."

"But why?" Her eyes connected with his, and Emmeline's heart stopped at witnessing tears slide down his face. The only other time she had seen Andrew cry was when Aiden died.

"I've been an arse. Gambling. He refused to cover my debts. I'm essentially homeless." He wiped the tears from his face. "Christ, I'm a bloody mess." He stood and groaned, "I shouldn't have come here."

"But you did. You may as well tell me why."

He ignored her and made his way out of the room and down the stairs. He paused before the door and turned to her, his face full of anguish. "I came to say goodbye."

Goodbye. Where was he going? "You are leaving London?"

"Yes. I'm setting sail tomorrow with Weston to the West Indies. It may be years before I'm back to stay."

Years? Her heart stopped or shriveled and died—she couldn't tell which. Nor did it matter. "I see."

He moved forward so he stood only inches from her. "Before I leave, I want to know why Aiden was unhappy. He never drank to excess, especially when riding and hunting were involved.

What did you do to him?"

Emmeline gasped and covered her mouth in shock. Was he blaming her for Aiden's death? He wouldn't be that cruel, would he? What had happened to the Andrew she had known . . . and loved?

He held up his hand. "Never mind. I don't want to know." With a look of contempt, he left her standing in the hall, her heart in her throat and tears raining down her face. Not only had she lost her husband but now the man who owned the other half of her heart as well.

CHAPTER FIVE

London 1816

RIDING IN THE carriage on the way to the Duke and Duchess of Westport's London residence with Emmeline were her mother and her cousin, Henry Weston's widow, Lady Liliana Langford. After Henry's nephew, Edmund Weston, arrived to take over the earldom, he had said harsh and hurtful words to Lilly. Refusing to stay under the same roof with such a despicable man, whom she'd just met and who accused her of nefarious deeds, she had moved into Emmeline's home with her. During her brief marriage to Henry, she and Lilly had become fast friends, and Lilly had known she was always welcome in Emmeline's home.

Lilly and Emmeline had spent the past nine months keeping each other company and preparing for the Season. It was past time Emmeline made a real appearance in Society, and Lilly insisted on joining her since her year of mourning was over.

They shared a special bond that would never be broken, no matter where they ended up in life. They both had the misfortune of being young widows and childless—no baby to raise and ease their broken hearts. And it didn't matter that Henry was sixty-six at the time of his death any more than it mattered that Aiden had been twenty-three. Dead was dead. Widowed was widowed. A lost love was a lost love.

Her thoughts now drifted to Andrew, who she knew was

back in London after all this time, and wondered if he would notice her tonight. And why would he look her way at her old age of twenty-eight? Not with the young debutantes and the ladies in their second or third Season available. He would need an heir now that he'd inherited from his father. Even if they somehow became close again and married, could she give him one?

Nonsense, she scolded herself. Many women had children well into their thirties. But would he think her worth the risk?

"You have become quiet suddenly," Lilly said.

"Forgive me. I was thinking about whether a certain gentleman would be in attendance tonight. He is in partnership with Langford and Caldwell, and since they are both in London, perhaps he is as well."

Her mother humphed. "You know he will be."

"He may be in attendance, but he may not want to see me."

"Do you think I don't remember two young gentlemen vying for your affections ten years ago? I will never forget you crying in my arms, trying to decide between the two. As I understand, he never wed. And you are a widow, beautiful and kindhearted. He will be there tonight. Approach him."

"But he's a duke now. *A duke.* He needs a young bride to give him heirs." She had only known him as the Earl of Quincy, but right before he'd returned to London, his father had passed making him the new Duke of Blackstone.

"Heirs," her mother flicked her wrist, "which you can give him. Nothing says he cannot marry a young widow."

"Thank you, Mother, but I think you are biased. He is good friends with the Earl of Langford. I highly doubt the new earl speaks kindly of me anymore."

"Why ever not?"

Inhaling deeply, Emmeline held her breath for five counts, then exhaled. She did this three times. "Because Lilly has been staying with me. Not to mention the fact that Langford hasn't been in London for several years, and when he was last, he wasn't very friendly to me. I'd married one of his closest friends. I think he blames me for Aiden's death. As though I caused the horse to throw him off to his death." Emmeline gasped for breath, removed her delicate handkerchief from her reticule, and dabbed at her teary eyes. "Perhaps the duke thinks the same about me."

Lilly leaned forward and grasped her hands. "Nonsense. Nobody blames you. How can they? From what you told me, they were with him during the tragic accident, not you. They were the ones who got inebriated during a hunting party and decided to race willy-nilly on horseback without regard to any of their lives. You were back at the estate having tea with the other guests."

"Oh, dear. We have arrived," Emmeline said as she held Lilly's hand, giving them the courage to do what others did so easily: enter Society. "We can do this. We will stick together, hold our heads high, and ignore any whispers if there are any."

"We can do this," Lilly agreed as she squeezed her hand.

Emmeline stepped inside the Westports' ballroom. Once they were announced, she linked her arm with Lilly's. It was the first significant social event she had attended in six years. Bees swarmed inside her stomach, and she was more nervous than when she'd had her come out at the Westports' ball her first Season. The night she met Aiden, Andrew, Weston—now Langford—and Caldwell. Who could have known when that night began that their lives would be intertwined forever? Her expectations had been high as a young debutante. She still had high expectations tonight ten years later.

Tonight, her future happiness and her heart were at stake. Her new purpose was to convince Andrew, the previous Earl of Quincy, now the Duke of Blackstone, that he still loved her. It would not be an easy feat after the events of the last time they saw each other and the things he had hinted at.

That night and his words were seared into her brain. She relived his words over and over again until she had begun to believe that she was perhaps responsible for her husband's death.

"Where did your mother go?" Lilly asked.

"To sit with the older ladies and watch us young folks dance and socialize. Let us take a turn around the room," Emmeline said. She guided Lilly and they joined a line of people promenading around the outer circumference of the ballroom. While they strolled, Emmeline reminded Lilly about the rules and etiquette required at a ball and about rogues.

"What about the rogues?" Lilly said in a panic.

"If I see any rogues heading your way, I'll warn you." Emmeline patted her hand. "You'll be fine." Her steps faltered, forcing Lilly to stop. Emmeline recovered quickly and they continued.

"What is it?" Lilly asked.

"Quincy . . . Blackstone. Dressed in navy. Staring daggers at me."

"Who is the man with him with the dark wavy hair and dressed in charcoal and black?"

Emmeline led them off to the side of the room. "Do you need spectacles?"

Lilly giggled. "No. I see perfectly. Why?"

"That, my dear Lilly, is Langford."

"Henry's nephew? The new earl? That's impossible. I met him. Surely I would remember what he looked like."

"Don't panic, but here they come." Emmeline squeezed her hand, causing Lilly to wince.

"Please let go of me," Lilly squeaked out.

"Oh, sorry. I didn't realize."

"Mrs. Fitzpatrick." Blackstone's gaze—intense and uncomfortable—never left her face. Emmeline didn't offer her hand, but he reached out and took it nonetheless and bowed most gallantly. She had the feeling he was mocking her.

He dropped her hand, and Emmeline curtsied, her eyes downcast. "Your Grace." As she stood, she looked at him, trying to decipher his mood while she drank in the sight of him. When she had seen him last, he'd looked dreadful and on death's door. He had been unhealthy and angry at his father and her. The man standing before her now was the epitome of health. His hair was lighter than she remembered, and his skin was tanned, no doubt from his time at sea. His green eyes were guarded but clear. He stood taller than most men and filled out his jacket well. From what she could tell, he'd put on weight and muscle. He'd been gaunt before he left London.

She presented Blackstone to Lilly and Blackstone re-introduced her to Langford. It was all quite awkward. Shortly later, after they made small talk, she found herself alone with Blackstone as Lilly and Langford danced. "I'm sorry about your father."

"Thank you."

"I heard you invested in Mayfair Imports and Exports, and the business is thriving."

"Yes. My father throwing me out was the best thing that ever happened to me."

"Yes, well," she said, fiddling with her fan as her nerves got the best of her. "I'm happy for you."

Leaning close, he whispered, "Are you?"

Why was he goading her? In the span of ten minutes, he had glowered, smirked, and sneered at her. Never mind what his eyes conveyed: a confusing combination of dislike, hunger, and indifference. How was she to know what he really felt? She didn't have the chance to answer his question as Lilly returned to her side, and Langford hurried away, looking angry.

"Why did he run off?" Blackstone asked with a knowing smirk. He bowed. "If you'll excuse me, ladies. I should seek out my friend." Emmeline's eyes followed him until he ducked through the glass doors to the veranda.

"Tell me what happened," Emmeline said.

It transpired that Langford had asked Lilly why Henry had married her, and Lilly had intimated that it had to do with his desire to have a more suitable heir. Emmeline laughed at that.

"What a little devil. I didn't realize you could lie so easily."

Emmeline and Lilly strolled arm and arm out of the ballroom

making their way to the drawing room in search of refreshments. After partaking, Lilly danced with the Duke of Westport. Emmeline did not have time to warn her about his lechery, and she felt terrible for Lilly as she watched him leer down the front of her gown and drool.

"May I join you?"

Instant awareness of Blackstone's deep, smooth voice wrapped around her, making her overly warm. "By all means."

"You and the countess seem quite close."

"It has been nice having her stay with me. I haven't had a close friend since Catherine and I were young."

"How is the Viscountess of Appleton?"

"She is well. Busy with her five children, three sons and two daughters, and living at their country estate. We correspond, but I haven't seen her in several years." A sadness fell over Emmeline as she missed her onetime closest friend. Thankfully, she had Lilly now. And to be honest, she and Lilly were closer than she and Catherine ever had been. Not to belittle the friendship she and Catherine had shared, it was just that it was different with Lilly. They had been living together for nine months and doing everything together. And they understood each other on a deeper level as only widows could.

Blackstone chuckled, "Appleton has his heir and then some."

"Now that you have inherited the dukedom, are you looking for a wife to settle down and produce heirs with?" Heat kissed her cheeks, and she wished she could take back her words. She had been so reserved the past six years. What possessed her to speak her mind now? But deep down, she wanted to know if he was looking for a wife and if she could be that person. Or, her heart constricted, did he have his future duchess already picked out?

Coughing into his hand, Blackstone muttered, "Warn a man before you ask something so personal. As for your answer, eventually. But right now, I'm getting acclimated to my new role and all it entails. Marriage can wait."

Based on his answer, she didn't know whether to be happy or

sad. Perhaps trying to get Blackstone to fall in love with her was futile. There were too many layers to break through. Anger. Blame. Forgiveness.

"Don't look now, but here comes Lady Langford. She looks upset."

"Can we leave now?" Lilly asked, her face red and her body trembling.

"Yes. We need to get my mother."

The carriage ride home was silent. Emmeline worried about Lilly, who looked like she could cast up her accounts at any moment. She stayed quiet, knowing Lilly would share in her own time. In the meantime, all she could do was be there for her.

Once they arrived home, the three ladies ascended the stairs to their chambers. After Emmeline was dressed for bed, she found she couldn't sleep and went to Lilly's room. She knocked on the door and whispered, "Lilly. Are you awake?"

"Yes."

"I'm glad," she said as she entered the room and crawled onto the bed. They talked for an hour about the Westports' ball before they were both yawning and Emmeline left. She climbed beneath the coverlet and closed her eyes, emotionally and physically exhausted, but that didn't stop Blackstone's face from appearing.

It had been two weeks since Emmeline's first ball where she had met Aiden and Andrew. Her heart fluttered for each. She'd experienced her first kiss with Aiden, while Andrew was more reserved. Or perhaps afraid to compromise her and cause a scandal. She dreamed of both men, which confused her. Her heart was fickle, and she wanted both of them. Her mind and body were just as bad. Experiencing desire was something new. Several times, she touched herself, wishing it were Aiden's or Andrew's hands on her body.

Her wanton behavior shocked and embarrassed her. Why did she have all these feelings and desires for both of them? Why couldn't she love one? Because no matter what happened, she could only marry one. Her heart cracked down the middle, protesting her thoughts. If only she could get her heart to choose. But it refused, and she knew whatever the future held, she would have to live with a broken heart and love with only half of it.

ANDREW RODE HIS gelding, Storm. He had sold Merlin after Aiden's accident—the poor beast reminded him too much of that tragic day. Storm had been birthed during a terrible thunderstorm, hence the name. Beside him was Langford as they made their way to Emmeline's townhouse to pay a visit during proper calling hours. Emmeline should have received a hothouse bouquet from him that morning, and he wondered what she thought of it. The flower choice was difficult for him, but he chose white roses in the end.

When it came to Emmeline, his feelings ran the gamut. And until he understood them for what they were, he couldn't move forward with his life. He could not pursue another lady if his long-ago love for Emmeline still existed. It wouldn't be fair to either of them. Especially after seeing the way she'd looked at him last night. Several times, he'd glimpsed love, desire, and vulnerability in her beautiful blue eyes. Eyes he could get lost in, and he had many times in the past.

When he'd accused her all those years ago of possibly being the reason Aiden was unhappy and inebriated, he hadn't meant it. *He* was the sole reason Aiden was dead. He'd always known that. The guilt of it had nearly ruined his life, but fortunately, he had eventually channeled it into positive work with Weston and Caldwell, and it had paid off. The three of them had amassed a pile of wealth. Though there were still times he was haunted by the accident and slipped up in drinking too much. However, he never gambled anymore and never would again.

One of these days, he would have to admit to Emmeline that he had killed Aiden. Every muscle in his body tensed at the thought. What if she hated him after she found out the truth? Could he risk it? His conscience demanded that he tell her. It was only a matter of when.

"Why so serious all of a sudden?" Langford asked as they arrived at the mews behind Emmeline's townhouse and handed off the reins to a stable hand.

Andrew dismounted and handed over Storm's reins. "No reason."

Laughter coming from Langford surprised him. "I know you better than you think. Emmeline's getting to you."

"True, I'll admit it. Seeing her again resurrected feelings I'd buried and can no longer ignore now that I'm back in London to stay." He looked at Langford. "Why have you come? To grovel at Lady Langford's feet after nearly accosting her?"

Langford huffed, "Christ, you make it sound terrible. "I tried to kiss her last night, nothing more. But yes, I sent Lilly flowers to apologize for my behavior."

"I wish you well." He also wished himself well.

After they were announced, Andrew sat in a chair directly opposite Emmeline. Without being obvious, he drank in her beauty. The pink of her gown highlighted her rosy cheekbones. Her dark hair was half up and half down, and how he wished he could run his fingers through the silky tresses as he'd done once before. Her pink lips were full and made for kissing—something he always regretted never doing. He'd never tasted her lips, tangled with her tongue, or felt the soft skin of her throat with his lips.

Thankfully, he held his hat in his hands on his lap. Otherwise, she would have a direct view of his erection. Tight riding breeches hid nothing.

Another gentleman was announced, the Marquess of Hollingsworth, and Andrew glared at him. He was an affable fellow, but Andrew was afraid he was here for Emmeline. How did one ask without appearing rude or jealous?

By the time they said farewell and left, Andrew felt worse than when he had arrived. The three men walked to the mews together in silence. Andrew and Langford rode to Hyde Park only to have Hollingsworth show up there as well.

"May I join you?" Hollingsworth asked.

"Only if you tell us which lady you are interested in," Langford said, echoing the sentiment Andrew felt, though he suspected his friend's mind was more on Lady Langford.

Hollingsworth had the nerve to chuckle, "Perhaps I was merely paying a social call with no ulterior motive."

"If we weren't in public . . ." Andrew threatened.

"If you must know, I called upon the countess. And please tell me you both are not vying for Mrs. Fitzpatrick's favors. We don't need history repeating itself."

"No." Andrew said, and his entire body relaxed. At least if he messed this up, he had no competition he knew of. Yet.

THE FOLLOWING MONTH had its ups and downs. There was little time to get Emmeline alone to request to court her properly. The countess kept close by her side at all times. That and Andrew didn't really push the issue. He was stalling, which was a terrible trait he had recently acquired.

Then one night when Langford had had business in St. Giles, he'd been run over and pinned beneath a carriage wheel, and it was the countess and Emmeline who had come to his rescue. Both Emmeline and Lilly belonged to the Ladies' Society of Mayfair, a charity that supplied the citizens of St. Giles and other surrounding areas with medicine, clothing, and food.

By chance they were in St. Giles making a delivery when they came upon the accident. Andrew was thankful they were there. Otherwise, Langford might have died. He recovered at Emmeline's townhouse for several weeks, and the friends spent time watching over him.

During the time Langford convalesced, Lilly was also being courted by Viscount Redford, and Andrew invited Emmeline,

Viscount Redford, and Lilly to Vauxhall Pleasure Gardens for a night of dancing. Andrew had the whole night planned. Stalling be damned, he would dance with Emmeline, and hopefully sneak off with her to the private gardens to steal a kiss or two.

The first part went to plan—they did dance and they did go into the private gardens. Andrew had even pulled Emmeline into his arms. But just as he leaned down to kiss her, they were interrupted. They had still never shared a kiss, and he hoped to remedy that soon.

To be fair, the interruption had been justified. Redford had accosted Lilly in the gardens and Langford had been forced to come her rescue. Not long after, Redford kidnapped Lilly, and tried to force her to marry him. It turned out he wanted her money. But Langford had saved her again and proposed to her. Now, they were married.

And now, not long after Langford's and Lilly's nuptials, Andrew found himself invited, along with Caldwell, to a house party in Bath at the Marquess and Marchioness of Waterford's country manor and accepted the invitation. Though he had only done so as he knew Emmeline meant to attend with her mother.

It was time to be bold and hopefully win Emmeline over.

As their carriage pulled up the drive of the Marquess and Marchioness of Waterford's country manor right outside of Bath, Emmeline said, "I can't wait to see Catherine. I was shocked when I received her letter stating she and the viscount would attend."

"I'm not, since she and the marchioness are first cousins," her mother said.

"That is true. I have a feeling Catherine asked Claire to include me knowing I've re-entered Society. Either that or they were short one single lady. A good party must have equal numbers of single gentlemen and ladies. Married couples are already a pair."

"Oh, my dear, you were invited because they want you to attend. You three had your first Season together."

Her heart hurt. "Yes. Now they are married, and each has a nursery full of children while I'm a childless widow. Claire probably just took pity on me."

Mother patted her hand. "Since when have you ever felt sorry for yourself? You stand up tall and hold your head high. And I know for a fact that Blackstone is attending."

Her heart went from hurting to skipping. "No doubt Catherine's doing."

Her mother giggled. "No doubt. Even from a great distance, your childhood friend is looking out for you."

The door opened, and the stairs lowered. "Here, let me." The gentleman they had just spoken of leaned into the carriage with his hand out. "Baroness."

Mother took his hand. "Thank you, Your Grace."

He smiled. "The pleasure is all mine."

Once her mother exited, Blackstone leaned back in, his hand out again. "Mrs. Fitzpatrick." The glint in his eyes took her breath away.

"Blackstone." When their hands touched, the connection they'd had ten years ago returned, and she had to fight back her tears of joy.

Andrew—she tried to think of him as Blackstone, but it wasn't easy—escorted them inside the manor, and the marquess and marchioness greeted them. Claire looked lovely, if a little tired, but she greeted Emmeline warmly.

"Mrs. Fitzpatrick, may I call you Emmeline?"

"Yes, please do."

She pulled Emmeline into a hug. "Call me Claire like you used to. It is so good to see you after all this time."

Emmeline hugged her back. "It is wonderful to see you. Thank you for inviting me and my mother."

"Catherine just arrived and is getting settled. I know she is beyond excited to see you."

"As am I." And she was. Seeing Claire now brought back all the memories of spending time together as children and during their first Season. It was a time worth remembering.

"Jacobson." Claire waved over a footman. "Will you escort Mrs. Fitzpatrick and Baroness Connolly to their rooms?"

"Yes, my lady."

Before Emmeline followed the footman up the staircase, she glanced over her shoulder at Andrew as he greeted their hostess. *Breathe.* Just because Andrew was here didn't mean he was here for her. Jacobson stopped at the first door on the right, three floors up. "Baroness, this is your room. Your things will be up shortly."

Mother turned to her and kissed her cheek. "I will see you soon. Please relax and enjoy yourself, and let nature take its course with Andrew. You two belong together. Any fool can see that."

Was her mother calling her and Andrew fools?

"This is your room, Mrs. Fitzpatrick," Jacobson said as he opened another door for her to enter.

"Thank you." Emmeline took in the lovely room, decorated in pale yellow and cream with subtle touches of blue. There was a large mahogany four-poster bed, a dressing table, a wardrobe, and a stone fireplace. Off to the side was a screen for privacy. It was a modest-sized room, and Emmeline knew she would be comfortable here for the next two weeks. Her hand flew to her stomach. Two whole weeks in the company of Andrew. If she couldn't get a marriage proposal during that time, she would have to give up on him and look elsewhere for a husband, even if the only husband she wanted was Andrew. She already knew she wanted children, so if she couldn't have Andrew, she would have to marry someone to give her those children even though it would break her heart for it to be anyone else.

She needed to come up with a plan. Perhaps Claire and Catherine could help her. They had married young, just as she had. But how had they gotten their husbands to propose? People got betrothed all the time. How hard could it be?

It's hard to know if Emmeline's five years of waiting—after her year of mourning—proved anything about the difficulty or ease of finding a husband. Once her mourning was over, she hadn't exactly entered Society looking for a husband, or much at all. Of course, during most of the six years since Aiden's death, Andrew had been in a dark place and then out of the country. She hadn't truly had the heart to seek a husband then since what remained of her battered heart belonged to Andrew, and wasn't transferable. But the time had come. Andrew was back and either they would have their chance or they wouldn't, but she couldn't wait any longer for the family she hoped to have.

Just then, Amanda entered the room with her trunks. "Nothing is planned until this afternoon," Amanda said as she unpacked her things and smoothed out all the dresses and ball gowns before hanging them in the wardrobe. "Would you care to rest?"

Now that Amanda mentioned resting, Emmeline realized she was tired after the long three-day journey. "I would like that." Stripped down to her chemise, she climbed beneath the counterpane and rested her head on a soft, fluffy pillow. It wasn't long before sleep descended.

"Emmeline, my love," Andrew said one afternoon in her parents' London townhouse gardens. "I have a question to ask." His face was flush, and sweat beaded his upper lip. It was warm in the gardens, but she believed the sweat was from nerves. "Will you marry me?"

Her heart stopped beating right then and there. She had dreamed of hearing those words from him, and nothing would make her happier. Except she also loved Aiden. She had thinking and soul-searching to do before she could reply. In her eyes, they were both perfect for her. She loved them both. As far as her heart was concerned, she loved them equally. Though her brain may be another matter. She'd already listed their good and bad qualities, hoping that would help her if it came to that.

Granted, only Andrew had proposed. However, she knew Aiden would propose, too, once he caught wind of this. She had never intended for two gentlemen to fall in love with her. Nor had she planned to fall in love with both of them. It broke her heart to know one of them would be hurt, that by her actions, one of them would be rejected. She would do anything not to hurt either of them.

Tears pooled in her eyes, and she dabbed them away. She couldn't decide now, no matter how it might hurt Andrew. Forcing herself to look him in the eye, she gasped at the love shining from those soft green orbs with hope and worry. It was all there for her to witness. If only she could put him out of his misery and whisper yes. "How I've dreamed of hearing you ask those words." She took his hands in hers and squeezed them. "Can I have some time to make my decision?"

Disappointment flashed in his eyes and on his features before he masked them. "Take all the time you need." He brought both her hands to his mouth and kissed each of them. "Please remember that I love you and have loved you since the moment I laid eyes on you. Your expressive blue eyes, unguarded features, grace, and beauty spoke to my soul. There will never be another for me. You own me. All of me."

Before she could respond, Andrew bowed gracefully and walked away, his shoulders back, and his head held high. The sadness and uncertainty she'd glimpsed in his eyes told her it took a strong will to walk away from her.

If only she could have said yes to ease his burden. When she'd prepared for her first Season, the most important thing on her mind was not having an attack of nerves from the crush of people attending all the events. She hadn't wanted to embarrass herself by covering her ears and humming to drown out the voices of hundreds of people, all crowding together. She was excited to try to find a husband, someone to love and be loved by, but she hadn't worried overly much about that. Now she worried about the man she would leave behind.

The next afternoon, Aiden called upon her, seemingly determined to have a private word with her without her mother chaperoning.

"May I escort Miss Emmeline for a stroll through the gardens?" Aiden asked her mother, looking rather shy.

"You may."

For the second day in a row, Emmeline sat on the same bench in the same spot in the formal gardens, glancing into the eyes of a man she loved.

"Emmeline, my love. Will you do me the honor of marrying me?" Aiden grinned, and his brown eyes softened. "I know I am not the first to ask for your hand. I only ask that you consider my offer." He dropped to his knees and took her hands in his. She swallowed the lump in her throat as tears pooled in her eyes. "I love you more than life itself. I don't possess a title, nor will I ever, but I can make you happy and care for you. Neither you, nor the children we have, will want for anything. I don't expect an answer now, but please say yes when you do."

And as she had yesterday, she found herself alone in the garden, crying tears of love, joy, and heartbreak.

CHAPTER SIX

A KNOCK ON the door and Amanda's voice calling out startled her from her dream. "Time to get ready for afternoon tea."

The dream made Emmeline want nothing but to stay in bed and ease the heaviness of her heart. Instead, she got out of bed, wiped tears from her eyes, and forced her melancholy aside. She refused to wallow in sadness about her past and her choices and instead enjoy her time away from London—her time with Catherine, Claire, and, more importantly, Andrew.

Stopping by her mother's room, Emmeline was surprised to find her mother had gone down to tea already. Perhaps she was late. She picked up her skirts and hurried down two flights of stairs, following the voices traveling down the hallway to a large green drawing room filled with twenty or so people. Her eyes found her mother sitting on a dark green settee with two older ladies she recognized as Claire's and Catherine's mothers.

She was glad her mother had ladies her age to spend time with. Emmeline made her way over to Claire and Catherine, standing near the open double doors leading to vibrantly colorful and fragrant gardens.

"Claire, Catherine," Emmeline said with a smile. "I'm so looking forward to spending time with you both."

"As am I," Claire said.

Catherine hugged her close. "It is so good to see you. I've

missed you terribly. You need to tell me everything that has happened in your life and in London." She leaned close to her ear and whispered, "The Duke of Blackstone is still as handsome as ever. Is there a chance?"

When Catherine stepped back, she held her hands and looked at Emmeline with sadness and hope. "Don't look now, but he's looking at you with hungry eyes."

She tugged her hands from Catherine's and covered her mouth before laughing aloud. The word *hungry* and how she'd said it tickled Emmeline. "Warn me before you say something inappropriate," she whispered close to Catherine's ear. "I forgot you have a habit of saying shocking things. I'm glad to see you haven't changed."

She smiled and patted her stomach. "Having five babies has made me fat, but otherwise, I'm the same. And as Charles says, it just means there is more of me to love."

"Please don't call yourself fat," Claire admonished. "'Pleasingly plump' is much better."

Once again, Emmeline had to cover her mouth, only this time her eyes found Andrew as he cocked one brow and grinned, no doubt wondering what had amused her. "If you will excuse me, I would like to see the gardens and take in the fresh air." As she stepped outside, she glanced over her shoulder and smiled at Andrew, hoping he would take the hint and follow her into the gardens. It was time she became brazen and took what she wanted. If she waited for him to make a move, years could go by.

Was she brave enough to seduce him? Invite him into her bed? Even if they never married, she wanted to experience lovemaking with him. It would give her memories to cherish for years to come if she married someone else she could never love. The remembrances of Andrew's lovemaking could sustain her and give her recollections to draw on and make the marriage act with her husband bearable.

Emmeline came upon a white gazebo at the end of a quiet pathway. No one else was around, so she climbed the two steps and walked inside, taking in her surroundings. Her heart beat a fast staccato as she knew Andrew was close. His boots crunched on the granite stone, giving him away. Her breath suspended inside her lungs as she waited for him to acknowledge her presence.

"Are you leading me astray?"

At the sound of his amused, deep voice, gooseflesh traveled up her arms, and her entire body tingled. "Do you feel as though I'm leading you astray?" Teasing with Andrew was something new. He'd always tended to be a little reserved and guarded with her, even when they had courted all those years ago. Perhaps it had been because of Aiden.

"Yes. I believe it to be true." He looked around at the scenery. "This is a beautiful place. Peaceful and private." He turned and looked questioningly at her. "I haven't seen you since Langford and Lilly's wedding. Have you been avoiding me because I almost kissed you that night at Vauxhall Gardens?"

His words surprised her. "No." Her cheeks warmed. "I wanted you to kiss me. We would have if not for Redford."

He came up behind her, close enough that she felt his warm breath against her exposed neck. Warm hands slid up and down her arms as he pulled her back against his hard body.

"Yes. We would have. And I wouldn't be wondering what you taste like now because I would already know," he whispered into her ear.

His hands still lightly caressing her arms, her stomach tightened, and heat spread between her legs. She had wanted to kiss him ten years ago before she'd married Aiden. And once she was out of mourning, she'd dreamed of kissing him. Those dreams and desires had her yearning for him. Had he brought up that near-kiss because he planned to remedy the situation? Dare she hope?

"Yes," she sighed, finding it difficult to breathe or think.

"Let's hope this time we aren't interrupted." He spun her around, his green eyes dark with desire as he stared so intently at her that she felt it inside her soul. His hands cupped her face, and he lowered his mouth to hers. She sighed and relaxed into him, finally knowing what his lips felt like upon hers. He took it slow for a moment, then wrapped his strong arms around her back, pulled her tight against his body so they touched everywhere, and he devoured her mouth.

A moan escaped her lips, her arms circled his neck, and she rubbed her breasts against his chest to ease their sensitivity and discomfort as arousal lit up her body.

He licked inside her mouth, his tongue tasting her. Her tongue joined his, and they swirled around and around languidly, teasing and withdrawing as though they had all time in the world. Then the kiss turned raw, demanding, and possessive. Emmeline had never experienced anything like it. As he possessed her mouth, her body wanted to crawl inside him and become one with him. Her hips pressed forward, seeking and making contact with the large bulge in his breeches, causing him to break the kiss, bury his face in the curve of her neck, and moan.

"You taste so good. I have waited for what seems like a life-time to kiss you. To be able to hold you in my arms," he whispered as he nipped her neck. "I want to lick every inch of your body until you scream out my name."

"Oh, God," she sighed as he placed featherlight kisses down her neck and slid one leg between her thighs, rubbing her core. "Andrew," she moaned. Unabashedly, she rubbed against his thigh, her body coiling up tight as she sought relief. One of his hands massaged her bottom while the other tugged down the front of her dress, his lips attaching to one nipple, biting down. Her knees trembled and threatened to buckle, and still, she clung to him as her orgasm came out of thin air and slammed into her. She buried her face in his chest to stifle her cries of pleasure as wave after wave rolled over her until her knees did give way, and Andrew held her up as he righted the front of her dress.

When Emmeline caught her breath and could stand alone, she cupped Andrew's face and kissed him deeply, trying to convey her feelings for him. "I wasn't expecting that. Thank you," she said as she nuzzled his neck.

"Thank *you*. I have dreamed of holding you in my arms for as long as I can remember. The other was a bonus."

"Blackstone," Caldwell's low voice came from nearby. "People are coming."

"Smooth out your skirts and your hair. We are about to be descended upon." He kissed her quickly. "I'm so glad I thought to have Caldwell stand guard," Andrew said softly as he walked to the other side of the gazebo, straightening his jacket and cravat and adjusting his breeches. Caldwell, his feet landing with a thud, joined them in the structure just before several people appeared on the walkway.

"Thank you," she heard Andrew whisper to Caldwell.

"You can return the favor for me sometime."

Laughter rang out. "I've been watching your arse for years, keeping you from the parson's noose."

"So very true," agreed Caldwell with a smile.

"Your Grace, Emmeline. Mr. Caldwell. What a lovely surprise to come upon you," Claire said with a smile, her arm linked with her husband's. Catherine and her husband followed close behind.

"Your gardens are lovely, and this gazebo belongs in a fairytale," Emmeline said. "I recently commissioned a small one for my garden and look forward to it being finished."

"My dear husband built it for me for a wedding present," Claire said, glancing lovingly at the marquess.

This caused Emmeline to experience a twinge of sadness and envy. She wanted to be able to look at Andrew and claim him in front of everyone. Let the world know she loved him without having to keep her emotions hidden. "Did he build it himself?" She would be surprised if he had. But then again, she did not know the marquess all that well.

Claire and her husband joined them in the gazebo. "He did," she replied, her face beaming with pride and love.

"Really?" Andrew said as he inspected the craftsmanship. "I'm impressed. You are talented, Lord Waterford. Have you built anything else?"

Andrew and Caldwell exited the structure and went outside to study how it was built.

"Yes," the marquess answered. "I built the orangery, although with help since that was a much larger project. I must get back to our guests, but perhaps I could give you a tour tomorrow?"

"Most definitely," Andrew said.

The others drifted off, and once Emmeline and Andrew found themselves alone again, they walked arm and arm leisurely back toward the manor. They stopped at all the roses and beautiful flowers to smell and admire the blossoms. "The gardeners must spend all day keeping these gardens so pristine. I don't think I've ever seen more beautiful ones."

"Perhaps someday I can show you Blackstone Hall," Andrew said as he waved his arm. "The gardens there rival these. However, I need to commission someone to build me a gazebo. My father always talked about building one but never did. I need to remedy that." He paused, and when he continued, his voice became deep and alluring, "Can you imagine what else we can do at my gazebo without anyone interrupting?"

Her feet barely touched the walkway as her heart pounded excitedly at the thought of visiting Blackstone Hall someday and what could happen in his private gazebo. She had to remind herself that Andrew had inherited his father's title and estates. Some days, she still thought of him as the Earl of Quincy and not the Duke of Blackstone. He was a duke and needed to marry and produce heirs. Did she dare hope that he wanted her to be that person? Or was he merely toying with her before he found someone younger? The flames licking inside her body were extinguished in a sudden torrential rain as she lost sight of her determination to get him to fall in love with her.

ANDREW ESCORTED EMMELINE through the gardens and back to the drawing room, and his body vibrated with awareness. Truthfully, it hadn't stopped since the moment he pulled her into his arms and kissed her. The memory of her soft, pliant lips and the feel of her tongue inside his mouth, teasing with his, had him nearly groaning out loud. He hadn't lied when he said he'd dreamed of kissing her forever, because it was true. And finally, thank Christ, it had happened in such a magical place. He didn't usually have flights of fancy. However, he had felt transported to a place where only they existed in a garden full of fairies. He chuckled at his thoughts as he tightened his hold on her. He never wanted to let her go.

His time with Emmeline in the gazebo would visit his dreams tonight. When he rubbed his leg against her womanhood, her eyes had glassed over while little pants and moans had escaped her delicious lips as she climaxed. He'd fought hard not to embarrass himself and come in his breeches. She had been a true vision. Never had he seen her look more vibrant and beautiful. He would spend every minute of every day giving her pleasure if he could.

His heart constricted. He had to tell Emmeline the truth of Aiden's death. But he would push it off as long as possible, spend as much time with her as he could. Because once she knew what had really happened, she would despise him, and he wouldn't blame her. So, for the time being, he would ignore the pain in his heart and his conscience and spend these two weeks with her, knowing it may be all the time they had.

"You are quiet," Emmeline's soft voice interrupted his thoughts. "Is something bothering you? Do you regret . . .?"

"No. Never will I ever regret the time I spend with you." Bloody hell, he needed to rein in his emotions. "I hope we can spend every moment of this house party together."

She gazed up at him, her face alight and happy. "So do I."

They were back in the drawing room, which had thinned out. The other guests were off on their own since there were no scheduled events until dinner and dancing. But Andrew knew the billiards room was available to guests. "Would you care for a game of billiards?" He remembered from long ago that she played. He hoped she still did.

"I haven't played in so long," she said with a smile. "But, yes, I would love to."

Leading the way to the game room, which Andrew had stumbled upon by accident earlier, he had to fight to keep his hands to himself. Since he'd touched her earlier and got a feel for her soft skin, he craved her even more. When they arrived, he found the Marquess of Hollingsworth and Caldwell playing.

"Caldwell," he said with a smirk, "it didn't take you long, after I mentioned a billiards room, for you to take over the table."

Caldwell's laughter spread throughout the room, "It was such a wonderful idea. I couldn't let the suggestion pass."

"I didn't see you earlier, Hollingsworth. I didn't know you were attending." Andrew led Emmeline to a comfortable chair and took the one beside her for himself.

"I'm still in the market for a wife, thanks to Langford," Hollingsworth said. "I was informed there would be several young ladies attending who hoped to make advantageous matches."

"And you consider yourself one?"

"Hilarious, Blackstone."

"What about Lady Priscilla? I thought your banns would be posted by now," Andrew said.

"Yes, well." Hollingsworth tugged on his cravat. "It appears she couldn't escape me fast enough. She ran off and married a naval officer with whom she had secretly exchanged letters. He is the cousin of an acquaintance of hers." He took a shot and missed. "My self-esteem has become non-existent as of late."

Andrew couldn't help himself teasing. "Perhaps you will find a lady who will overlook your damaged person and advanced age."

Hollingsworth missed another shot. "If you don't shut up, I will lose this game. And since when is thirty-five old?"

Flinging out his arm, Andrew said, "Just hurry up and finish the game. Mrs. Fitzpatrick and I would like to play."

"Please take your time," Emmeline interjected. "There are several hours yet until dinner and dancing."

Thirty minutes later their game ended with Caldwell winning. Hollingsworth was a terrible billiards player.

Andrew stood and held out his hand to Emmeline. "The table is ours."

Hollingsworth and Caldwell poured themselves drinks from the sideboard. "Don't mind if we stay and watch," Hollingsworth said with a smirk as he sat in the chair vacated by Andrew, and Caldwell sat in the one Emmeline had occupied.

"Not at all. Perhaps you will learn something." He winked at Emmeline. "Emmeline used to be a fierce competitor."

Laughing, she picked up a mace. "That was a long time ago," she said as she concentrated on striking her white ball with the foot of the mace. They agreed the game would end when the first player reached twenty-one points. Emmeline focused on hitting her white ball into the red ball and sinking it into the pocket, which would give her three points.

"You missed," Andrew chuckled. "I remember a time you could make that shot with your eyes closed."

"Yes, well. I told you it's been quite a while since I played. Aiden wasn't a fan of billiards."

Andrew winced and shrugged his shoulders before he took his turn. "No. He wasn't. Which is why you and I played." He hit his white ball with the opposite end of the mace and put her white ball into the nearest pocket, earning himself two points. He tried not to appear concerned after her mention of Aiden but suspected he wasn't entirely successful.

"Nice shot," she said.

The game dragged on, but Emmeline didn't seem to mind. When they had finally finished several games—she won two and Andrew won three—they both went to their respective rooms. Dinner couldn't come soon enough.

CHAPTER SEVEN

BACK INSIDE HER room, Emmeline washed up to prepare to dress for dinner. She and Amanda decided on an elegant medium-blue ballgown embroidered with flowers and swirls in pale-blue silk thread down the skirt and across the hemline. The high-waisted bodice and scooped neckline were trimmed with tiny embroidered flowers and seed pearls. The short sleeves also had a touch of embroidery and pearls. Matching gloves and slippers completed the look.

There was a knock on the door, and the baroness entered, dressed in a navy gown and turban. Emmeline's mother's hair had grayed and thinned at a young age, so she always wore a turban, even in the privacy of their home. Lilly—now Lady Langford twice over—had once commented that she didn't know whether Mother even had hair or what color it might be, but Emmeline knew her mother's turbans helped her feel stylish and more confident.

"My dear," her mother said as she looked her over. "You look breathtaking. Blackstone will be unable to speak when he sees you. Come, we don't want to be late." She led the way to the door and paused before opening it. "Have you managed to get him alone and seduce him yet?"

Emmeline nearly choked at that. Even if she had seduced him, she would not share that tidbit with her mother! Good God, what a conversation that would be. She would, however, appease her. "We strolled through the lovely gardens and visited a gazebo the marquess built with his own hands."

Her mother looked disappointed. "Well, there is still time."

"We just arrived today. Of course, there is time." A little stab of guilt pained her insides. She did want to seduce Andrew but not to force him to marry her. Widows were allowed certain freedoms in the eyes of the *ton*, and it would not be such a scandal or ruin anyone's reputation if it somehow became known. No, she had no desire to trap him. But if he felt compelled to offer for her afterward, she would not refuse the man. She loved him, and that would never change. And if he never proposed and they only slept together, at least she would have the memory of being with him to draw from for the rest of her life.

The large drawing room was crowded with guests waiting for the dinner bell. Emmeline took a glass of ratafia from a passing servant. When she turned around to speak with her mother, she found herself alone. Her mother had a knack for disappearing in a crowd. Seeing Catherine standing with her husband, she made her way toward them instead. "Viscount, viscountess," she said as she curtsied.

Catherine took her hands in hers. "Please call me Catherine and my husband, William. In the country, we are not so formal as in London."

"Catherine, William," she said with a smile.

"My dear," William said to his wife, "I will leave you two to reminisce."

"He didn't have to leave," Emmeline said as William retreated.

Catherine smiled. "William is shy and would prefer to be off alone or with other gentlemen. He is uncomfortable around ladies. Especially when they start talking about ladies' things."

Emmeline didn't quite know what to say to that. "Are you happy? You seem very happy to me."

Catherine beamed. "Yes. William and I are very much in

love. He is not so shy with me."

"That is good. I'm happy for you," Emmeline said, then took a sip of her punch.

Catherine touched her hand. "What about you? I'm surprised you haven't married again yet. Six years is a long time."

Ignoring the knife stabbing her heart, Emmeline didn't see a reason not to tell her friend the truth. Catherine had gone through her first Season with her and all her struggles in choosing between Aiden and Andrew. "Honestly, I simply stayed home, not socializing much at all these past six years, at least until recently. Not because I couldn't move on from losing Aiden, although it was hard, but I chose to spend my time with my mother and a small circle of ladies in Mayfair doing charity work. Going out at night to balls and musicales didn't interest me for one reason and one reason only." She paused, placing her hand on her chest, hoping to slow her heart down before it beat out of her. "Andrew struggled after Aiden's death and refused to see me—for years. His father nearly disowned him, and finally, three years ago, he joined Langford and Caldwell in their business." Her eyes glanced around, and she lowered her voice for Catherine's ears only. "I loved Aiden with everything I had and never regretted one moment of our marriage. But after my year of mourning ended, I realized my love for Andrew had never disappeared, either. I didn't want to spend time dancing and conversing with other men I had no interest in, nor would I ever. I've been waiting for him to return home and come to his senses."

"I had a feeling that was why," Catherine said as she smiled sympathetically. "I must admit, if it weren't for Caldwell being with you two this afternoon, I would've sworn something intimate had happened between you and Blackstone. Both your complexions were flushed and the looks you shared . . ." She fanned her face with her hand. "Flaming hot."

Emmeline's cheeks heated. "Caldwell was our lookout," she whispered. "We did embrace and kiss." Sighing, she pursed her lips. "My first time kissing him."

"No," Catherine gasped.

"Yes." Her lips curved up into a dreamy smile, thinking back. "Words cannot adequately describe how it made me feel."

"If you don't mind my saying so," Catherine looked around and opened her fan, leaning close, blocking most of their faces, "you are not inexperienced, and it has been some time for you. You must be elated at the prospect of an affair or, hopefully, a marriage to Blackstone."

"I would prefer marriage but would settle for an affair if that's all he's capable of." Her hands trembled. "Is it shocking of me to think about an affair?"

"No, it is not. You have been widowed for a long time. And if you manage to procure a marriage proposal from Blackstone, can you imagine the screams throughout the London drawing rooms from all the mamas and their daughters looking to snare the duke?"

Unease settled in her stomach. "I don't care about Andrew being a duke. I would love him if he had no title and were penniless. But I understand he is this Season's most sought-after eligible bachelor." As the words left her lips, her eyes landed on Andrew, dressed impeccably in dark grey and looking handsome as the devil, ambling toward her and Catherine.

"Here you are," Andrew said as he grinned and lowered his head. "Mrs. Fitzpatrick, may I have the honor of escorting you into the dining room?"

Both Catherine and Emmeline giggled. "We were so engrossed in our conversation that we never heard the dinner bell," Emmeline said as she dipped her head. "Thank you. That would be lovely."

"Here comes my dashing husband," Catherine said as she took his arm. "Let us talk again soon." Her eyes moved from Emmeline to Andrew.

Andrew leaned close to Emmeline's ear. "Why do I have the feeling you two were discussing me?" The heat from his breath caused her body to tingle in the most intimate places.

She batted her lashes because she felt like a young debutante. "What an inflated sense of importance you have, Your Grace."

Chuckling, he said, "It has nothing to do with my own importance and everything to do with how you blushed when I approached. And the viscountess looked at me and then you with a knowing smile and a twinkle in her eye."

"She never could hide her emotions, but she can keep secrets."

"Come, let us join the dinner crowd." Placing her hand on Andrew's forearm, she felt heat travel up her arm and curl around her heart. As they stood at the long rectangular wooden table, Andrew paused, his brows raised. "Will you look here? We are seated next to one another." He winked. "I wonder how that happened?"

As if she didn't know. Either Claire took it upon herself to have foresight, or Andrew had asked her to put them side by side. Either way, she would not question it and would enjoy her time with him. As he helped her sit, she looked around the table and witnessed several Marriage Mart Mamas glaring at her and several of their daughters pouting. Poor Andrew must hate all the attention he had received since his return to London. Her heart sank. Or perhaps not.

No. She knew him well enough to know that he hated the attention. He always had for as long as she'd known him—ten years, to be sure.

"My sense of importance has just deflated," Andrew said softly with an exaggerated frown. "What has caught your attention besides me?"

She tried very hard not to laugh, and she succeeded. "Mrs. Smythe and the Countess of Chelsea glaring daggers at me. Not to mention their daughters' sulking." She lowered her voice to barely a whisper. "The daughters are lovely and should make advantageous matches, but unfortunately, their mamas scare off potential suitors."

"That can be an issue." He draped his napkin across his lap as the first course arrived—fish stew. "I don't believe their mamas will be too much of a detriment, as I witnessed several young bucks following them around after I first arrived." He looked at her and waggled his brows. "Love is in Bath."

His large hand curled around her thigh under the table, and she bit her lip to keep from moaning as her body responded with instant desire. It was also good that she hadn't taken a spoonful of stew yet, because she would have spewed it across the table at the Countess of Chelsea. Could he perhaps have been referring to them when he said, "Love is in Bath?"

Several courses came and went, and at every opportunity, his hand slid beneath the table, stroking her thigh. The same need for his touch traveled through her entire body each time. When desserts of fruit, nuts, custards, and confections came to the table, Emmeline was unable to eat another bite unless she loosened her stays and doused her body with cold water. "Do you suppose the gentlemen are going to have port and cigars? Or are we going straight to the ballroom for dancing?"

"I'm hoping for port and cigars. I can't possibly be expected to dance after everything I ate."

"Me too. A little time in the drawing room to digest would be nice."

"Since when do ladies talk about their digestion?" he said with a grin.

She wanted to smack him. "Since this lady felt like it. Do not look, but Caldwell is seated next to Lady Clarice Chesterfield. Remember the scandal that ensued the summer Aiden died?" She watched Andrew closely when she mentioned Aiden, otherwise she would have missed his entire body tightening up muscle by muscle. Until today, she hadn't notice how tense he got when Aiden's name was spoken. It pained her to know he was still dealing with Aiden's death.

"No, I don't."

"Her parents, the Earl and Countess of Portsmouth, made

several bad investments and were in dire straits. They used poor Lady Clarice. They dangled her beauty, kindness, and charm in front of all the wealthy gentlemen seeking brides during her first Season." She softened her voice. "It was as though they sold her to the highest bidder. Every rich aristocrat, older, widowed, single and looking for a young bride to raise his children, or looking for an heir, lined up to pay homage to her parents. Also, gentlemen who'd had trouble finding a bride for whatever reason also came to London. They had their pick of a dozen suitors. But the earl and countess were smart, and they chose the oldest and richest. Instead of a dowry paid to the groom, I heard the groom paid a dowry to the bride's parents and to the bride as well, so when he died, she would be rich in her own right. Which I know happens all the time, but they announced it openly in the *Daily Times*."

"Christ." Andrew coughed into his hand. "Warn me before you say something like that."

"I will next time. Anyway, her parents sold . . . procured a wealthy and ancient husband for her. The Marquess of Chesterfield."

"Ah, yes. I do remember now."

"He died two years ago. No children. A distant nephew inherited the title and estate. I heard that Clarice receives two thousand pounds annually until she remarries."

"I never took you for a gossip."

"I'm offended. All of this could be read in the papers. What else was I to do when holed up inside my townhouse for years but keep up with the current affairs of the *ton*?"

Shaking his head, he said, "I don't know what to do with this information, and why were we discussing Lady Chesterfield anyway?"

"Well, it's only that Caldwell looks smitten with her. Hasn't been able to keep his eyes off her face or . . ." Emmeline glanced pointedly down the front of her dress.

"I see. Or rather, don't want to see. But Caldwell is seeking company for tonight and nothing more."

"How scandalous," she whispered, wishing Andrew would visit her room tonight seeking her company. Moments later, the ladies retired to the drawing room and the gentlemen remained to enjoy their port and cigars.

ANDREW WENT TO Emmeline in the drawing room once the men rejoined the ladies, then escorted her into the small ballroom. When the dancing began in the ballroom with thirty people in attendance—not including the older guests, such as her mother and other chaperones—Emmeline and Andrew stood in a slightly crowded corner. Tapping her feet to the music, she hoped Andrew would ask her to dance, though from experience, she knew he wasn't much of a dancer. Not that he couldn't dance, but she remembered he preferred not to take to the dance floor. Tonight, she sincerely hoped he would indulge her and dance. Just then, the orchestra began the opening chords of a waltz. She held her breath, hoping . . .

"Would you care to dance?"

Her pulse jumped. Finally, she would waltz with him. "Yes."

They joined the other couples on the polished wooden floor. Andrew placed his large hand on the center of her back while his other hand held hers. The heat from the hand on her back burned through her clothing. Her hand not holding his rested on his upper arm, near his shoulder. His solid muscles rippled beneath her hand as they moved across the dance floor to the lively tune. Talking wasn't always easy during a waltz as they twirled around the room, but they made the best of it and succeeded quite nicely.

"May I ask a question?" she said, suddenly feeling shy in his arms.

"Anything within reason," he replied with a wink.

"You're a good dancer. Light on your feet. So why don't you

like to dance?"

"Ah, a mighty fine question. It is something I've never been comfortable with. I don't mind a waltz, but the country reels and intricate line dances don't interest me. I prefer to sit them out."

"I understand. Many dislike them. I love all dances, but the waltz, with the right partner, can be beautiful."

He grinned and winked at her again. "Am I the right partner?"

In every way that matters. She swallowed down the words she wanted to say. "For right now, you are," she teased, and she enjoyed the sound of his quiet laughter.

"I deserved that."

"Tell me how it feels to be back in London. How are your mother and sisters coping with the loss of your father?"

His body tensed, and she regretted asking him. But truthfully, she wanted to know, and she wanted him to know she cared about his family.

"Mother took it hard. My father was only fifty-eight years old and in good health. The family physician believes he had a stroke. My mother's sister, also a widow, moved with her to the dower house. I believe they are enjoying the peace and quiet of the countryside."

"And your twin sisters?"

"Amy and Amelia were both devastated. Their brood of children, husbands, and estates keep them busy. They married brothers, so they are still close and live an hour's ride from each other. I imagine that gives them solace from their sadness."

"What about you?"

His eyes saddened. "When I returned to London from the West Indies, I looked forward to spending time with my father. You know about our history and how disappointed in me he was. We corresponded, however, and I knew he was proud of me and forgave me for what I had put him through. I was excited to see him. I missed him by eight days." He cleared his throat. "Eight heart-rending days."

She gently squeezed his upper arm. "I'm sorry. I know you

had your differences, but he bragged about you to my mother. Just because I didn't socialize didn't mean my mother stayed home. Besides reading the *Daily Post*, she kept me abreast of the goings-on in town."

"Thank you for telling me."

The music ended, and Andrew escorted her off the dance floor. He turned and bowed. "Today was wonderful spending it with you, but if you'll excuse me, I believe I will retire early."

"Goodnight." She curtsied as her heart folded in on itself.

As HE WALKED away from Emmeline, Andrew felt like a bloody arse. He couldn't help it, though. He didn't want his sudden, somber mood to seem reflective in any way of what he felt for her. Except when he entered his small chamber, his mood worsened. He'd been playful tonight and flirting with her, which felt amazing and natural, except when his guilt had crept up when they danced. Guilt surrounding Aiden's death. He hated keeping the truth from her any longer, but he needed more time to solidify their relationship, so when she found out, perhaps her heart would be too invested to hate him.

An empty decanter sat on a chest of drawers, so he rang for Clayton. When he arrived, Andrew said, "I believe you packed my favorite brandy. Could you fill the decanter?"

"Yes, Your Grace."

He disappeared, only to return minutes later and empty a bottle of brandy into the crystal decanter. He poured half a glass and handed it to Andrew.

"Is there anything else you need?"

"No. I'm fine for tonight."

He bowed. "Goodnight, Your Grace."

Andrew sat in an overstuffed chair before the cold hearth, staring into his glass of brandy, contemplating his life. He had spent a lot of time regretting several decisions and choices he'd made in the past. He was so very thankful for the good ones he'd made regarding his close friends and their business venture they so graciously let him buy into. Since inheriting the dukedom, he didn't need the funds from Mayfair Imports and Exports, so he had begun donating much of it to charity and had set up a fund for his future wife and children. He wanted funds not entailed to the dukedom to be readily available to them if anything happened to him.

Since his father's death, he had thought a great deal about his mortality and the mortality of others. Well, to be truthful, it had really started with Aiden's death and the darkness that followed him around like a shroud. He didn't want any more regrets. He didn't want Emmeline to be a regret. He didn't want to look back on his life and say, what if I had done this? He didn't want to die never having made love to her. Being selfish was not in his nature, except when he had been a gambler and fallen into an abyss of debt. If he went to her room and made love to her, would that be selfish? It would be fulfilling a dream for him, but would it be fair to Emmeline to put her in that position? A position to risk her reputation if anyone found out or if she became with child before agreeing to marry him.

Downing the contents of his drink, he pushed his physical needs aside and went to bed with visions of Emmeline in his head.

CHAPTER EIGHT

WHEN AMANDA ARRIVED with a breakfast tray for Emmeline, the following morning, she sat up in bed, her stomach in knots about the day's upcoming events. And, of course, the prospect of seeing Andrew again after how abruptly he'd retired to his room last evening. Would they be paired up for the scavenger hunt today? From past experience, a scavenger hunt was always a good opportunity for two people to sneak off and steal a kiss or two. Giddiness had her feeling like she was eighteen again.

"I was thinking of the pretty green day dress with matching spencer and hat for today since you will spend a good deal of time outdoors." Amanda opened the wardrobe and pulled out the dress." I will return after I press out the wrinkles."

Once Amanda returned and Emmeline was ready for the day, she went downstairs to the drawing room. Gripping her wide-brimmed hat in her hands, she scanned the room for Andrew. When she didn't see him, her heart sank to her toes.

But then, "Mrs. Fitzpatrick," said the man of her dreams in a deep voice from right behind her. "You take my breath away with your beauty."

Warmth kissed her cheeks, and her stomach flip-flopped from his nearness. She loved Andrew's flirting and was still getting used to that side of him.

Pivoting around, she found herself getting lost in his handsome face, his green eyes alight with mischief and a wide, authentic smile on his lips. "Andrew," she breathed out, suddenly finding it hard to take in air. "You look dashing today." She batted her lashes, hoping she was succeeding in flirting. "Is there a lady you are trying to impress?"

"Yes. There is a lady. Perhaps you have seen her. She is this tall," he held his hand up to the top of his shoulder, "has the most glorious thick, ebony hair, and usually wears it up like yours. The blue of her eyes resembles a cloudless sky on a warm summer day. And her smile," he covered his heart with the palm of his hand, "touches me here." He looked around the room with a sigh. "Have you seen such a lady?"

"Perhaps I have. I am also looking for a gentleman who has piqued my interest." She raised her quivering hand to the top of his head. "He is about your height and build. His light brown hair comes to his chin and is wavy and thick. Sometimes, he pulls it into a queue with a strip of leather. The green of his eyes reminds me of a field of tall grass after a light rain." She lowered her lashes to give herself a moment as emotions overwhelmed her. "He resembles you. You could be his twin."

"Shall we head to the picnic area?" he asked, his voice deep and throaty and his eyes dark with desire. "My hands are trembling. I need to touch you, and I think I'll perish if I don't soon."

Taking his offered arm, she wrapped hers through his as he led the way out the double glass doors and through the gardens to a flat green lawn before either of them spoke. Words were unnecessary as their bodies occasionally brushed against each other, causing more intimate friction. Emmeline's heart soared. Until recently, she hadn't suspected he was capable of teasing, flirting, and showing emotions of caring for her. Even when he offered for her hand all those years ago, she felt as though he had held back a part of himself from her. She understood he was protecting his heart back then. How could he not when he wasn't the only man courting her? She didn't blame him for keeping part of himself hidden from her. However, deep down inside, she had always thought he was capable of more emotion than he had shown her. And now she knew the truth. He had a deep well of feelings, passion, and love inside him.

"Look." She pointed up ahead. "Several people are already here. And there are blankets scattered about. Let us claim one for ourselves."

Taking her arm from his, she hurried toward a blue plaid blanket spread beneath a large English Oak shading the space. She laughed as she sat on the blanket, wiggled her behind to make an indent in the grass, then spread her skirts over her legs.

"What is the hurry?" Andrew asked as he smiled and dropped down beside her.

"I want to sit in the shade."

He chuckled as he bent one knee, wrapped his arms around it, and looked around. "We are not the only ones hoping for time alone before the picnic begins."

"Yes." She blew out her breath. "It appears that way."

He nudged her gently with his elbow and winked at her. "No pouting. I promise you and I will sneak a kiss or two or three during the scavenger hunt."

Heart scorched her cheeks as their shared kiss and more from yesterday came to the forefront of her mind. "I will hold you to that promise." Had that breathy voice come from her?

Chuckling, he said, "See that you do. Do not look now, but we have visitors."

Looking up, she saw Caldwell and Lady Chesterfield approaching.

"May we join you?" Caldwell asked.

"But of course," Andrew said as he rose to his feet and bowed. "Nice to see you again, Lady Chesterfield. It has been many years, if you don't count yesterday."

"Your Grace." She curtsied. "It has. Please call me Lady Clarice. Chesterfield makes me feel ancient."

"Lady Clarice it is."

"Thank you for letting us join you," Caldwell said.

"Lady Clarice," Emmeline said with a smile. "It is nice to see you. It's been many years for us as well."

"It has. I'm glad to see you have re-entered Society."

"You as well," she said, feeling a kinship with another widow close to her age.

"Well, now that social etiquette and pleasantries are done with," Caldwell drawled, "what do you think about the scavenger hunt?"

"What is there to think about?" Andrew replied. "A hunt is a hunt. It's always the same objects to find. Just once, I want the host and hostess to shock us and have us find something scandalous. But I doubt it will be the marquess and marchioness unless they are not quite as straitlaced as they appear."

"Straitlaced!" Emmeline said. "Claire was never straitlaced, and the marquess is just a bit subdued and naturally reserved. There's nothing straitlaced about them."

Andrew cleared his throat and chuckled. "I stand corrected."

"Speaking of our host and hostess, here they come." The gentlemen rose and helped the ladies up from the blanket as the marquess and marchioness walked across the lawn to their guests. Emmeline didn't want to let go of Andrew's hand but resigned herself to waiting until later to hold it again. The four of them made their way toward several long tables with food and drinks set up beneath several canopies, along with several round tables and chairs.

"Welcome, everyone," Claire said with an excited voice. "As you all know, today's events are a picnic, followed by a scavenger hunt, pall-mall, and other lawn games if you wish to partake in them. And tonight, there will be charades, chess, billiards, and cards."

The marquess took over. "Luncheon is ready to be served, and my lovely wife will pass out the scavenger hunt list when the luncheon concludes. The hunt will begin when you have the list in your hand. You have an hour and a half to complete the list and meet back here."

Andrew led her to the food table, handed her a plate, and took one for himself. They went down the line, adding various meat pies, salad greens, fruits, nuts, and jam and bread, followed by queen currant cakes and other confections. They made their way to a table where several other guests sat. After greetings went around, he held her chair out as she sat down, placing her napkin on her lap.

"The food on my plate looks delicious," Andrew said as he picked up a meat pie and grinned at her with the pie close to his mouth. His eyes darkened as he stared at her lips, causing her insides to hum. Right before he took a bite he whispered, "Although I'm ravenous for something. Or should I say . . . someone?"

Instant heat coursed through her body, wetness pooled between her thighs, and she squirmed in her chair as she leaned close to his ear. "Do not say things like that unless you mean them." Oh my, she was shamelessly flirting with him, which only added to her desire.

He murmured close to her ear, "I assure you, I mean them and *so* much more." His hot breath wafted across her ear and neck, causing her to shiver in a most decadent way. "I want to taste every inch of your body and lick . . ."

She swallowed the gasp forming in her throat before she drew unwanted attention their way. "Promise?" she breathed out as she leaned away from him.

His brows waggled up and down several times, making her laugh. "I promise."

Emmeline could hardly contain the excitement Andrew's words caused her as she nibbled on first a veal pie and then some fruit. Her insides were jumbled up, which made her appetite vanish. At least her appetite for real food. So she sat and listened to the animated conversation going on around the table, without actually hearing it.

Finally, Claire's voice rang out, "Listen up, everyone, Viscountess Appleton is handing out the list for the scavenger hunt. Find yourself a partner, and let the hunt begin."

"Come on," Andrew said, taking the list from the viscountess and standing with his hands on the back of her chair. "Let's go."

"I'm ready." She rose, and they went and stood beneath a shady tree away from the crowd for privacy.

"There are ten things to find," Andrew said, holding the handwritten list. "How about we start in the middle?"

She pointed at number six. "I think I know this one. *I come in many colors. I open and close and resemble the wind.* I think it's a fan. We must go back to the house so I can go to my room and retrieve one."

"Look at this one," Andrew said as he pointed to number five. "*I have feathers and fly, but I am not alive.* It's a shuttlecock. We're near the lawn games, so let's find that one first."

They walked to where the lawn games were spread out not far away. "Over there," Andrew said as he pointed to a pile of shuttlecocks. He picked one up and put it inside his jacket pocket. "I'm surprised no one else figured this one out. But, oh well. Let's go get that fan."

They entered the residence through the double glass doors into the drawing room. "Wait here," Emmeline said. "See if you can solve any others, and I'll be right back."

She returned not five minutes later holding a blue lace-trimmed fan. "Did you solve any more?"

"Perhaps this one. *What sails the seas becomes scarce and has seeds.*"

"An orange," she replied. Andrew held his hand out to her, and she took it quickly. They traveled back through the gardens, down a stone path to the side of the manor where the orangery the marquess built stood in all its beauty. Several teams were inside, picking oranges off the numerous orange trees.

"We may as well join the others inside," Andrew said as he opened the door to the orangery, and a blast of warm air hit them. People quickly hid their finds, and Emmeline stifled a laugh. It wasn't as though the riddles were all that difficult. Each team would probably get each clue and find the object. But who could do it the fastest? She picked up an orange that had already been picked from a tray, and they exited.

"I have an idea." Andrew grabbed her hand and led them down a path to the gazebo they had visited yesterday.

Emmeline's pulse soared. "What about the game?"

Andrew pulled on her hand and tugged her up the stairs. "I believe this is the perfect moment to be alone without any eyes on us. And I promised you a kiss or two." He walked her backward until she leaned against the railing facing him. The hungry look in his eyes had her insides trembling. "Do you mind forfeiting the game?"

A giggle escaped her lips. "Not at all." Feeling confident, she wrapped her arms around his neck and leaned into him, inhaling the masculine scent of sandalwood she was beginning to associate with him and him alone.

Wrapping her up in his arms, he lowered his lips to hers. Her toes curled as he devoured her mouth. Not a part of it was safe from him. He sipped, licked, sucked, and tasted all of her. Her knees nearly buckled under his assault. And that was before his hands began roaming up and down her back and her sides, his thumbs brushing the outer edges of her breasts. She was so thankful she had discarded her spencer in her room when she'd procured the fan.

He broke the kiss, his teeth and lips caressing her neck. Her head fell to the side, giving him better access. She wanted to feel his heated mouth everywhere on her sensitive skin.

Moans sounded from both of them. "Your skin is so soft and tastes like warm sunshine."

One hand pulled the front of her bodice down, exposing her breasts to the warm air. He bent his head and took one nipple into his mouth as he palmed the other with his large hand, squeezing and tugging. She gripped his shoulders for support as her knees buckled. His tongue swirled around and around, and his teeth closed around the taut peak, making her see stars in daylight. Just as she was losing herself completely to his touch and her body felt entirely liquified, he backed up and righted the front of her gown. He stepped back further, dragged his hands through his hair, and groaned, "Forgive me."

It took a moment for Emmeline's mind to catch up to the sudden withdrawal of Andrew and what he'd been doing to her body. She cleared her throat and placed her hand on her pounding heart as she gasped for much-needed air. "There is nothing to forgive. I'm no virgin."

His head fell back and he laughed, deep and throaty. "Thank God for that. But still, we needed to stop before I pulled up your skirts and thrust my . . ." He tugged on his hair.

Having gotten her aroused body somewhat under control, she said, "Shall we finish the scavenger hunt?" Her words were barely more than a whisper as her breathing had not returned to normal.

He held his hand out to her, his face and eyes suddenly guarded, and it pained her. "No. Let's return to the picnic area and wait for the other teams to finish. I could use something to cool myself off, and the lemonade tasted good."

"Yes." Something cold was just what she needed to slake the lust still humming throughout her entire body. Andrew, his talented hands and exquisite mouth, shocked her at how quickly her body responded. It felt as though her body and his knew they belonged to one another.

As THEY SAT beneath a canopy, sipping lemonade, Andrew's mind wandered. Sleep had eluded him the previous night as visions of Emmeline, naked and in his bed, had him in a constant state of arousal. He'd taken to easing it with his hand, but it was useless.

His body and mind craved her and her alone.

Even though he'd been in love with her for ten years and had always craved her, he hadn't shied away from brief affairs. He had to feed his body's physical needs. The ladies he'd had affairs with always knew beforehand that he wasn't looking for a wife or a longtime mistress. Unfortunately, more than one claimed to have fallen in love with him, and he felt lower than a slug each time he walked away, but he couldn't commit to any of them. His heart had always belonged to Emmeline, and that would never change.

But though he loved her with everything he had, he would give anything to have his friend, Aiden, still alive and breathing, even knowing that his heart, body, and soul would never be whole because she would then still belong to Aiden.

It took years for him to realize—really understand—that Aiden wasn't ever coming back. Dead was dead. The guilt he battled daily from his involvement in his death would never go away either. Perhaps when he confessed his sins to Emmeline and had her forgiveness, he could finally breathe easy and forgive himself.

He didn't believe Aiden would want him to suffer. He truly believed Aiden would be happy for both of them if they embraced the love that had started so long in the past. It wasn't as if Aiden hadn't known about Andrew's love for her. And he'd always been a kind friend and a good man.

As far as Emmeline's love for him went, he hoped she loved him. He hoped her love was true enough to overcome his treachery. Aiden would be alive if not for him. But he couldn't think about that now. He wished she would fall so deeply in love with him that the past wouldn't matter. That when she found out he'd killed Aiden, she would still love him anyway and forgive him.

His stomach tightened up with excruciating pain as he finished his cool drink. Guilt manifested into real sickness with him at times. This morning, he had tried to eat something from the breakfast tray Clayton had brought him, but he'd failed. The morning meal was rarely something he partook in. Luncheon, dinner, and occasional suppers were when he ate, as the guilt from his inevitable bad dreams had usually abated by then. Not that the guilt ever went away. But it eased its talons enough that he could take in food without the nausea.

When the scavenger hunt began, he'd had every intention of finishing the game, but when he remembered the gazebo from the day before, his feet had moved that way of their own accord. He needed to hold her close to his heart as much as he needed air to survive. But he had not intended to take it so far and was ashamed of putting her in such a precarious situation. Yesterday, he had Caldwell looking out, giving them certain freedoms, but not today. Today, anyone could have come upon them, and she would have been exposed from the waist up. Staring into his cup of lemonade now, he could see his hands trembling. He had lost all reason, and if he didn't get himself under control, Emmeline would pay for his actions. He needed to control his urges and lust when in public places. He could not touch her again until they were locked inside one of their bedchambers, safe from the eyes of other guests and those prone to gossip.

He kept reminding himself that he loved her too much to risk her reputation, but in the heat of the moment, his brain had malfunctioned, and natural desire and need took over his body. Emmeline was the only one who affected him so. Love was powerful, making him wonder if he would survive the rest of the house party unscathed—or, more importantly, survive Emmeline.

"You have become quiet," Emmeline's soothing voice pulled him out of his thoughts. "Are you well?"

"Please forgive me." He forced his lips to curve up and resemble a smile. "My mind wandered."

Her luscious mouth said, "Oh."

He reached beneath the table and squeezed her thigh to ease her discomfort. "Once again, forgive me. I would never want you to feel uncomfortable because I was listening to my mind.

Regarding us, you have nothing to worry about. I hope you know how I feel about you." Her expression looked even more uncertain than it did moments ago. He wasn't helping the situation. He may have turmoil within his brain, but he needed to keep it from affecting Emmeline. She didn't deserve to suffer from him projecting his guilt and frustrations outward. He knew she had her own demons to fight regarding Aiden. And some, if not all, of it was his fault for what he'd said to her before he left England. He'd been in a dark place and she hadn't deserved to be sucked into his darkness. He owed her one hell of an apology for his behavior and he wondered if the time would ever be right.

"Would you care to return to the manor and visit the library? I would love a moment of calm and quiet to read a book and relax before dinner and more games. We could order tea."

Her eyes flickered between his face and the other people gathered around them. The trepidation he witnessed briefly crossing her face stabbed his heart. He was hurting her without meaning to, and it twisted up his insides. "If you prefer not to, that's fine. Would you rather play battledore and shuttlecock or pall-mall?"

"Goodness no," she said with an exhale of air. "I am not interested in either one of them."

"Good. I don't feel like playing either."

"I believe I would like time in the library, and tea sounds divine."

Rising from his chair, he pulled hers back and held out his hand to help her stand. "The library it is."

They walked in companionable silence, with just a hint of unease. Knowing he was the cause of that unease saddened Andrew.

Before they entered the library, he spoke with one of the footmen and requested a tray be brought to them. The library was cool and dark, with the curtains drawn to keep the sunlight from harming the volumes. He went to the three large windows and opened the curtains so they could see enough to read.

Turning to Emmeline, who was scanning the shelves, he said, "Please remind me to close the curtains before we leave."

Glancing over her shoulder, she smiled. "I will." Her hand delicately pulled a book from a shelf. "I have always wanted to read this book."

"Which one?"

"*The Lady of the Lake*, by Walter Scott."

"Good choice. I've read it."

"You have?" Her eyes lit up with surprise.

Chuckling, he took a seat on the settee without choosing a book. "Spending so much time at sea, the captain's quarters always have a supply of books to read."

She sat beside him, leaving a good amount of space between them, and he tried not to let it bother him. "I thought you would be on deck at all hours of the day and night perched up at the helm."

"At times, yes. At other times, down below, going over maps and tide charts. When there are storms, that's when all hell—excuse me—breaks out. But trust me, there were times at night when I was in my bed and couldn't sleep when a book eased my lonely soul."

"I never thought of that. Is reading how you dealt with the loneliness?" Her concern touched him.

"Spending weeks or months at sea is trying and lonely, but fulfilling as well, knowing the cargo in the hold represents money for the sailors to support their families." He snorted. "And I'm not going to lie, it also feels good to be able to line my pockets, donate money to charity, and invest for my future wife and children. But to answer your question, yes, reading helped me."

"What about not seeing your family for so long? That couldn't have been easy."

"In the beginning it was good to be away. To clear my head and get away from my failings. After my father and I mended our relationship, I did miss my family. As for my mother, I regret what I did to leave in the first place. I missed her and felt guilty for leaving under such damaging circumstances. I put a strain on my parents' relationship that I never meant to. My mother was furious with my father for what he did and said. But I'm glad he threatened to disown me. Who knows what would have become of me otherwise? I could be long dead."

He paused and swallowed the lump in his throat. "As for my sisters, they have been married for over ten years, and I haven't seen them but a handful of times since then. I miss them, but they have made new families for themselves."

She looked at him with such sadness in her eyes that his stomach tightened. "Please don't mention your death. I can't even think about what it would be like if you had died. I don't think I would have survived losing you, too, after losing Aiden."

Now he felt like a bloody arse for saying that. He hadn't been thinking about it from her perspective. "I'm sorry to upset you. It wasn't my intention."

She reached for his hand and held it. "I know. Ever since Aiden's death, I've been afraid for everyone close to me. Deep down inside, it always felt as though I must have done something wrong for Aiden to be taken from me. And I continue to believe it, though I know I shouldn't, thinking at any moment someone else I love will die." Her hand released his, and she wiped the tears from her cheeks. "I hate that I'm crying."

He moved close, placed an arm around her shoulder, and held her. "It's my fault you are crying. I should not have brought up death. Christ." He ran his free hand through his hair. "I'm such an idiot. I seem to be asking for your forgiveness repeatedly lately."

"No need. You can't possibly know what's going on in my head and how I've dealt with Aiden's death. Sometimes I think I shouldn't be so emotional six years later. But then, what do I know? Some people mourn for a lifetime."

Every muscle in his body tensed up at hearing her words. Could it be that he was the only one in love? He felt sick. Was his mind playing tricks on him, thinking she'd responded favorably to his advances in the gazebo? No. No. That wasn't right. She had responded to him, just as eager to be in his arms as he was to be in hers. Perhaps she lusted after him and nothing more. He needed to shut his mind off before it ruined their budding relationship.

"I need to say something that is long overdue." He removed his arm from her shoulder, and took both her hands in his and looked directly into her beautiful but guarded eyes. "The night I visited you before I set sail from London with Langford, I spoke hurtful and hateful words to you." He squeezed her hands as her eyes glistened with tears, and he fought back his own. "I accused you of making Aiden unhappy which contributed to his death." His voice shook. "You made him the happiest man alive. I lashed out, wanting someone else to share my pain and guilt. I'm sorry and do not expect your forgiveness for what I've caused you with my intolerable behavior."

She squeezed his hands as tears trickled down her rosy cheeks. "I forgive you. I always knew your words came out of your own grief."

Pulling her into his arms, and cradling her close, his heart was a tad healed for her forgiveness. There was still much healing to do because there was so much more he needed to beg her forgiveness for. In time, he would confess all. Meanwhile, he would cherish every second he had with her from this moment on. No more wallowing in self-pity and making her sad. He would spend the rest of the house party catering to her every whim and need. Starting with the tea tray the servant had placed on the table only moments ago.

"May I pour?" he asked.

Laughter spilled out of her as she wiped away the last of her tears. "Do you even know how?"

Now, it was his time to laugh. "Contrary to what ladies might think, gentlemen know how to pour tea—at least this gentleman does. You forget I grew up with twin older sisters who insisted I join their tea parties when we were in the nursery."

"I wish I had seen that," she said, amusement shining in her eyes.

"No, you don't. They would make me wear their dresses and call me Lady Andrea." The sound of her laughter lightened his heart.

"Indeed I do. I wish I could have seen you as a cute little blond boy wearing a frilly pink dress and a bonnet on your head."

"I never said I wore a bonnet."

"A proper tea party is never complete without a bonnet."

He chuckled. "You would be correct." He picked up the teapot and poured the hot liquid into two teacups. "Cream and sugar?" he asked with a smile.

"Sugar and a splash of cream." She looked impressed with him.

Once he had added her accoutrements, he handed her the cup and saucer and asked, "Would you like a biscuit?"

"Not just yet. Thank you."

"As you wish." He relaxed back into the settee and sipped his tea with sugar only. The warmth soothed him, as did the woman beside him. He had no idea why he'd almost had a breakdown this past hour. He'd not been fit for company, yet she'd stayed with him. "I must apologize again for letting my mind suck me into a dark place. It wasn't fair to you. It won't happen again."

"Andrew," she said with a stern voice he didn't think he'd ever heard from her. "Do not hide from me, please. If you are troubled, I would rather you share with me or someone else, perhaps Caldwell or Langford, than have it wallow inside you until you burst. I, of all people, know what it's like to keep my feelings of angst to myself until they eventually come out and hurt someone else. For me, it's my mother. Thank goodness she understands and still loves me. It's hard dealing with issues from our past. We want to think we are invincible and don't need anyone to help us, but sometimes we do. Sometimes, we need help dealing with our demons."

"You are a wise woman." She understood what he was still

going through. It didn't surprise him, since she had dealt with the death of a husband. And three close friends had abandoned her at her time of need. He had gone off drinking and gambling, and Caldwell and Langford had buried their grief in their business and took to their ships, and then he'd joined them.

"You should go rest before dinner," he said as the clock chimed and he noticed how time had gotten away from them.

"Oh my, look at the time." She stood, and he did as well. "Are you coming?"

"No. I believe I will stay here." He kissed her cheek. "I will see you for dinner."

"Yes."

His eyes followed her as she gracefully exited the library, taking all the light and warmth from the room.

CHAPTER NINE

EMMELINE DECIDED TO wear her hair down to dinner. Amanda pulled strands from either side of her face to the back of her head and added pearl pins. Her long, thick tresses were curled and fell in waves around her shoulders and down her back. She looked in the mirror over the dressing table and tried to see herself as Andrew saw her. Her face was unlined and still youthful looking, but the wisdom in her eyes gave her age away. Her figure was trim but had nice curves in all the right places and an amble bosom. She'd lost weight when Aiden died and never put it back on. She believed Andrew saw her as an attractive woman. Not as fresh and young as the debutantes, but young enough. And she had one thing they did not—knowledge and experience on how to pleasure a man in the bedroom. And she honestly couldn't wait to share a bed with Andrew, to experience lovemaking with him. Part of her wondered how it would be similar or different to her experience with Aiden, but she couldn't let her mind dwell on it. It wasn't fair to any of them. Aiden was Aiden. Andrew was Andrew. And she wasn't the same person in her marriage to Aiden as she was now. Oh, she was still herself deep down inside but also altered. How could she not be after going through what she had?

In some ways, Andrew was different as well. At times, he was more brooding, and at other times, he was more playful and flirting. However, she could see that something bothered him deeply, though he tried to hide it. But she could tell no matter what his personality reflected when he was hurting or angry or sad. Or all of them at once. He sometimes let his guard down, and his eyes became a window into the upheaval inside him. When that happened, she wanted to take him in her arms and hold him until whatever plagued him relented and released its hold. She hated him being in turmoil, because she knew all too well what it felt like. All the emotions she saw cross his features had crossed hers.

Even if she hadn't given real credence to Andrew's hurtful words before he went to sea, she still felt partially responsible for Aiden's death and had the guilt to prove it. They should not have attended the hunting party, not after the emotional loss of her miscarriage, and she should have insisted they stay home. Aiden hadn't taken the loss well. They'd argued over several things leading up to the house party—stupid things. Sadness, pain, and loss made people say and do things they would regret and apologize for later. But when it came to her and Aiden, there were no apologies. There had been no chance. Though she had long since forgiven Aiden for any hurtful words said in his own grief.

But if she genuinely wanted to move forward, she needed to forgive herself, as well.

And forgiveness was an ongoing struggle. Even months after his accident, she had still been numb all over. Then, one day, she'd woken up angry at him for getting drunk and racing an unfamiliar horse. Then another day came, and her heart was pierced in two by guilt, and she wished she could have gone back to the numbness. Because of the guilt, she simply felt too much. Emotions had paralyzed her for more months, and she could barely function.

Eventually, she'd found her way to move on, dedicating her time to the Ladies' Society of Mayfair. That charity work had saved her sanity and eased the pain in her heart. Seeing others suffer put her own life in perspective. And when her cousin's widow, Lady Langford—or just Lilly, as she'd insisted on being called—came to stay, they helped each other heal even more. The two of them had braved London Society together. And now Lilly was married to the new Earl of Langford, her old friend Edmund Weston.

Yesterday was the first time Emmeline and Andrew had been together since Lilly and Langford's wedding, though they had begun to grow closer before the uproar at Vauxhall. However, she now needed to convince both Andrew and herself that they deserved happiness and love no matter what had happened in the past. The past was over. They needed to focus on the future, and she prayed her future was Andrew. And deep down inside her heart she believed Aiden would be happy for both of them.

"Your hair looks gorgeous," Amanda said as she stood back.

How long had she been lost in thought? "Thank you."

Standing in her chemise, Amanda dropped the deep-blue evening gown over her head, tugged it into place, and fastened the pearl buttons. Amanda tied the sash in a lighter blue behind her back into a perfect bow. Once her slippers and gloves were on, she wrapped a matching shawl over her shoulders and left her room to go to her mother's across the hall. She knocked.

"Come in."

"Mama, are you ready?" Emmeline frowned when she saw her mother in bed, sitting up against pillows with a tray on her lap. "Are you ill?"

"Just a migraine. I'm keeping to my room tonight, but you go and have a wonderful time, and you can tell me about it tomorrow."

"I can stay with you."

"No need. Stacy is taking good care of me. She snuck me an early dinner tray, and I plan to sleep off this terrible migraine. I'll be right as rain tomorrow. Go." She shooed her with her hand. "Go seduce Blackstone."

She exhaled loudly. "Mama, please stop saying that. Someone

is liable to hear you."

"Perhaps the duke will, and then come to his senses."

Emmeline fought not to laugh. She didn't want to encourage her mother. "Feel better." She hated leaving her mother alone when she felt unwell, but she knew she needed quiet, darkness, and sleep.

Entering the drawing room, she casually looked around, trying not to be obvious as she sought out Andrew. And when she found him conversing with several other gentlemen, he nodded in acknowledgment of her arrival. He looked positively dashing, dressed in a dark brown superfine coat, matching breeches and shiny brown shoes, with a brown and cream paisley waistcoat, cream linen shirt, and cravat. Butterflies took flight inside her stomach. The only thing she could think of that would be better than seeing him dressed so handsomely was seeing him unclothed. Her cheeks warmed at picturing him naked. Imagining was all she could do since she had never seen him without clothes. But not for long, she hoped. Perhaps she could convince him to come to her room tonight.

"Care to share why you are blushing a becoming shade of pink?"

The man himself. Startled at being caught visualizing him naked, she flinched. "How did you sneak up on me?"

Chuckling, he replied, "You were lost in thought. I didn't mean to startle you."

"You didn't," she said, trying to cover her moment of wanton reflection gracefully.

He leaned close, his eyes full of mischief. "If you say so. I'll ask again, why are you blushing?"

At his question, her cheeks heated even more. "It is not something I wish to share."

"It must be something private then."

His dark mood from earlier today had clearly disappeared, and the playful Andrew was here. Well, she could be playful, too. "Oh," she batted her lashes, "it was very private."

"You must tell me." His voice seemed to have suddenly lowered several octaves.

Her inner wanton imagining was quickly rising to the surface. She would think about whatever was coming over her later. "If you must know, I was thinking how dashing you look this evening."

"And that made you blush so deeply?" he teased.

Leaning very close so no one could hear, her lips touched his hair, and she inhaled his sandalwood scent and whispered, "No. That is only part of my thoughts. The other part was thinking you would look even better . . . without . . . clothing."

His hand flew to his mouth as he smothered a choke, cough, or laughter—she couldn't tell which. All she knew was that she had shocked him with her honesty.

Taking her hand in his, he hurried them out the double doors to the veranda and the gardens beyond until they reached a private area of the gardens surrounded by shrubbery and flowering plants. It gave the illusion of being in a magical forest. Facing each other, he had both her hands in his, his thumb stroking where her gloves met skin. The connection traveled throughout her entire body, and she found herself leaning forward and holding her breath.

"When you see me naked, I pray I don't disappoint." The green in his eyes had gone dark and intense with desire. And she couldn't look away as the breath she had been holding escaped her lungs. "I have pictured you without clothes for the past ten years, and when I do finally get to gaze upon your luscious, naked body . . ." His voice cut off for a moment. "I will be the most fortunate man alive . . ." His voice cracked, and she could see him struggling with emotions. "I will treat your body with reverence. Worshiping it and licking every single inch of your skin. When I finish, I will know your body better than you or anyone else."

His words had her heart pounding and heat flaring between her legs. There wasn't a speck of her body that didn't tremble in anticipation of his words. Desire awoke deep inside her belly, craving his touch. "Come to my room tonight," she said before she lost her nerve.

One masculine brow rose in silent question to her statement. "I will do my best not to be seen, but even the best-laid plans can go wrong. If I'm seen, people will talk and gossip."

Her stomach did a silent tumble at the idea of people gossiping about her. But if she was being truthful with herself, she knew it was time to throw caution to the wind and live again, whatever the cost.

"I have lived my entire life cautiously and it is time I took control and did what I want to do." She cupped his closely shaved cheeks with her hands. "I am no debutante or blushing bride. I know firsthand the pleasure two people can experience when their bodies come together, and I want that with you." Rising on tiptoes, her lips brushed his briefly. "I want the ethereal connection that comes when two bodies, two souls come together in magical bliss." She kissed him deeper. "I want you to take me to the place where lovers go to experience the fulfillment of the flesh." Her lips took his again. His tongue joined with hers, and he made love to her mouth. She experienced his desire, his need, his want. Everything he craved was gathered up in that kiss. The connection of their mouths, tongue and lips told her everything she needed to know. Andrew wanted her as much as she wanted him. Words were obsolete. His actions proved everything.

Breaking the kiss, Andrew placed his forehead against hers and groaned. "I don't know if I can wait."

Feeling bold, she grazed her hand across his groin, finding his manhood straining against his breeches, and she swallowed down a moan. "I'm just as ready."

He stood back, his eyes wide as he ran his hands down his face. "Don't say things like that. I'm barely holding on."

Teasing, she batted her lashes again. "I know. My hand found the truth. I can't wait to take it into . . ."

"Blackstone," Caldwell's voice rang out through the quiet garden, cooling Emmeline's body instantaneously. "The dinner gong rang ten minutes ago. People are wondering where you two have gone."

"We are here," Andrew said as they hurried down the garden pathway, approached the veranda and faced Caldwell.

His eyes took them in, and he grinned. "No one is looking for you. I lied. But still, dinner is served."

Andrew shoved Caldwell in the shoulder. "Don't do that again."

Emmeline inhaled and exhaled. The panic she'd felt at Caldwell's words evaporated. He hadn't changed at all in the past six years. He had teased her and Aiden relentlessly when they would sneak off for private moments. It appeared he was going to do the same with her and Andrew. Not that she minded, as it brought back good memories of her and Aiden.

Her heart stopped. Perhaps being reminded of memories of her and Aiden when she was with Andrew wasn't a good thing.

Dinner was an informal affair served from a buffet where guests could eat as they pleased. The games and charades began while Emmeline and Andrew were still picking at their plates, so they passed on charades and sat down to play backgammon. They played several games with Andrew winning them all. Emmeline's mind had been playing around with what she hoped would happen tonight with Andrew. Her body had as well. Her nerves hummed and her skin tingled, making her want to strip off her clothing and rub her naked body against Andrew's equally naked body to ease the sensation. All that stimulation made it impossible to concentrate on backgammon, making it easy for her to lose.

"One more game?" Andrew asked with a lopsided grin. "I know a proper gentleman shouldn't take pleasure in beating a lady at a parlor game, but I'm not feeling very proper tonight."

Her cheeks warmed at his insinuation. "No. Let's sit here and watch the guests make fools of themselves playing charades." So that's what they did. They watched charades, laughing at the antics of the other guests. As the games began to wind down,

Emmeline retired with a promise from Andrew that he would visit her around midnight.

SITTING UP IN bed, the hour close to midnight, Emmeline's body trembled with nerves. When would Andrew come? Would he come? When she'd retired to her room an hour ago, several people were still gathered in the game room playing cards and chess. Perhaps he could not get to her room without being seen. Eyes heavy, she closed them for just a moment, and the next thing she knew, the bed was dipping. When she opened her eyes, it was to see the handsome face of Andrew illuminated by the one candle she'd left lit on the bedside table.

"I'm sorry to be so late. Several young bucks didn't see fit to retire tonight. I fear large quantities of drink and coin passed hands during their game of whist." He kissed her lips. "I gave up and left them to their own devices. They will no doubt be there in the morning having fallen asleep due to their overindulgence."

"Do you always worry about others?"

"I do when it comes to gambling. I don't want anyone to go through what I did. Gambling is all fun and games until someone bets their future away. I was lucky. Others are not." He kissed her again. "But enough of that."

He rose from the bed. His eyes were in shadow, but she could still tell he was unwaveringly staring at her as he began to undress. His coat first. Then his waistcoat. Next came his cravat, and then he slipped his linen shirt over her head, and her mouth watered at the sight of his well-defined chest, arms, and abdomen. He sat on the bed to remove his shoes and stockings. Dressed only in his breeches, he peeled the covers back, exposing her in her sheer, pale-blue night rail. She'd worn it just for him. She had packed it in the hope that this would happen.

His eyes traveled from her loose hair draped across her pillow to her toes peeking out the bottom of her night rail, and she shivered in her awareness of him. He hadn't even touched her, and she was ready for anything he wanted to do to her.

He scrubbed his hand down his face. "You are . . . so beautiful. I've pictured you this way many times in my head, but reality far surpasses anything my imagination envisioned."

The bed dipped again as he kneeled beside her, hitting her with a devilish grin and smoldering eyes. Tingles danced up her spine as she stared back, knowing he witnessed her desire for him in her expression and in her eyes. Reaching out her hand, she placed it on his chest, sprinkled with light hair, right over his heart. The beat of his heart accelerated the longer her hand lay flat against his skin. The knowledge that she caused it was exhilarating. The proof of how badly he wanted her gave her courage. Coming up to her knees, her eyes still connected to his, she pulled her night rail over her head with hands that trembled ever so slightly, making her realize she was perhaps not as courageous as she believed.

Andrew exhaled and his eyes narrowed, taking her in from head to toe, causing gooseflesh to break out all over her skin. Suddenly feeling vulnerable, she covered her breasts with one arm and dropped the other to cover her sex.

"Don't," he drawled. "Don't hide your beautiful body from me." With gentle hands, he pulled her arms away until she was bare to him again. "Nothing is more precious to me than you. And knowing you are willing to share yourself with me in the most natural, loving, and sensual way," he paused as his voice cracked, "means everything to me. I am undeserving of you."

The words he spoke and how he said them touched her. Yet he still had clothes on, making her uneasy in her nakedness. Her hands unbuttoned the front placket of his breeches. "You need to shed these."

No sooner had she finished the last word of her sentence, than he'd jumped off the bed, pulled his breeches and undergarments off, and climbed back on the bed, barely giving her a glimpse of his engorged manhood. He gently pushed her shoulders, laying her down, and his body followed, coming down heavily as he took her mouth.

He feasted—tongue, lips, and teeth. His mouth fit hers perfectly. His tongue sparred with hers in a never-ending battle for control, a battle neither of them wanted to end. His teeth nipped her bottom lip occasionally, making her that much more aware that what transpired between them was real. The slight pain mixed with pleasure added to the intensity of the feelings bombarding her body. Every tingle, every twitch, every shudder made her know she was alive, and she owed it all to Andrew.

"I'm afraid to open my eyes to find out I'm dreaming," she moaned as his lips broke free from her mouth. His teeth scraped down her neck, and she felt the pull between her thighs setting her on fire.

"I know the feeling," he groaned as his mouth found her nipple. His tongue swirled around her pebbled peak, and she arched her back, trying to get closer. "I have dreamed about you aplenty." He took her nipple into his mouth and suckled, causing her to gasp. "Have you dreamed about me?"

Had she? More than she wanted to admit. "Yes," she breathed out as his teeth clamped down on her nipple, nearly making her scream. She needed to even up the sweet torture. Her hand moved between them, and she took his large, thick erection in her hand and stroked him from bottom to tip and back again. Her lips curled into a smile as his body tensed and shuddered.

"Oh, God. Do that again," he said, his voice deep and throaty.

And so she did several times until he stilled her hand with his. "Stop . . . I can't hold on."

The one thing about being a widow instead of a virgin is she knew what he referred to—something she hadn't understood on her wedding night. *Do not think about your wedding night.*

Before she could remark on his comment, he had kissed his way down her stomach, and her eyes scrunched tightly. She stopped breathing as she waited, and anticipation built. The thrumming in her body increased. His lips found her sex, and he licked between her folds, sucking her nub into his mouth.

Shocked. Emmeline was shocked. Even though she heard this whispered of in private drawing rooms . . . Aiden had never.

Andrew's hands nudged her legs open wider, and he buried his face between her thighs. Embarrassment tried to push itself into her mind but was lost to the demands and needs of her body as Andrew did wonderful and unspeakable things to her. Things that had her legs wrapped over his shoulders, and her entire body weighed down heavily with desire until she crashed. It hit her like an untamed, stampeding horse. Her body trembled and tightened. She fisted Andrew's hair, holding him between her thighs as his mouth and tongue gave her the most exquisite, torturous orgasm she'd ever experienced. When she reached the other side, her legs slid off his shoulders, her arms flopped across the bed, and she didn't believe she could move . . . ever again. She felt languid and satiated like she'd never been before.

Andrew climbed up her body, placing butterfly kisses here and there until his body covered hers, and he chuckled into her ear. "Did you enjoy that, my love?"

The truth was she'd enjoyed what he did. More than she'd ever thought was possible. How did one answer such a question? Not to mention, how did one function after being pleasured so completely?

"Hmmm, it was fine." She went with an elusive answer after his playfully smug question.

Leaning up on his hands, he smirked. "Fine? Just fine?"

Laughter bubbled up from deep inside her. "Do you need your sexual prowess complimented so your self-esteem doesn't become an issue?

His lips took hers in a punishing kiss, then he pulled away abruptly. His chest heaved as he inhaled deeply. "My self-esteem is just fine. Your screams were all the verification I needed that I saw to your complete and utter pleasure."

She nudged his shoulder with her hand. "I did not scream. Do you think my mother heard? She is across the hall." Oh dear, how embarrassing if she did. Not that she had to worry about keeping it a secret from her mother. She would be happier than happy. No one occupied the room beside her, so she was safe there.

"I hardly think your mother could hear you across the hall. But . . . I'm not finished with you yet."

And he wasn't.

His fingers skimmed up her thigh, and she couldn't believe her body quivered with need again so quickly. He spread her folds, circling her nub with his thumb as he inserted one finger inside, then another, sending her hips rising off the bed of their own accord. He replaced his hand with his cock, pushing slowly an inch at a time. His mouth returned to hers, and he kissed her deeply. Not carnal and wild as before but gently, reverently. He sipped from her lips as if they held the sweetest wines in the world, and then his tongue mimicked the actions of his member once he was seated to the hilt.

Emmeline moaned from the fullness of Andrew being inside her. He was thick and long, and it took a moment for her body to adjust, but adjust it did until the fullness felt like it belonged inside her. Their hips moved together as he pulled in and out faster and faster. Her legs wrapped around his waist, his hips thrust over and over, his lips broke from hers, and their eyes locked together as they climbed toward release. She crested over the precipice, biting her bottom lip to keep from yelling out. At the same time, Andrew groaned and quickly pulled out, spilling his seed onto the sheets. He wrapped his arms around her and pulled her close then groaned, "The sheet's wet."

She couldn't help it and she giggled. "Move us over, there's plenty of dry bed behind me.

He repositioned them and sighed. "Much better."

Laying in Andrew's comforting arms now, her head resting on his chest, Emmeline sighed with contentment and exhaustion. Neither spoke again. Words were not needed after what they had experienced together. They both knew what had transpired between them was beyond exceptional.

As she drifted off to sleep, she pushed back against the guilt trying to wiggle its way into her mind.

ANDREW KNEW THE moment Emmeline drifted off to sleep. Her breathing evened out, and her head and hand resting on his chest sank further into his body. The emotions and feelings inundating his mind and body were almost too much to handle. He had known for ten years he loved her. But until they'd made love tonight, he had not realized how intense that love was. Never in his wildest imaginings had he known such a connection between two souls could genuinely exist. And she felt it, too. He was as sure of it as he was sure he had two hands.

When midnight had passed tonight, he almost hadn't come to her. He'd feared it was too late, and he didn't want to disturb her sleep. Thank goodness he hadn't listened to reason and had come anyway, regardless of the late hour—or rather early morning, as it was. It had been a long time since he'd been able to elude the pain and guilt of the past. But cradling Emmeline close to his heart had erased it. He wasn't fool enough to think those emotions wouldn't come back to him in the morning, but for now, he would relish the freeness and weightlessness his body and soul were experiencing.

Making love to—no, not to . . . *with*—Emmeline transcended the stars. His mind and body still had trouble comprehending how their bodies came together so perfectly. Where she ended, he began, and vice versa.

Two bodies joined together as a whole.

Two souls fading and blending to become one.

Two hearts beating in perfect rhythm.

If only he had known ten years ago what he knew now. He never would have stepped aside for Aiden. Pain pierced his heart.

No. He couldn't change the past. And truthfully, he wouldn't wish to. Ten years ago, perhaps he and Emmeline wouldn't have been ready for what existed between them now. Perhaps they needed the years of life's experiences, good and bad, to become the people they were now. To become people who were vulnerable and willing to put the pain of the past aside and love in the present.

Little mewling sounds came from Emmeline. It could be considered light snoring, but it was too pleasing a sound to really compare it to snoring. He kissed the top of her head and closed his eyes.

Not that he wanted to sleep. He wanted to hold her close and watch her sleep for the rest of the night. But his body and mind were drained. And nothing good would come tomorrow if he stayed awake. He would be too tired to enjoy the day's events and activities. Too exhausted to enjoy Emmeline.

CHAPTER TEN

"GOOD MORNING," EMMELINE'S maid said as she tossed the curtains aside, letting in the bright sunshine. "It is a lovely day to relax outdoors before traveling into Bath for dancing. There is not a cloud in the sky."

"Indeed." Emmeline blinked as the sunlight filtered inside the room. Sitting up, she stretched, noticing little aches in certain areas of her body, reminding her of last night. It had been six years since she'd lain with a man, and her body was not used to the vigorous activity. The subtle achy twinges had her heart soaring. The only thing better would have been to wake up in each other's arms. But that was impossible. Perhaps in time. Many widows had their lovers spend the night. But she wanted more from Andrew. She wanted all of him.

"Let's get you ready for the day. Everyone is gathering on the veranda and in the gardens for breakfast. Your day is free until three when we need to get you ready for tonight," Amanda said as she opened the wardrobe, eyeing the day dresses. "Would you care to wear the peach day dress with matching spencer and bonnet?"

"That would be perfect." Once she was dressed she sat at the dressing table while Amanda worked her magic taming her hair and making her look presentable. It was not long before she approached the doors to the veranda, and the aroma of breakfast wafted her way, along with the hum of voices and laughter. Her stomach took that moment to grumble, and she made her way to the serving tables and fixed a plate of eggs, ham, and toast with a dollop of whipped butter and jam. She scanned the gardens, smiled in acknowledgment to her mother sitting with her friends, and spotted an empty chair at a small table with Catherine and her husband near the rose bushes.

"May I join you?"

"We were just leaving, but please sit," Catherine replied. "We promised to help Claire organize things for this evening's trip to Bath. Enjoy your breakfast."

"Thank you," Emmeline said as she glanced around the gardens, looking for Andrew. He stood on the veranda by the doors with Caldwell. Their eyes connected, and he winked. Heat scorched her cheeks as she remembered what he had done to her last night with his mouth. She covered hers to stifle her gasp as he moved toward her, his eyes intense and predatory. His body moved with a natural masculine grace most gentlemen did not possess.

"May I?"

She wanted to ask *May I what? May I kiss you? Make love to you?* As far as she was concerned, he could do anything to her.

But he didn't wait for her reply, taking the seat vacated by Catherine. "You look flushed," he said, placing his elbows on the table, leaning forward, and lowering his voice. "I didn't mean to leave without saying goodbye, but the sun was rising, and I was afraid to be seen." He lowered his voice to a mere whisper, and her eyes were riveted to his mouth. "I knew if I woke you, I would not leave until I'd made love to you in the dawning light."

Swallowing down her moan, her eyes left his lips and moved to his green eyes, which were now a deep forest green rimmed in black. "How disappointing." They were both shocked at her words.

His brows rose, and he grinned. "Perhaps tonight."

Her lips curved into an easy smile, and warm happiness

spread throughout her body. She feared that if anyone looked too closely at the two of them, they would know what they had shared, but she couldn't let the joy go. For the past six years, she'd had very little true happiness in her life, and she refused to let it go or hide it inside now.

"Perhaps . . . do you think it is obvious?"

Relaxing back in his chair, his arms across his chest, he said, "Is what obvious?"

Her eyes darted around the gardens. Nobody noticed them except her mother, who studied her intently from across the way. She would know. A mother, or at least *her* mother, always knew. But there was no need to be embarrassed because her mother at least would be thrilled for her.

"Us. What we shared." As she said the words, her cheeks burned even hotter.

"You look positively gorgeous when you blush. And knowing that what we did put that color there makes me thrilled." He gestured to her plate. "You should break your fast. You used an awful lot of energy last night."

Just when she thought it was safe to put a forkful of eggs in her mouth, he had to say that. "You are not making it easy. Perhaps you could be silent so I can eat without choking."

"Whatever pleases you."

TEN CARRIAGES ROLLED down the long drive of Waterford Manor toward Bath at six o'clock sharp, transporting all occupants of the house party to the Upper Assembly Rooms for the Dress Ball. Emmeline was in a carriage with Andrew, Caldwell, and Lady Clarice. Catherine obviously had a hand in the carriage assignments. It was only a couple of miles to the Assembly Rooms, and Emmeline listened to the conversation between Caldwell and Andrew with only half an ear. Her mind was occupied with the dancing and what she hoped would come afterward when they returned to Waterford Manor.

"We are here." Andrew's voice pulled her out of her musings, and he assisted her in exiting the carriage. Her hand connecting with his had heat traveling up her arm and curling around her heart. A heart he'd claimed completely last night. A heart she willingly gave to him. A heart she hoped he didn't break. Her heart was more fragile than most, and she didn't think she would survive if he broke it.

He escorted her into the Upper Assembly Rooms. Andrew paid the cost of attendance for the four of them, with funds the marquess had supplied him for that purpose, and they entered the large ballroom to a considerable crowd milling about. The time was just past seven. They had two hours of dancing until tea at nine and then dancing until eleven.

For two hours, the orchestra played minuets. They danced several times but also took turns around the ballroom, watching others partake in the dancing. "Is all well with you?" Andrew said with concern. "You appear a little distant this evening."

Knots formed inside Emmeline's stomach. She hadn't realized her fear of her love for Andrew, and her panic that he was capable of breaking her heart, was resonating from her. The last thing she wanted to be was distant and give Andrew reason to think she regretted last evening or didn't want to repeat it. "Forgive me. Nothing is wrong. Perhaps I'm tired."

He raised a brow in silent question. "I know we discussed what happened between us this morning at breakfast, and you had no regrets then. Has something changed?"

Yes. She had fallen more in love with him than ever before, and it frightened her to the point that her heart nearly burst from her chest. "No."

"Emmeline." he closed his eyes, inhaled and exhaled. "Please answer me one question: Do you regret last night?"

Oh dear, what was wrong with her? Was she trying to ruin their relationship as it was just beginning? "No," she whispered. "Never."

His face lit up with his devastating smile. "Neither do I. So then, would you care for refreshments?"

When tea ended, the orchestra picked up the tempo with more enthusiastic country dances. They danced a set or two, and as her feet connected with the dance floor and her body twirled and sashayed, the heaviness in her chest eased. When the dancing ended she was both disappointed and excited to see how the rest of the evening would unfold.

At eleven o'clock on the dot, the carriages arrived, whisking the guests back to Waterford Manor.

Lying in bed, Emmeline's ears strained for any little sound. A creak from a floorboard, a door opening and closing, feet shuffling quietly down the hallway, anything to confirm Andrew would come to her tonight. But there was nothing. With her heart pounding and hands shaking, she was ready to scream her frustrations out. Until she heard the faintest sound outside her door. By the glow from the candle on her nightstand, she watched, her pulse jumping as her bedroom door opened, and Andrew snuck in quickly, closing the door silently behind him and locking it.

"Forgive me for taking so long. The same gentlemen from last evening had it in their minds to corner me to pick my brain about the shipping industry. They are hoping to make their fortunes in the import and export trade. I wish them luck."

Her eyes were riveted to him as he divested himself of all his clothing. The bed dipped as he joined her, pulling her into his arms and kissing her with a ferocious hunger they both shared. She would never tire of kissing him, tasting him, or enjoying the pure bliss he gave her body. Reaching down she curled her hand around his member and smiled when he moaned into her mouth. She moved her hand up and down his shaft repeatedly, feeling it enlarge even more.

Andrew tore his mouth from hers and placed barely there kisses down her neck until he reached her breasts and used his tongue to swirl around and around her pert nipple. When he sucked it in his mouth, her hips rose off the bed and she released his member. Her body wanted Andrew inside her and now. She pushed him onto his back and straddled him, taking his entire length at once.

Andrew's eyes, dark with desire, met hers as his large hands gripped her hips urging her to move up and down his shaft. Faster, harder, until Lilly's head rolled back as her body crested in pleasurable release. Her moans merged with Andrew's groans as pleasure overtook them both.

Moments later, entwined in each other's arms, satiated from their vigorous lovemaking, Emmeline felt content for the second time in as many days. Andrew's body, warm and strong, held her close, and she sighed in relaxation. Making love with Andrew was fulfilling, exhausting, and pure magical bliss.

She fought to keep her eyes open because she knew when she awoke next time, she would be alone. But it was no use. Sleep pulled her under, and when she awoke, sunbeams were sliding between the curtains, and she sat up, alone in her bed, and stretched, then lay back down and snuggled under her coverlet again. The muscles in her body eased, and she relished the mild soreness reminding her of last night's pleasurable events.

"Morning, ma'am," Amanda said as she entered the room and opened the curtains. "It is another rare sunny day. The carriages will be leaving at eleven to go into Bath. You are promenading through Sydney Gardens and having breakfast in the gardens when the promenade concludes. Then you are free to shop along Bond and Milsom Streets and visit the Pump Rooms. Which is where the carriages will pick you up to bring you back here."

"My goodness, Amanda, how do you know all this?" Emmeline said as she pulled the coverlet up close to her chin to hide her nakedness.

"The itinerary was posted just now. The hosts changed the schedule once they saw the sunny, warm day."

"Leaving at eleven," Emmeline remarked. "Would you go down to the kitchens and bring me toast and tea?"

"Yes, ma'am."

Once Amanda left, Emmeline hurried from the bed, threw on her night rail and dressing gown, and sat on the bed awaiting her breakfast tray. Her stomach growled, and she realized she was famished. She didn't usually wake up hungry, but after last night's lovemaking, she had an appetite.

Her mind wandered to what Andrew was thinking right now. Did he remember last night with great enthusiasm? Was he looking forward to repeating it with her tonight? How silly she was being. She wasn't a doubter or one to have fits of uncertainty, nor was she a worrier. Somehow though, when it came to Andrew, she was all those things and more. She didn't like it one bit. It made her feel weak and timid, and she was neither. He also made her second guess herself in his eyes. Was she enough for him? Did he love her? Was he only whiling away the time until he found a young debutante to marry? Someone pure, innocent, and very young. Someone who could give him many heirs.

Wrapping her arms around her stomach, she groaned out and chastised herself, "Stop it. Stop it right this moment."

Amanda entered with her food and sat the tray beside her on the bed. "What would you like to wear today?"

Emmeline nibbled on toast with marmalade. "The pretty pink silk day dress with the matching pelisse and wide-brimmed bonnet."

"Good choice. And your cream parasol, which complements the dress nicely, will keep you shaded while out of doors along with your bonnet."

A few minutes before eleven, Emmeline went downstairs to the hall, which bustled with everyone chatting. She had a moment of anxiety, finding everyone speaking at once unsettling, but it quickly eased. Finding her mother, she made her way to her. "Have you everything you need for today, Mama?"

Her mother looked at her, somewhat confused. "And why wouldn't I? I've gone on many outings in my day." She paused and looked her over with a mother's critical eye. "Are you feeling well?"

"Yes. Just excited for today."

"Oh, look. It's time to leave," Her mother said, taking her arm as the crowd was exiting the house and piling into numerous carriages. Emmeline found herself inside a coach with her mother, Catherine, and Catherine's husband. She had yet to see Andrew. Just as their vehicle lurched forward, she spotted him entering a coach with Caldwell, Lady Clarice, and Mrs. Charlette Beauchamp.

Not until this house party had she met Mrs. Beauchamp. She was the widow of a decorated war hero who'd fought alongside the Duke of Wellington and was a close friend to Lady Clarice. Both ladies were several years younger than Emmeline and no doubt seeking husbands. They could become friends as long as Mrs. Beauchamp didn't have her sights set on Andrew. However, she didn't know what to make of Lady Clarice. She was an enigma. Emmeline first thought Caldwell was smitten with her, but she took that back after Andrew's comment about her warming his bed. They appeared friendly but not in love. She, for one, could not entertain sharing a bed with someone merely for the sake of one's own pleasure. Her heart needed to be engaged. Which, of course, it was with Andrew.

The carriages pulled up one by one and unloaded their passengers in front of the Sydney Hotel. One must go through the hotel to enter the pleasure gardens. Emmeline looked around for Andrew. She loved her mother but would rather parade through the gardens on his arm. Just when she had given up, she saw him strolling her way. She sighed with relief. At the same time, her heart accelerated.

"Mrs. Fitzpatrick," he said, bowing gracefully. "Would you do me the honor of allowing me to escort you through the gardens? People are lining up for The Promenade."

She curtsied. "The honor is mine, Your Grace." She looked questioningly at her mother, who waved her off. "Go. Do not fret about me."

Before placing her arm on Andrew's, she opened her pretty

cream parasol trimmed with lace. "Shall we?"

"We shall," he replied with a grin that made her heart surge.

The gardens were crowded with people of all social standings who came for the daily breakfast and dancing afterward. Bath was such a pleasant surprise to Emmeline, and after this visit, she planned to come back. It had much to offer and didn't have the oppressive feel of London or the overly quiet solitude of the country. Not that she had a country estate of her own, of course.

"What beautiful gardens," Andrew said as he slowed his pace.

"They are," she agreed as she also slowed. It was either that or step on the heels of the two fashionably dressed young ladies, not from their party, strolling in front of them. They both looked over their shoulders now and again, blushing and giggling. They looked around seventeen. Did they keep looking because of Andrew? Did they know he was a duke? It appeared as though they did from the coquettish looks they sent him.

"You appear to have two pretty admirers in front of us."

"I see that," he chuckled. "Too young for my taste, my dear." He waggled his brows at her. "I have the lady I desire already on my arm."

His words nearly had her tripping. "I believe they have set their sights on you."

"Yes, well. No doubt either of their mothers or both sent them my way, hoping for a match." He lowered his head and murmured. "Innocent virgins don't interest me. Not in my bed nor as my wife."

This time, her steps did falter.

Steadying her, he said, his voice laced with humor, "Is something amiss? You're usually so graceful."

"You rogue. Behave, or I shall seek out my mother and walk with her instead," she teased.

He gasped, his free arm covering his heart. "You wound me, my dear. Perhaps Mrs. Beauchamp would enjoy my naughty behavior if you do not?"

She opened her mouth to speak but nothing was forthcoming.

Realizing his error, he patted her hand. "Forgive me. I shouldn't have teased you by saying that. It's not the same thing as walking with one's mother."

"All is forgiven. After all, I started it." As soon as the promenade ended, they made their way to the food tables. Andrew got coffee, and Emmeline picked up a cup of tea. They both indulged in one of Sally Lunn's famous buns.

They took their drinks and buns to a quiet area near the canal, and Andrew, ever the gentleman, removed his jacket, placing it on the grass beneath a large English Oak so she wouldn't soil her dress. "Thank you, my gallant knight."

"You are ever so welcome, my fair lady."

With Andrew holding her food, Emmeline sat down, adjusted her skirts, and took in the scenery as he handed her tea and bun to her. Several boats were on the canal with fashionably dressed patrons aboard. It would be fun to take to the canal if they had time. "It's beautiful and peaceful here."

He joined her on the ground, managing not to spill a drop of his coffee, sitting close, their bodies touching everywhere possible. She knew he did it on purpose, and she didn't mind. It was safe, comforting, and arousing all at the same time, even if it wasn't proper. "It is. Are you comfortable?"

"Yes. Very."

"Emmeline?"

"Yes, Andrew?"

"You do know where this is going, don't you?"

She knew where she wanted their relationship to go. Was he of like mind? Before she could answer, Andrew moved over, putting an appropriate amount of space between them. "We have company."

"Indeed."

"It's just Caldwell and Lady Clarice."

"So this is where you went off to," Caldwell said as he spread his jacket on the ground. He helped Lady Clarice sit and joined her. "I heard several mamas speak your name to their daughters.

You were smart to leave the crowd."

"And you had to find us?" Andrew said with one cocked brow.

Caldwell laughed, "I may not be a duke, but I am also sought after by some of the mamas who don't care about titles but do enjoy money. And I have plenty of money. One young lady practically chased me. If she hadn't tripped on her skirt, she may have caught me."

Andrew shook his head and laughed. "I would pay good money to see you run from a young debutante."

"Are you enjoying Bath, Mrs. Fitzpatrick?" Lady Clarice asked as she picked blades of grass and twirled them between her fingers, having long since finished Sally Lunn's delicious and gooey bun.

"Yes. And please call me Emmeline."

"Thank you, Emmeline. I spent some time here years ago with my husband. He'd taken ill and swore the restorative water and the Roman Baths would cure him."

"Did they?" Emmeline asked.

"For a time. But he was old. People die."

"What a mood crusher you are, Lady Clarice," Caldwell remarked with a grin, a wink, and a nudge.

"I hear music. The dancing must be starting. Shall we?" Andrew said as he stood, holding out his hand for her. She took it, and he pulled her to her feet and picked up his jacket, brushing off the grass and dirt before putting it on.

"Oh my," Emmeline said with trepidation as they approached the dancing, presently a country reel. "I believe those mothers and daughters are looking straight at you."

"A little bold, don't you think?" he said.

"You should dance with several of the young ladies. It will boost their standing with the other gentlemen to be seen dancing with a duke."

"I'm not dancing with them. I don't know them. If it were someone I knew and could help her without entangling myself, I would consider it." He held out his hand. "Shall we?"

She smiled, and took his hand. "We shall."

The dance was not conducive to conversation. They moved forward and back, twirled around, broke apart, and came back together, only to do it again. Emmeline liked the excitement of country reels, but they were nothing compared to the waltz. Memories of dancing the waltz with Andrew the other night flashed in her mind. She didn't expect a waltz in the middle of the day with the sun shining, which was unfortunate.

The dance ended, and they walked to a table with punch and lemonade, which had already been poured into cups. They both picked up a lemonade. "Don't look now," Emmeline whispered, "but the Countess of Hartford is almost upon us with her daughter, Lady Beatrice."

Andrew groaned.

"What a pleasant surprise to see you here, Your Grace," said the countess as she curtsied. "I hope your mother is well and enjoying living in the country."

Andrew smiled tightly and bowed. "She is doing well, all things considered. I will give her your best."

"Please do, Your Grace. You remember my daughter, Lady Beatrice."

Andrew bowed over her hand as Lady Beatrice curtsied gracefully. "It is a pleasure to see you again, Lady Beatrice. Are you enjoying Bath?"

Before Lady Beatrice could answer, the countess chimed in. "She would enjoy it more if you found it in your heart to dance with her, Your Grace."

Andrew's eyes locked with Emmeline's, conveying his hesitancy. Before he could respond the countess added. "It's one dance, Your Grace. It will do wonders in helping my daughter attract a suitor." She touched her fan to his forearm. "Please, you must help out a family friend."

Even before Andrew relented to the countess, Emmaline knew he would. Once she mentioned their family connection, she knew he would agree to one dance. He was too honorable not to.

Andrew bowed to Lady Beatrice and held out his arm. "Will you do me the honor of dancing with me, Lady Beatrice?"

"Yes," she said softly, blushing as she placed her small, gloved hand on his arm, and they walked off. Emmeline tried not to acknowledge the pain in her heart as he walked away with a stunning young lady looking comfortable on his arm. Lady Beatrice did not take after her mother. Lady Beatrice had long, thick, and wavy blonde hair. Her facial features were delicate, and her green eyes were stunning. Emmeline predicted she would not have a second Season.

CHAPTER ELEVEN

"WHAT A SHOCK to run into the Marquess and Marchioness of Waterford's house party today. And to have the good fortune of Blackstone amongst the guests." The Countess of Hartford said to Emmeline, snapping open her fan and waving it. "He is still dreadfully handsome. My daughter has had her eye on him since the Season began. It is too bad you have been monopolizing his time. But you can't possibly expect him to be still interested in you? You are ... may I be blunt? ... past your prime."

The rude and hurtful words had her insides seething, and Emmeline wished she could grab Lady Hartford's fan from her hands and slap the biddy on her cheek with it. It was no less than she deserved for insulting her. Instead, she would use her words. "If you hope to endear your daughter to Blackstone, insulting me will not help. I am his closest friend, and he heeds my opinion. He will not court or marry anyone I disapprove of. Lady Beatrice may be the sweetest, most polite and kind person, but her mother is not, and His Grace will not chain himself to a lady whose mother is gossipy, nasty, and invading." Her curtsy barely existed. "Good day, Countess."

Trembling all over, barely able to see from her anger and, worse, mortification, she wove through the crowd until she found a large tree and leaned her back against it. It took over eight times of inhaling and exhaling before she calmed. Never had she been insulted like that. It made her wonder if others felt the way the countess did. Were they whispering and laughing behind her back? Thinking her a fool as she paraded around on Andrew's arm? She had many insecurities regarding him and her age, but she had finally thought she had put them to rest. Obviously not, if it only took one remark from a spiteful countess to have her shrinking inside and her confidence scattered into the wind. Well, she wouldn't let her actions or words taint what she had with Andrew.

"Here you are," Andrew said as he stood before her, taking her in. His brow cocked. "What is wrong?"

Shaking her head, she said, "Nothing."

He leaned close and murmured, "I don't believe you." He crossed his arms and rocked back on his heels, his eyes piercing hers. "Tell me what Countess Hartford said."

She shrugged. "What makes you think she said anything?"

"Because I know her. My mother disliked her, but she never got the hint and visited often after my father passed. She would come with Lady Beatrice and prattle on and on about merging our families in marriage." He leaned closer and said through clenched teeth, "It is never going to happen."

Emmeline let out her breath. "She told me I was *past my prime*." Emmeline knew twenty-eight wasn't past prime. Many ladies married for the first time at that age and proceeded to give their husband heirs. However, Countess Hartford had tapped into Emmeline's own insecurities about her age and used them against her.

"What?" His voice rose and attracted the attention of several people nearby. "I'll tell her who is old, shall I? Emmeline, do not believe anything that gossipy wart-faced lady says. Eight and twenty is not old. You are more beautiful and more youthful than any other lady here." His fingers caressed her cheek. "You are the only one for me. When we are seventy, I will still love and want you." He held out his hand. "Come. Let us go shopping and then visit the Pump Rooms. The carriages are picking us up there in two hours."

Emmeline took Andrew's arm as they left Sydney Gardens behind and walked toward Bond and Milsom Streets. Andrew led her inside a jeweler's, and her pulse soared. "What are we doing here?" she asked.

"I thought I could cheer you up by buying you something pretty to wear on your wrist."

The lemonade she'd recently drunk sloshed around inside her stomach. All she thought about was what they had shared the previous two nights. Did he feel obligated to buy her expensive jewelry because she slept with him? She took his hand and led him to a quiet corner.

"If you are buying me a trinket because I slept with you, please don't bother. I gave myself to you freely."

"Emmeline, my dear," he whispered, an expression of contrition on his face. "Please forgive me if you thought such a thing. I've never purchased jewelry for anyone unless you count my sisters and nieces. I saw the store and thought that since you wear bracelets, perhaps you would like a new one. It was an innocent thought. Please let me buy you a trinket. It is the first time I can do so when you are free to receive my gift."

Feeling silly and embarrassed, she curled her lips into an apologetic smile. "I'm sorry. I believe lack of sleep the past two nights is affecting my thoughts." He was right. The Andrew she knew would never feel obligated to buy her favors, so why was she even thinking such thoughts? When it came to him, sometimes her confidence and clear thinking disappeared.

He winked and grinned as though he had done something naughty. "Come. Let's look at what the store has to offer." Emmeline and Andrew stood looking over several pieces on display. "Do you like that one?" Andrew pointed to a beautiful piece, and before she could reply, he spoke to the proprietor. "The lady would like to see the gold and diamond bracelet with the pearls. And the matching earbobs as well."

"That is too much, Your Grace."

"Nonsense, my dear. Anything for you."

"If I may suggest," the shopkeeper said. "There is a matching necklace as well. Shall I get it?"

Emmeline noticed that the moment she referred to Andrew as *Your Grace*, the proprietor's eyes had widened. He no doubt hoped for a most profitable sale.

"Yes. We will take all three pieces."

Andrew tucked the box into his jacket pocket after the proprietor wrapped the jewelry in a black velvet box tied with red ribbon. When they were outside, he leaned close. "I can't wait to see you in nothing but these jewels tonight," he said, his voice raspy and laced with lust.

His comment, the way he said it, as though he were seducing her right there on the street, had her entire being tingling with awareness. "You are a complete rakehell, Your Grace. Come, let us continue," she said as she wrapped her arm through the crook of his elbow. Thankfully, her knees didn't buckle as her body still hummed for him and what he would do to her later within the confines of her bedroom. "Now behave before someone hears you say something scandalous."

This time, he laughed. "I'm sorry, Emmeline, but you look good enough to eat, and I am famished."

Ignoring the meaning behind his words, she continued pulling him along. "Shall we visit the Pump Room?" From what she'd heard, the Pump Room was not just a place to go and drink the restorative waters, but also a social place to gossip and mingle with the residents of Bath and those visiting on holiday.

When they arrived, Andrew and Emmeline made their way to the water table, filled glasses with the liquid, and crossed the room. Emmeline's mother separated from a group of women she was with and made her way to them.

"There you are," her mother said to her and Andrew. "Your Grace." She curtsied. "I wondered when you'd make your way here."

"Have you been here before, baroness?" Andrew queried as he sipped from his glass.

"Several times in the past when the baron and I were newly married."

"I didn't know that, Mama."

She raised one perfectly shaped brow, enhanced by her blue turban, which matched her dress. "You don't know everything about my life, my darling daughter."

Emmeline smiled. "You are correct. Have you been before, Your Grace?"

Grinning at her over the top of his glass, Andrew said, "Not in many years. But it appears much the same as I remember."

A short time later the carriages arrived, and everyone returned to Waterford Manor.

Since it was a day full of adventures, that evening's dinner was an informal affair. Everyone appeared tired after their busy day. Once everyone who hadn't retired for the evening congregated in the drawing room, Andrew asked, "Would you like to venture into the gardens?"

"That would be lovely." Wrapping her arm through his, Emmeline allowed him to lead her into the dimly lit gardens. They meandered through the stone pathways, occasionally stopping to smell the jasmine. The sound of the nighttime insects buzzed a sweet lullaby and Emmeline's worry about her age after the hurtful countess called her "past her prime" eased, and she felt lighthearted in the bountiful gardens on Andrew's arm. As they approached the gazebo, they heard voices drifting their way. Voices belonging to Caldwell and Lady Clarice, and they paused, not wanting to intrude.

They could hear the deep timbre of Caldwell's voice but not understand his words. Suddenly the breeze picked up blowing in the perfect direction because now their words were clear, as if they were standing beside them. "Why are you telling me this?" Lady Clarice asked.

"I don't know. I suppose I just needed to relieve some of the guilt and tension strangling me since I've been spending more time with Mrs. Fitzpatrick lately."

"I can't believe she doesn't know Blackstone is responsible for her husband's death. That the three of you lied to her."

Emmeline gasped and pulled her arm from Andrew's. A sick feeling took over her body. She turned and looked directly into his eyes—eyes that looked cautious and guarded in the dim light of the gardens.

"Andrew?" She choked out his name as she tightened the shawl around her shoulders. Her body trembled uncontrollably, and her skin prickled with chills.

"Emmeline. Let me explain." His hands reached out to grab hers, but she wouldn't allow it. "Caldwell, Langford, and I may have left out some details, but we were protecting you from more pain."

"More pain?" she yelled, even though it came out stifled as her throat clogged with anger and frustration. "My heart is being stabbed right now with more pain in finding out you've *left out details* for years. Years, Andrew. What am I supposed to do with this newfound understanding? Pretend I didn't hear? Pretend the truth wasn't kept from me? What didn't you tell me?" Her heart was dying inside her chest. Turning black and hardening. All her joy at being with Andrew was slowly disappearing and she didn't know how to stop it.

"Please let me explain." The panic in his voice almost got to her. She would allow him to explain, not for him, but for her. She needed to know the truth once and for all. Her future depended on it.

"Go on."

"It is true; we had been drinking. We each had a flask of whisky that Aiden supplied. And since none of us were great hunters, we decided to ride off alone. We reached an open field that went on forever. I asked if anyone wanted to race." He paused, ran his hands through his hair, and then tugged hard enough that he winced. "Aiden said he would. I don't know what was wrong with him that day, but he didn't appear to be his easygoing self. He seemed angry at the world. Angry at me, as if I'd done something to offend him. He also said that since I was a better rider than him, he would take my horse to compensate. I tried to persuade him, since he wasn't a good horseman, but he'd set his mind on riding Merlin, who was hard to handle, and I ended up riding Langford's mount.

"Hard to handle. But you told me he was docile right after the accident. Why did you lie? Why did you let him ride him knowing it would be dangerous?" By now her heart was pounding inside her chest so hard it hurt, and she could barely breathe to get words out.

Andrew ran his hands through his hair and groaned. "I don't know. He insisted, and I didn't want to cause any more strain in our friendship. And then the race started. Merlin took off, and Aiden used his crop on him, which I knew was bad. I pushed the horse I rode hard and came up beside Merlin, who was very agitated. I called to my horse." His voice drifted off, and his eyes blinked back tears.

Emmeline barely breathed.

"Merlin came to a sudden stop, Aiden went flying. Merlin reared up and came down on top of Aiden." He scrubbed the tears from his cheeks. "Christ, I'm so sorry. It happened so fast I couldn't do anything to help him."

His voice seemed far away, echoing from inside a tunnel as he explained that heartbreaking day. His telling of that tragic accident, and keeping nothing out this time, had her hand covering her stomach as she fought not to lose her dinner on the gravel path.

"I have felt guilty. The guilt ate me alive, and you know it. It nearly ruined my life. I dreamed for many years of a life with you, being married to you, but never at the expense of my best friend. I never wanted his death." Andrew's pain radiated through his voice. She wanted to feel sorry for him, but it was all she could do not to step up to him and beat her fists against his chest, much like she had done the day Aiden died.

"Ruined your life," she mumbled. "Your life?" Her words became louder as she swung out her arms to encompass the gardens, and she spun around. "You are alive and breathing. You lived to see another day . . . years even. I don't feel sorry for you. He *is* dead because of you. I hope never to see you again."

Her throat was raw, her heart eviscerated, and her body and mind barely functioned. She hunched her shoulders as her feet shuffled through the small stones leading back toward the manor. Andrew called after her, but she ignored him. She needed to get to the safety of her room before she broke. It was coming, and there was not a thing she could do to stop it.

She could blame Andrew all she wanted, but it was his betrayal of her that hurt, not his role in Aiden's death—not really. Her heart knew the truth about that. Aiden had been dealing with her miscarriage and drinking too much because of it.

Finally behind the closed door of her room, she collapsed face-first on the bed and let the tears come, tears that encompassed too many things in her life. She cried for Aiden and her unborn baby, and she cried for the loss of Andrew. She honestly didn't know how she would face him again, or go on from here without him.

CHAPTER TWELVE

STANDING IN THE garden, his eyes riveted to Emmeline's back as she left, broke something inside him. He had always known when he confessed the truth of that terrible, heartbreaking day that she would reject him, but he had hoped for more time. Fate was not on his side once again regarding Emmeline.

"I heard Emmeline yelling. Did something happen? Where did she go?" Caldwell said, looking concerned.

He turned his back on them so they wouldn't see him crying. "She was here."

Caldwell came up behind him and placed his hand on his shoulder. "Is all well?"

"No," he stuttered, forcing his feet to move down the path, deeper into the garden toward the orangery, ignoring Caldwell calling after him. He was not fit for company. Ugliness ate at his insides; all he wanted to do was lash out—or cry like a baby. Once at the orangery, he sat on the grass outside, leaning against a large tree.

One moment tonight, they were dancing, laughing, and making plans for another night of lovemaking, and the next Emmeline was telling him she never wanted to see him again. Oh, he didn't blame her. He should have told her everything when Aiden died.

The truth of the matter was that he was ashamed of his actions. If he had told her the truth from the beginning, perhaps she would have forgiven him by now. As it stood, he didn't know if she ever would. First thing tomorrow, he would ride out, go to his country seat, and hopefully heal his broken heart. He would give Emmeline some time to heal and then go to her and beg her forgiveness. Life was nothing to him without her. Either he would find a way to earn her forgiveness or he would die old and alone. He refused to marry another no matter what people said was required of him.

"Now that we are in the carriage alone and on our way back to London, will you tell me what happened?" Emmeline's mother asked with concern. "I know it has to do with Blackstone. I have not seen you this upset since Aiden's death, and I am going out of my mind with worry."

When she'd returned to her room last evening, Emmeline sent a note to her mother requesting they leave first thing the following morning and one to their hosts explaining they must go to London. She gave no reason in either missive, and she could no longer put off her mother. "Last night, I found out something that played into Aiden's death." She went on to explain most of what had transpired between her and Andrew.

"Darling." Her mother, sitting beside her, placed a hand on hers. The warm comfort eased her a tad. "I cannot tell you what to do or how to handle the duke. The only thing I ask of you is not to take lightly what you and Blackstone share. I can see the love you both have for one another, a love that started ten years ago and never died. I know he has spent nights in your room. This must be difficult for both of you after your shared intimacy."

Visions of Andrew in her bed, his scent clinging to the pillows and sheets, had plagued her last night, making sleep impossible. Perhaps if they hadn't shared their bodies, the loss would not be so devastating. She didn't believe she could ever lie with another man. Not only was her life with Andrew over, but her dream of being married with children was over.

She would die an old childless widow.

WHEN ANDREW LEFT the house party, he went straight to Blackstone Hall. He hoped spending time in the country would ease the turmoil running rampant through his mind. All he could hear was Emmeline's words telling him, "I hope never to see you again." The devastating pain he'd witnessed on her face plagued him daily.

The day Aiden died was a day that played over and over again in Andrew's mind. Even six years later, he tried to manipulate the accident in his mind so Aiden lived. So Aiden was alive today. But he could not change the past. He had to live with it. He had to live with his decision to race Aiden. And his decision never to tell Emmeline the whole truth.

At Blackstone Hall, he punished himself by working in the stables. His stable hands were horrified that their duke was mucking out stalls, filling the feed buckets, and hauling water from the well, but he needed the physical work. Otherwise, he would not be able to sleep. Exhaustion was the only way he slept, the only thing that eased his dreams.

He hid from the world and exhausted his mind and body for a month before he traveled back to London, hoping to make things right with Emmeline.

EMMELINE SPENT THE month after her world collapsed in her library, reading away her heartache. When reading failed to help, she embroidered new handkerchiefs and pillowcases. She'd never been so proficient with her embroidering, even though her heart wasn't in it. It was mindless activity that she wanted.

Finally needing a break, she ventured out to the Duchess of Greenville's home for a meeting of the Ladies' Society of Mayfair. They were packing baskets to be delivered the following day. Emmeline and Mrs. Bishop volunteered to go with Mitchel, Her Grace's volunteer driver, to St. Giles. After several hours of organizing, planning and refreshments, she bid the duchess farewell.

"Your Grace, another successful day."

"Yes, Emmeline," said the duchess. "I've missed you these last weeks, and I'm glad you have returned. Thank you for agreeing to go tomorrow. Mitchel will pick you up at half past eight."

Her driver had dropped her off today at the duchess's house and she had sent him home, preferring to walk the short distance home after the meeting. As she strolled through the streets of Mayfair toward her townhouse, Emmeline wondered what she would do for the rest of the day. The weather was lovely, and she could ride in the park, except riding by herself didn't appeal to her. She could call upon Lilly and Langford, but they were in the country, having recently returned from their honeymoon. Perhaps she could visit them soon. However, she doubted they would want her around much as they started their new life as a married couple.

Melancholy settled in, and Emmeline hated it. She'd spent years after Aiden's death feeling sorry for herself, and she refused to revisit those years. If only she could convince her heart and mind. Her heart pained her constantly, and her mind screamed at her to forgive Andrew, but she didn't know how.

MITCHEL PICKED HER up on time in the morning, and Flynn rode along as their escort. Emmeline was bundled up against the rain.

They picked up Mrs. Bishop before venturing into St. Giles. Emmeline stared out the carriage window as they left London proper behind and ventured into the poorer sections of town. Each time she traveled into the slums, she thought she would get used to the stench, the sights, and the sounds, but she didn't. They bombarded her much like the first time all over again, and she had to fight down her anxiety. She refused to let it win. This charity had been her saving grace for the past six years, and she needed it as much as those living in poverty needed their donations. When the Ladies' Society of Mayfair started, they would deliver baskets once every two weeks. They were making several trips to the rookeries each week now.

Emmeline told the duchess she would go twice a week from now on as she had nothing else to occupy her time. Anything was better than sitting at home and thinking about Andrew. Their carriage today was crowded with over thirty baskets and bags to be delivered. Mitchel had the addresses of where they needed to go. Once he stopped the coach, Flynn would open the door, escort them to the stoop, and help deliver the goods to the correct person.

The day was long and emotionally draining, and by the time Emmeline returned home, her body ached from being inside the carriage and carrying the heavy goods. Her body was chilled from the cold rain which penetrated through her cloak. As she wearily climbed her own front stairs, she recognized Andrew's carriage and driver in front of her neighbor's house. She wasn't fooled. He was here to see her, not her neighbor.

Harrison opened the door. "The Duke of Blackstone is here to see you. He is in the drawing room."

Her heart raced upon hearing Andrew's name spoken out loud. She had wondered when he would seek her out. Then she remembered how angry she had been with him. "Please tell him I will be down shortly, and have tea delivered." She handed Harrison her wet cloak and gloves, hurried up two sets of stairs, and entered her chambers, ringing the bell for her maid. Her warm bath would have to wait until later. She removed her damp traveling clothes. Wearing only her chemise, she used a cloth, soaked it in the basin, lathered it with flowery-scented soap, and wiped down all her exposed skin, taking the dust and grime from the streets with it.

"Ma'am," said Amanda as she entered the room. "I just heard the Duke of Blackstone is here. What shall you wear?"

"The garnet day dress. Please bring a new chemise as well. Mine is damp."

After she dressed, she sat at the dressing table. "Could you take my hair down? I shall leave it loose as it is also damp." Once Amanda brushed her hair, Emmeline put on the matching slippers to the dress and slowly walked down one flight of stairs to the drawing room. Outside the partially open door, her hand covered her pounding heart as she tried to calm her nerves. As much as she wanted to see Andrew, she also didn't want to see him. Part of her was still so angry at him. It had been a month since she had seen him, and she was shocked he'd called upon her so abruptly. She had said she never wanted to see him again, and at the time, she'd meant it . . . but now?

She breathed in and out several times to calm herself, then she pushed the door open and stepped inside. "Your Grace, to what do I owe the pleasure of your company?" He faced the window, his arms behind his back, and he pivoted around at the sound of her voice. His features were guarded as he swept his eyes up and down, taking her in. Two things became noticeable at once: he looked tired, and he looked uncertain. She understood perfectly.

"I was in the area and wondered if you knew Langford and Lilly arrive in town tomorrow."

She frowned. "No. I did not. But a note would have sufficed. You didn't have to travel out on such a nasty day. I'm quite convinced Lilly will send me a note when she arrives at Langford House tomorrow." She tried to ignore the fast beat of her heart at the handsome sight of Andrew looking dashing in his riding clothes, even if he was exhausted. No matter how angry she was at him, her heart would never forget him, nor would her upbringing let her be rude and throw him out. So she did the only thing she could think of. "But as you are here, would you care to join me for tea?" She sat on the dark blue settee and arranged her skirts. "Please sit."

"Thank you." He took a wing-backed chair facing her, his hat in his hands, and she noticed his hands trembling ever so slightly. So she wasn't the only one affected by this little impromptu visit. "I didn't expect you to receive me."

She tilted her head, her heart thumping wildly as she wondered how this visit would play out and what the outcome would be. Because honestly, she had no idea what she would do or say. "Why did you come?"

He shrugged his shoulders. "Perhaps to see if you would receive me?"

"I see."

"I don't think you do," he said with sadness.

"Enlighten me." So many emotions were swirling inside her body and mind that she didn't know if she'd survive this visit unscathed. They were old friends, awkward strangers, and intimate lovers all at the same time.

"I miss you." His words were so soft they barely reached her ears.

"Nothing has changed since last we spoke." Except she missed him every minute of every day. Her heart craved him. But her mind was still so very hurt and angry. She wasn't a callous person who held grudges—except something deep inside her where she loved Andrew had altered that day. She had been fighting it and trying to heal the wound ever since. Indeed, she was angry at Langford and Caldwell as well, but knowing them, they were likely following Andrew's lead that day when the story was told. Either that or they were protecting him from her. After all, it was Andrew's horse Aiden rode and Andrew's words that spoke the lie about his horse. They just didn't contradict him.

"I'm sorry to hear that," he said, his voice edged with fatigue. His usually bright-green eyes were dull, and his face looked drawn as if he had lost weight.

Tears clogged her throat and stung her eyes, but she refused to let him see her cry. She needed to remain strong for the sake of her sanity. Thank goodness a footman took that moment to enter the room and place the tea tray on the highly polished wooden table in front of her. She picked up the pot and poured the tea into two cups. "Sugar?"

"Yes."

She prepared his tea, then leaned forward, holding out the cup and saucer. He took it from her hands and leaned back in his seat. "Thank you."

After adding sugar and a splash of cream to her tea, she picked it up and took a sip. "There are biscuits. Please help yourself."

"I'm fine. Thank you."

She had been positively famished when she'd arrived home, but no longer. Hoping the tea would settle her stomach, she sipped it slowly.

"How have you been?" he asked over the rim of his cup.

Before she could answer, her mother entered the drawing room. "I thought I heard a man's voice . . ."

Andrew rose and bowed. "Baroness, how lovely to see you again."

"Your Grace." She curtsied. "What a pleasant surprise. Please sit."

Her mother joined her on the settee and poured herself tea in the extra cup on the tray.

"Langford and Lilly will be back in town tomorrow," Emmeline told her mother.

"That is wonderful news. I miss Lilly so much. It is not the same as when she lived with us."

Emmeline stared thoughtfully into her cup of tea. She was happy for Lilly and her marriage to Langford, but she did miss her terribly. She was always a breath of fresh air on the dullest of days. An uncomfortable silence descended on them, and she wondered when Andrew would take his leave.

"May I have a private word with you, Emmeline?" he finally asked.

Her mother rose from the settee, and Andrew did as well. "I will leave you two to speak." As she exited, she left the door ajar just a crack.

"May I?" He indicated the settee with his hand.

She scooted over as far as she could to make room. He didn't look pleased, but he sat down, respecting the space between them.

"I'm hoping we can discuss what happened and move forward."

She was unprepared for this conversation, but now that it was forced upon her, perhaps it would ease the constant tightness in her chest. "That night in the garden when we overheard Caldwell and Lady Clarice talking," she said softly, "it was as though it was the day Aiden died all over again. The pain and anguish slammed into me. I never saw it coming. And your deceit wrecked me. It made me second-guess our friendship and our relationship. To be honest, I'm still struggling."

He reached for her hand, and she let him hold it. She tried not to acknowledge how much she missed his touch and how the warmth from his large hand eased the coldness inside her body. Before she could pull away, he did. "Words cannot express how sorry I am for what pain I caused you. I should have told you everything the day of the accident. Why I didn't, I can't say—except I was trying to make Aiden's death easier on you. And I know Langford and Caldwell felt the same." He paused. "Though, believe it or not, we have never talked about what happened. I imagine that does not help anyone move forward. We were all devastated that day. You the most."

"I've struggled with my own guilt from that day."

Andrew looked at her in silent question.

"It's a long story, but I'll shorten it. I miscarried one week before the house party."

His hand reached for hers again and gently squeezed.

"Aiden didn't handle it well. He was angry and overindulging in spirits. We quarreled—something we seldom did. I blamed myself for insisting we attend the party even though I was still recovering physically from the loss. I wanted him to be with his close friends. I thought it would help him recover mentally. Except, if I hadn't insisted we go, he would still be alive."

"Emmeline, I'm so sorry. I didn't know." The compassion in his voice touched her.

"No one did, except for my mother."

"Is there anything I can do for you now? Is there anything you need from me?"

Love. I need your love. But it was not something she would ask for. She felt ashamed now for how she'd treated him, and she wouldn't blame him if he never wanted to see her again. The cause of Aiden's death was a combination of Aiden's own recklessness, and racing inebriated.

Yes, Andrew had instigated the race and let Aiden ride his wicked horse, but he hadn't intentionally planned on seeing Aiden dead. "No," she finally said. She didn't know why she was still holding on to her anger at Andrew. She'd never been indecisive before.

"If you need anything, anything at all, please send word." His hand lightly touched her hair as he stood and took his leave, his sorrow only fueling hers.

No sooner had he exited than she curled up on her side, her face in her hands, and she broke down and cried.

➤➤➤✦◀◀◀

"I'M SORRY, I forgot my hat . . . Emmeline!" Andrew gasped. Pushing the table aside in a panic, he knelt before her and gently stroked her hair and back. "Please don't cry," he murmured. "If I could take all your pain away, I would. Please. I hate to see you like this." He moved to the settee and maneuvered her so he held her in his arms, her face buried against his chest.

Her body shook with deep sobs, and his heart ripped in two. He would do anything for her. Anything. He held her, his hands stroking her back while he murmured soothing words into her ear. Tears stung his eyes at the magnitude of her anguish, and when they trickled down his cheeks, he ignored them. They shared in their renewed grief for Aiden, and he would not choose to be anywhere else in the world but right here with her. No matter what she said or how many times she pushed him away, his love for her would never die, and he would spend eternity trying to prove to her that he was worthy of her even if he wasn't.

"Emmeline, love," he murmured as her sobs turned into hiccups, and then slowly, her breathing evened out, yet he still cradled her to him. "What can I do?"

"Just hold me." She wrapped her arms around his waist and snuggled deeper into his chest. "I want the pain to go away. I'm tired of it."

"Oh, my dear. What I wouldn't do to take it all away." Hearing her cry tore at his insides. Holding her close to him now, he realized how fragile she was. He had only seen her broken once before until today, and he'd hoped never to see her broken again. She deserved all the good that life had to offer. She had the biggest heart of anyone he knew. His hand ran through her silky tresses, hoping it comforted her. Time stood still as he soothed her until she disentangled herself from him. She walked over to the window, and he felt a deep chasm build between them.

"Forgive me for being such a watering pot."

"There is nothing to forgive." He forced himself to stay seated and not go to her, wrap her in his arms again, and hold her close to his heart. The need to go to her had his body quivering. The intensity of his emotions for her frightened him some days.

And today was one of them. He had to remind himself she had broken down. She needed him to be strong, not the other way around. Even if truth be told, he was weak without her. He needed her like air to breathe. Like food for nourishment. Like the beating of a heart to survive.

"Still. Thank you for comforting me."

Standing, he moved several steps forward but avoided getting too close. "Nothing you can say or do to me will change how I feel about you. I will always be here to comfort you if you so need. And even though I'm undeserving of you, I hope you will one day trust me again, so we can be together."

"Why do you say you are underserving?"

He exhaled. "Because you are kind and generous. Thoughtful and compassionate. Loving to all who know you." He paused, unable to think of how he might be worthy of her. "I'm moody, selfish, self-destructive, and I have many other bad qualities to name. I am entirely underserving of you."

"You are wrong." She still didn't turn around, and his feet stayed stuck where they were, and his breathing labored. "You may have been those things once, but not anymore. When I see you, I see a kind, compassionate, and loving gentleman. You treat everyone from the lowest servants to young debutantes to the elderly matrons with kindness and respect. People admire you for what you have accomplished in your life. You have proven yourself worthy of any person's respect." She inhaled loudly. "I want to forgive you, be with you, but I need time."

And there it was. Her words hit him in the chest, causing it to constrict in excruciating pain. His eyes narrowed on her, and everything else in the room faded to black. His eyes only saw what he so desperately craved and wanted. Instead of his heart pounding and his breathing increasing, everything slowed down to the point he didn't think he still lived.

She hadn't said there was no hope for them and he tried not to get too optimistic. All the secrets were out in the open, and something still kept them apart. Without saying goodbye, he turned on his heel, grabbed his hat off the chair, and inhaled deeply. He shuffled on heavy feet out of the drawing room, took his cape from Harrison, and left. He would do what he had done the past three years and bury himself in his work. He had work aplenty between Mayfair Imports and Exports and his ducal commitments to keep him busy.

CHAPTER THIRTEEN

"WELCOME HOME," ANDREW said to Langford and Lilly when they received him in their drawing room several days after they'd returned to London. He kissed Lilly on the cheek. "You look lovely. Married life agrees with you." He looked at Langford and smirked. "Even if you married this reprobate." He collapsed into a chair across from the settee they occupied.

"How kind of you to insult me in my own home," Langford said with an easy chuckle. "So tell me, what brings you here today?"

He toyed with his hat in his hands as nervous energy flowed through his body, making it hard to be still. "No reason. Can't I welcome my friends back from their honeymoon?"

"No other reason?" Langford's brows rose.

Sighing, Andrew threw his hat on the empty chair next to him. "I was hoping Emmeline would be here." Lilly and Langford shared a look that had his heart lodging inside his throat. Deuced uncomfortable.

"You just missed her," Lilly said with sympathy. "I'm sorry."

He flung up his hands. "Don't be." He was trying to be patient and understanding by giving Emmeline the time she needed. But after the first night they'd made love, a part of himself had joined with her, and now he wasn't whole without her. It was damn hard to function with a piece of yourself missing.

"Give her time to work through . . . what is troubling her," Lilly said.

"I'm trying," he said. "Never mind about me, how was the honeymoon?"

They exchanged a look of love. As unhappy as he was with his situation, it was good to see Langford and Lilly happy. They deserved it after all they went through. It no longer mattered that Lilly had been married young to Langford's uncle, the previous Earl of Langford. Or that when he'd passed a year later, Langford and Lilly had clashed during their first meeting, despising one another immediately. Thankfully, their animosity toward each other hadn't lasted long as the forces of nature took over, and they had fallen in love. Truthfully, he'd never seen his friend happier or more content.

"Rome was crowded but amazing. I could envision all the gladiators fighting in the Colosseum. Too bad we didn't live back then. We would've been fierce gladiators," Langford said.

"I think I'll pass on being a gladiator. You do realize they all died eventually. Either in battle, run over by chariots, or mauled and eaten by tigers. And don't forget by the whim of the emperor's thumb." He paused. "Those men and women were also slaves."

"I get your point." Langford chuckled. "Anyway, Venice was beautiful."

"It was my favorite place we visited. So romantic," Lilly said.

"So I've heard," Andrew remarked. "Will you both join me in my box at the Covent Garden Theatre tomorrow night?"

"Yes," Lilly and Langford said at once.

EMMELINE WAS GLAD Lilly and Langford had returned to London. She could spend time with Lilly, and hopefully, Lilly could help her solve her issues with Andrew. When it came to him, she couldn't think or see clearly.

She had purposely arrived early for tea that afternoon because she suspected that Andrew would also visit them, and she couldn't face him yet after crying all over him several days ago. She was in the drawing room, with windows facing the street, when he'd arrived on horseback. Panicking, she hurried down the hall to the library and snuck out the door when he was inside with Langford and Lilly. Fortunately, it had been a dry day, and she had walked. No carriage had been parked out front, which might have given her away.

She did not feel up to attending the Weston Musicale that evening, so she stayed home. This turned out to be fortunate, as a note from the duchess arrived asking if she could go to St. Giles. There was an emergency. Mitchel would come within half an hour to pick her and Lady Morton up.

Dressed in a drab, brown dress and matching cloak, she waited in the hall for Mitchel. When she heard the coach arrive, she told Harrison she shouldn't be too late and not to wait up. Regardless, she knew he wouldn't retire until she'd returned home safely.

"Evening, Mrs. Fitzpatrick," Mitchel said from atop the box, the reins to the matching four in his hands.

"Good evening, Mitchel," said Emmeline as Flynn folded down the stairs and held out his hand to assist her into the coach. "Thank you, Flynn."

She found Lady Morton inside and sat beside her, noticing two large carpet bags on the opposite seat. "Have you any information?" The duchess's note had been brief. Sometimes, she explained their assignment, and other times she did not.

"Yes. A young widow by the name of Melody Abbott was beaten by her landlord. The duchess sent Doctor Smith to tend to her. She wants us to take her and her baby to Amelia House. It wasn't the first time he attacked her, and her neighbor and friend reached out to the duchess. Their landlord is a large burly man who takes what he wants. In his own twisted way, he has taken a liking to Mrs. Abbott. Tonight, apparently she fought back. She is in bad shape. The duchess wishes one of us to stay with her tonight and care for her and the babe."

The duchess had recently acquired a large home in Cheapside and had started taking in women and children with nowhere to go. Or, as in Mrs. Abbott's case, those who had someone abusing them. The home was named Amelia House after the duchess's sister, who had found herself with child. The father refused to marry her, and disgraced, she had run away. Her family had tried to find her, and when they finally did, they discovered she had died of dysentery at six months along. Heartbroken, the duchess had started the Ladies' Society of Mayfair to help those in need, feeling that if she could keep one pregnant woman in need alive, everything they did would be worth it. Besides delivering necessities, they were increasingly taking in single mothers with their children living either on the streets or somewhere unsafe.

Through the Society, Emmeline felt as though her life had a purpose. Spending all her time socializing and being frivolous when there was so much poverty and suffering seemed so pointless. When she met the Duchess of Greenville and heard about the group, she'd joined the Society immediately. Lilly also belonged, and hopefully, now that she had returned from her honeymoon, she would continue her work. Langford refused to let her travel into the rookeries, but there were other things she could do.

As the carriage left the respectable streets of London behind and entered the narrow, dark, and dirty streets of St. Giles, it slowed down. The streets were clogged with drunks, prostitutes, and thieves. Even with the coach windows closed, the sounds and stench of the filth pummeled Emmeline's senses.

They stopped in front of a tenement. Flynn opened the door and lowered the steps, helping each lady exit. Flynn escorted them into the dilapidated building, climbed the creaky sagging stairs to the second floor, and entered number twenty-five.

The candlelit apartment consisted of a tiny room with a sofa, a small hearth in which cooking was done, and a bedroom. Emmeline, not having the stomach for blood, hesitated a moment before entering the bedroom, where she found the doctor bandaging the small, young mother whose baby slept on the mattress beside her.

"Doctor Smith, I'm Mrs. Fitzpatrick. I believe we've met before."

"Yes. Mrs. Fitzpatrick, I remember."

Emmeline noticed the mattress took up almost the entire room. The baby, wrapped in a blue blanket, slept soundly beside her mother and looked about six months old. Melody appeared to be perhaps eighteen. Her auburn hair was long, tangled, and dirty. Emmeline wondered how she had come to be in this predicament and whether she was a widow. Most likely, she had run away from home after finding herself with child and taken on the façade of being a widow. It was a story that played out time and time again, and Emmeline's heart squeezed in pain for her.

"Melody." She approached the side of the bed and took one of the girl's hands in hers. "I'm Mrs. Fitzpatrick, and Lady Morton stands in the doorway. The Duchess of Greenville sent us. If it pleases you, after the doctor has seen to your injuries, we have a safe place for you and your baby to live, and we can take you there now."

The young woman's head turned to look at her; her eyes were swollen half-shut, but Emmeline could see confusion, disbelief, or both in them. "How do I know you aren't taking me to a brothel and forcing me to . . ."

"Believe me, that is not what is happening. We belong to the Ladies' Society of Mayfair. Surely you have heard of us. We come to this area several times a week." Melody nodded. So she had heard of them. Good. "I promise you will be safe."

"Thank you."

Doctor Smith packed up his bag. "I'm finished. If you need me, have Her Grace send for me." He went out the door so fast Emmeline barely had time to thank him.

"Is there anything here you want to take with you?" she asked the young mother.

Melody looked around the room. "My journal on the nightstand."

"I will get it." Emmeline picked up the journal and spoke to Lady Morton. "Please send Flynn in, please."

Minutes later, Flynn carried the young mother, wrapped in a blanket, down to the carriage while Lady Morton cradled the baby and Emmeline held the journal in her hand. Then Mitchel drove them to Amelia House. By now, it was after midnight, and Emmeline covered up a yawn. She hadn't been sleeping well and found herself exhausted.

Mrs. Brock met them at the door when they arrived. She was a lovely woman of around fifty years who had previously worked as the duchess's housekeeper and now ran Amelia House.

"Welcome." She led Flynn to the third floor into a small, clean, furnished room. He gently placed Melody on the bed. Beside the bed was a crib for the baby, and Lady Morton laid the baby down.

The women brought here were here to heal, get healthy, and be strong. They were also trained as parlor maids, kitchen helpers, ladies' maids, seamstresses, or whatever they preferred. With the help of the Society, they found jobs and never had to return to St. Giles if they chose not to. Unfortunately, some of them, when they were better, went back to the slums as it was the only life they knew and felt comfortable with.

Emmeline hoped Melody would be one of the fortunate and select the best path forward. Many of those with children did because too many died of disease at an early age and they wanted a better life for their little ones.

The sun was rising when Mitchel drove her home. Exhausted as she was, she didn't see the lone horseman following them not far back. Her feet shuffled up her front stairs as Harrison opened the door for her.

"Welcome home." He took her cloak before she disappeared

up the stairs, her feet shuffling toward her chambers with one destination in mind—her bed.

With Amanda's help, she removed her clothing, washed up, put on a night rail, and climbed beneath the counterpane with a deep sigh. Sleep. She could sleep for days.

AFTER HE'D RETURNED to London from his country estate, Andrew, with the help of the Duchess of Greenville, had begun following Emmeline when he could as she traveled into the slums of London. When he'd first approached the duchess, she refused to supply him with the information but finally relented. She recognized a man concerned for a lady's safety. Making a sizable donation to Amelia House helped his cause as well.

Tonight had been never-ending. Sometimes, he took an unmarked coach, but tonight, he'd been on horseback and was deuced sore as he headed home to Blackstone House. He'd nodded off in the saddle several times throughout the night. But he'd refused to leave until he saw Emmeline safely home. He couldn't be with her each time she traveled, but he tried. The night trips were easier than some of the daytime ones.

He admired Emmeline for her charity work, but it frightened him all the same. With a business and warehouse on the docks, Andrew regularly witnessed the seedier side of London. If Emmeline knew all that happened in the areas she visited, he didn't think she would ever return. Theft. Murders. Kidnapping and enslaving of women to work in brothels. Assaults and rapes. The list went on and on. Unimaginable horrors.

He shivered as he left his horse at the mews behind his home in the care of a stable boy. He could sleep all day and wished he were able to. He had a meeting with his barrister in a couple hours' time, and he'd planned to spend time at the docks today going over the receipts from their latest shipment.

Each of the friends had a job within their company. Caldwell oversaw their fleet of ships and their travel routes. Langford planned and organized the cargo, what they imported and exported, and managed the loading and unloading of the ships with Caldwell's assistance. Presently, Andrew was in charge of the receipts and money as numbers came easy to him. But it was on their list of things to do to hire an assistant to oversee the office. Since he and Langford had inherited their titles recently, their time was in demand and often required elsewhere.

What with meetings and numbers and the lack of sleep, Andrew felt the day could not end soon enough. And on top of all that, that night he had the theatre. He would never cancel because he'd invited Langford and Lilly, but he'd also invited Emmeline. To his utter shock, she'd accepted his invitation. Seeing her from afar was all well and good, but he craved her nearness even if she didn't want it.

Finally, after a grueling day, Andrew, dressed in dark blue and cream, was ready for the theatre. His carriage picked up Langford and Lilly, then drove to Emmeline's townhouse. The distance between all three homes was not lengthy. It could be walked on a nice day. As Andrew exited the carriage, Emmeline came out the door and took his breath away. Her evening gown was deep green paired with a cream shawl. Her dark hair was piled high on her head, with cascading curls brushing her neck and shoulders. She was a vision, and his heart stopped.

"Good evening," he said while assisting her inside the coach.

"Good evening, Your Grace," she replied as she took the empty seat facing front. Andrew entered, taking the seat beside her.

The coachman flipped up the stairs and closed the door. When everyone was settled, Andrew tapped the roof, and the well-sprung, comfortably cushioned carriage lurched forward.

Several minutes into the ride, uncomfortable silence took up residence inside the coach, and, just to say something, Andrew muttered, "Shakespeare's *Romeo and Juliet*. I do love a well-done tragedy."

"Yes, it is a tragedy," Emmeline said in agreement. "But also a great love story for the masses. Two young people fall in love, their families enemies. Life for them together seems untenable, which turns out to be true, and they both die by their own hand. They love in life and death together, forever."

"It is a beautiful, tragic love story," Lilly said.

Langford huffed. "It is a tragedy, and I reminded my lovely wife to bring a spare handkerchief."

"I brought an extra one as well," Emmeline remarked.

EMMELINE COULDN'T BELIEVE he'd invited her to *Romeo and Juliet*. No one could sit through *Romeo and Juliet* without being passionately invested in the budding love between the main characters and emotionally battered by the end of the play. He didn't know it was one of the last theatre productions she and Aiden had attended. Her emotions would be raw from the play and her memories, and she hoped she didn't embarrass herself with a breakdown.

She hated how things had turned around for them. Her heart broke anew every day, wanting what they'd shared back. She was trying to forgive him. She even understood why he'd omitted the truth. But she was warring with herself every day . . . forgive him . . . don't forgive him. It was causing stomach issues, headaches, and fatigue. Her mother was beside herself with worthy over her health. It was a miracle she was attending the play this evening. And wouldn't it be easier if she just forgave him and they could go back to how they were at the house party? In truth, she had accepted his invitation tonight in the hope of starting the forgiving process.

"We have arrived," Andrew said. Once the door opened and the stairs lowered, Blackstone exited and leaned forward, his hand out. "Shall we?"

"Thank you." With the contact of their hands, warmth traveled up her arm and spread to her heart. There was never any question that they suited one another in the bedroom. And in other areas. She freely admitted she'd loved him—and still did. She hated herself because something deep inside her was holding her back, and no matter what she did, she could not stop it from sneaking up on her at the most inopportune times. She woke up each day with a plan to free her anger. She would go outside, inhale deeply, and then exhale until she had no breath left inside. Then, she would release all the anger, anguish, and resentment she had kept inside. Let it exit her body, join the wind, and carry it from her far, far away, never to return.

It never worked. She visited her garden and exhaled, but nothing was expelled but empty hot air. Her heart remained shattered from Andrew's lies, and her mind ached.

"Are you still with me?"

The sound of Andrew's concerned voice caused gooseflesh on her bare arms and eased her heart. It was a warm night, so she only brought a shawl to keep the chill away. "Yes, I'm here. I appreciate your concern."

"I'll always be concerned for your wellbeing."

"Thank you." She knew he spoke the truth now.

The Theatre Royal, Covent Garden had burned to the ground in 1808 and was rebuilt a year later. Emmeline was amazed at how quickly it had been managed. The theatre was beautiful. They entered from Bow Street into a large stone entrance hall, and someone rudely called out to Andrew just as they approached the grand staircase.

"Your Grace." The Countess of Hartford curtsied, and Emmeline swore her knees creaked. "How lovely to see you back in London." She tugged her daughter forward, who looked like she wished to be anywhere but there. "You recall my daughter, Lady Beatrice, who is having her first Season. I believe you danced with her in Bath."

Ever the gentleman, Andrew smiled and bowed over Lady Beatrice's gloved hand. "Yes. How could I forget such a lovely young lady? I hope you're enjoying your Season and have many suitors vying for your attention."

The countess's smile faltered for a brief moment. Lady Beatrice's once bored expression changed as she smiled, making her even more breathtaking. "You are too kind, Your Grace." It was apparent, by her wistful expression, that Lady Beatrice's affections were engaged to some suitor, and Emmeline hoped it would work out well for them. But with a mother like Lady Hartford, it was anyone's guess what would happen to Lady Beatrice.

After the mother and daughter left, the four of them climbed the stone stairs to Blackstone's private box, Andrew muttering, "Good Lord, what must I do for Lady Hartford to leave me alone? I'm not interested in her daughter, as lovely as she is." When they arrived, he insisted on helping her sit.

As the lights in the theater were being extinguished, she placed her hand on Andrew's arm, as he was seated next to her. "I don't know how you can be so polite to that woman."

He looked at her hand on his arm and shrugged. "Longtime practice, and my mother taught me well."

She removed her hand from his arm after feeling the heat from his body radiating into hers. His sandalwood eau de cologne enveloped her in its warm, woodsy scent, making her glad they were sitting beside each other. She always loved how he smelled. If she'd possessed one of his worn shirts, she would sleep with it at night and inhale it whenever she missed him.

"Are the seats to your liking?" Andrew asked, appearing unsettled. Did she do that to him? If only things were not so confusing between them.

"They are perfect." The curtain opened and Emmeline leaned forward in her seat and hung on every word and scene that unfolded before her. She could barely breathe when Juliet was on her balcony speaking to Romeo. Her favorite scene in the play. And as much as she wished the dying would not happen and

Romeo and Juliet would live happily ever after, it wasn't to be.

Her tears started when Tybalt stabbed Mercutio with a rapier and then Romeo killed Tybalt. They got worse when Romeo, believing Juliet to be dead, drank poison and died. Then Juliet awakened to find Romeo dead and stabbed herself with his sword to join him in the afterlife. Her tears intensified and she covered her mouth with her handkerchief as sobs escaped from deep inside her chest.

As the curtain closed, Andrew gently touched her thigh. "Is there something I can do to ease your distress?"

She gulped down her sobs. "No. I'm fine. "It doesn't matter how often I read *Romeo and Juliet* or see the play; I hope for a different ending and am heartbroken when there isn't one." She leaned around Andrew and saw Lilly in the same predicament as she, handkerchief out as she dried her tears.

As they exited the private box, she took Andrew's offered arm, and he escorted her to his carriage. Langford and Lilly were dropped off first, and when they pulled up to her townhouse she realized she didn't want to be alone. Her emotions were raw from the play and she didn't want Andrew to leave. Silly as it was, she could use his closeness tonight, even if she was still working through other feelings. "Would you care for a nightcap?"

One brow rose inquisitively, and he quirked a crooked grin. "I would like that very much. Thank you."

Harrison met them inside the door and relieved Andrew of his cape, hat, and gloves.

Once in the drawing room, Emmeline splashed brandy into two crystal glasses. "Please have a seat." She handed him his glass and indicated the settee. They sat at the same time. She turned to face him and held up her glass. "To good health."

"To friends," he said as he clinked his glass to hers, and they both sipped. The smooth burn going down her throat and into her stomach was most welcome. Brandy was her one vice, and she enjoyed it nightly. One small amount eased and soothed her before bed.

"I owe you an apology," she said while looking down into the amber liquid that dipped and swirled courtesy of her trembling hands. "I've been dreadful to you. I should have accepted your apology and moved on. I made a mess of our relationship, and I'm sorry. Nothing like a star-crossed lovers play to open my eyes to what is right in front of me." Afraid to look at him and see his expression, she continued staring into her glass. As much as she wanted another sip, she was frozen and couldn't move. "I don't want to waste any more time being angry at you. That is, if you still want me?"

Out of the periphery of her vision, she saw him down his drink and place the empty glass on the table. He swung his body toward her so their knees touched. His hand reached out, touching her chin and drawing it up so she would look at him. Her head rose, but her eyes slowly closed. She was both frightened and elated to move on from the past weeks. Her heart sped up, causing her pulse to jump and her breath to suspend inside her lungs.

"Look at me." The rhythm of his voice was so soft and endearing to her. Her lashes fluttered open, and she got lost inside his understanding eyes. "I'm sorry as well. You know I'd never intentionally do anything to hurt you." He took a deep breath, "And God, yes, I still want you."

Without breaking eye contact, she cupped his face in her hands and kissed him. Home. She was instantly home. Andrew took over the kiss, devouring her, his tongue tasting all of her. His hands settled on her hips, pulling her onto his lap so she straddled him. As he did, he lifted her skirts, so she came down with only her pantaloons and his breeches between them. He growled into her ear, his hands now squeezing her bottom. "You feel so good."

Her body was alive and on edge. She rotated her hips and ground into him, gasping as he kissed down her neck. One hand left her backside, and he pulled down the front of her gown, exposing her breasts to the cool evening air. Her head rolled back as a moan escaped her. Soft lips closed over one pebbled peak, and he sucked it deeply into his mouth. The connection caused her to tingle between her legs, and she squirmed around on his lap. "I'm not going to last," he groaned. He lifted her off his lap just enough that he could fit his hand between them, unbuttoning his breeches, releasing his hard cock. He found the opening in her pantaloons and sat her down, his member sliding into her channel. "Jesus! You feel so tight, so good."

Resting her hands on his shoulders, she rose up and down, swirling her hips as she did, loving the sounds Andrew made. Half groan, half growl, all animal. It fueled her desires. Faster and faster, she rode him, desperately wanting him deeper inside. Arching her back, her hips thrust forward. His cock hit that spot inside her body, and she screamed out as her orgasm slammed into her, rendering her lifeless and gasping for air. Her body draped over his, curling around him, as he thrust his hips up one last time before he tensed and groaned, spilling his seed inside her, which was a first. He had always pulled out before.

He blew out his breath. "That was amazing. I don't think I can move."

She snuggled closer. "Neither do I. But I don't think my mother will appreciate finding us in such a way in the morning when she comes downstairs."

Chuckling, he said, "No, I don't suppose she will." He peeled her off him and helped her stand on wobbly legs and pull up her bodice. "Let me take you to bed."

She tucked him inside his breeches and buttoned him up. Then she brushed her skirts down and took his hand with a come hither smile. "Come with me?"

Up two flights of stairs, she opened the last door on the right. "Welcome to my boudoir."

Laughing loudly, he suddenly stopped. "Where are your mother's chambers?"

"At the end of the other hallway. She won't hear us."

"Good."

Before she could move, he pulled her into the room, closed

the door, locked it, and proceeded to strip her of every piece of clothing she wore, and she reciprocated. Both naked, they fell onto the bed, laughing and kissing. The laughter quickly turned to moans and gasps. Emmeline's hand caressed down his stomach until her hand curled around his thick erection; sliding her hand up and down, she smiled at the sounds coming from the back of his throat. She scooted down his body and licked the drops off the tip of his manhood. His hips jerked, and he fisted her hair in his hand.

"What are you doing?" he said, his voice raspy and tight.

"Pleasuring you." She looked up and met his intense stare, her insides quivering. "Do you like it?"

"Hell, yes," he groaned as she licked him up one side and down the other. When she took him into her hot mouth, he saw stars. He survived her delicious torture for several minutes, then tugged gently on her hair and murmured, "Stop."

She crawled up his body, looking shy and uncertain, her cheeks bright red. "Did I do something wrong?"

He hugged her close to his side. "No. It was perfect. Have you never . . ."

She didn't let him finish. "No. Never. The same with you . . . kissing me down there."

He rolled on top of her and took her mouth in a deep, languid kiss where he sipped and nipped her mouth and lips. He would never tire of kissing her. Her taste was intoxicating—the sweetest nectar in the gardens.

Dragging his lips down her neck, across her breasts, and down her stomach, his destination was almost in sight. Kneeling between her open legs, he covered her sex with his mouth, and her body quivered as breathy sounds escaped her lips. He spread her wider and feasted. Emmeline's pleasure was the only thing that mattered to him. Her moans quickly intensified. Her fingers slid through his hair, gripping him to her. Soft legs trembled and vibrated as she found her release.

He licked her slowly until she calmed, then slid up her body, taking his cock in his hand, and entered her in one deep thrust. This time, they both moaned together when he was seated deep inside her warm heat. "I could stay like this forever," he murmured into her ear right before he claimed her mouth in a sensual kiss. All the love he had in his heart was conveyed in the kiss. At least, he hoped it was. His hips pumped faster and faster; her hands gripped his shoulders, her eyes closed, and she panted. She was close. So was he. Several more intense, deep thrusts and they both screamed out in pure bliss.

Rolling off her, his body spent and heavily sinking into the mattress, he whispered, "Thank you. That was beautiful."

Her head turned to him, and she smiled shyly, her face pink. A deep sigh escaped her mouth. "Yes. What you said."

His heart weighed heavily inside his chest because he needed to leave the warmth and contentment of her bed. Rolling off, Andrew began to dress. "I'm sorry, I must leave. I have a very early meeting with my assistant." He leaned over her and kissed her deeply. It took all his willpower to pull away. "I'll drop by tomorrow afternoon." He kissed her again. "Sleep well, my love."

CHAPTER FOURTEEN

S INCE HE'D SENT his carriage home, he walked from Hyde Park Street, where Emmeline lived, to Grosvenor Square and Charles Street, where he resided at Blackstone House. The moon was half full, giving off just enough light along with the gas lanterns lining the street, making the walk easy. Not far into his walk, something caught his eye behind a fence, and he paused to listen. Footsteps crunched on the stone, quite unusual this time of night.

He hated to leave and not investigate. It could be a thief breaking into the townhouse there, which, he groaned at the realization, belonged to the Earl and Countess of Hartford. It was just his luck.

He eased quietly toward the fence and scanned around. "Show yourself." More footsteps moved farther away until he heard a gate open and close somewhere else on the property. Whoever it was, they were gone now and unlikely to cause any trouble tonight, so he continued walking home with a grin plastered on his face, remembering Emmeline straddling him and how he had come harder and more explosively than he ever had.

Sitting in his office the next morning at eight, Mr. Thomas Ingram, his assistant, arrived on time. "Please sit." He indicated a brown leather chair facing his large oak desk. "Winters, please bring coffee." His butler exited.

Several minutes later, Winters arrived with coffee and a note. Andrew opened the note that bore the Langford seal. Along with Langford's note was a gossip rag dated that morning. He read the note and the circled article three times. His heart raced, and his hands trembled.

"I'm sorry to postpone our meeting, Thomas, but I must attend to something."

Andrew hurried out of his office, yelling to Winters, "Please see Mr. Ingram out and have my horse brought around." He took the stairs two at a time, fighting the panic threatening to engulf him as he hurried to his chambers and quickly changed into his riding clothes. When he exited his townhouse, his horse was saddled and waiting for him.

He mounted Storm, wondering where he should go first. To Emmeline? To Hartford Manor? Or to White's and get inebriated? He chose Emmeline. She was more important than anyone or anything else.

Harrison opened the door as he approached. Could the butler see through walls? "She is outside in the gardens, Your Grace," he said indifferently.

With quick strides, he entered the drawing room and went out the double doors. He scanned the gardens and found her sitting inside her new gazebo on a bench, her hands on her lap and her head down.

Every muscle and tendon in his body had tensed up painfully tight during the ride here. He was ready to explode and take his anger out on the first person who so much as crossed his path and looked at him condescendingly. Unfortunately, he had come into contact with no one, and the anger still churned inside his body. Before he approached Emmeline, he paused and fought the demons down. He could not take out his anger and frustrations on her. She had her own to deal with if she'd read the gossip rag. And if she hadn't yet, she would soon enough.

"Emmeline," he said as he approached, his feet noisy on the gravel path. Her head swung toward him, and his heart lodged up in his throat. She looked pale, and her eyes were puffy and red-rimmed as if she had been crying. She had seen it then. He entered the gazebo, sat down, and took her hands in his. "What utter nonsense they printed. As soon as I leave here, I'll confront the Hartfords and put an end to these utter lies. I will force the paper to retract the story. No one makes up lies about me. Especially when it affects you."

Tears pooled in her eyes, and one trickled down her cheek. He used his finger to wipe it away. Would he ever stop making her cry? "Who the bloody hell came up with me and Lady Beatrice together in a compromising situation in the garden at midnight anyway? Never mind—I can guess. But I will not offer for the chit because someone made up lies. I just don't understand how they knew I would be near their townhouse last night. Perhaps the countess simply saw me walking home and used the opportunity to force a suit. It's no secret she's been pushing Lady Beatrice on me ever since my father's death. Perhaps seeing us at the theatre sparked Lady Hartford's scheme." He inhaled much-needed air after ranting on so. "Say something. Please."

"I knew something would get in between me and my dreams, *our* dreams of a future together. Fate is cruel. Life is unfair." She paused and shuddered. "Haven't we been through enough? How can the countess hate us so much as to do this?" Both the words and the numbness with which she spoke them caused his heart to crack in two.

Pulling Emmeline into his arms, he rubbed her back, trying to soothe both her and him. By nature, he was not a man who hated. He may dislike a person, but hate? That deep, dark emotion hurt both the hater and the hated. It could eat away at your insides and bring you down. He had seen it happen.

But now, he was overcome with hatred for the Countess of Hartford, and his insides boiled. God help her when he exploded and took his wrath out on her. Nothing and no one would keep him from marrying Emmeline. If they had to, they would elope to Gretna Green today. He would feel bad for Lady Beatrice, knowing she had nothing to do with this, but that wouldn't stop him. He would find her a suitable husband to keep her from ruin if he had to, because he knew without a doubt that even if the gossip rag retracted the statement, the poor chit was as good as ruined.

"Believe me when I tell you, I will make this disappear." He kissed her on the cheek and left to visit Hartford Manor.

Once in front of their whitewashed brick, four-story town-house, he handed the reins to his horse off to a footman, hurried up the stairs, and knocked on the door.

It was answered immediately, and he placed his calling card on the silver tray the butler held in his hand. "Tell Hartford I expect him to see me immediately." He gave their butler points for not looking affronted.

"Yes, Your Grace," he said as he bowed. "Please remain here, and I will return momentarily."

Andrew watched the butler ascend the stairs, go down a hall, and return straightaway. "His Lordship will see you now. Please follow me."

Once inside Hartford's study, the earl looked up from his desk. "Please have a seat, Your Grace." He indicated one of two leather chairs facing his desk. "To what do I owe the pleasure of your company?" The earl appeared calm and composed, which surprised Andrew.

He tossed the gossip rag—the same one Langford had sent him not two hours ago—onto his desk. "Have you seen this?"

Hartford picked up the scandal sheet and read the circled article. The more he read, the redder his face became and the more his hands shook. He placed the sheet down, went to the door, opened it, spoke to someone on the other side, and then returned to his seat. "Is this true? Have you compromised my daughter?"

"No. I have been nowhere near your daughter except for the times your wife has tried to force her on me. And those times were witnessed by crowds, such as last evening at the theatre. I don't appreciate being accosted when in the company of my friends." His voice was louder and harsher than he intended.

The earl frowned. "Apologies for Lady Hartford's behavior. But who would make up such a story?" He gasped. "My daughter will be ruined whether it's true or not. You will have to marry her, Your Grace."

"No. I. Will. Not." He punctuated each word by itself and gave Hartford his most ducal, *don't test me* stare.

Hartford stood up, almost knocking his chair over. He placed his hands on his desk and leaned forward, looking panicked. "You have to. There is no reason you cannot. You are unmarried and must marry to produce heirs to carry on your name and the dukedom." He pulled at his thinning hair. "My daughter is innocent in this, and you mean to ruin her life."

Andrew stood, crossed his arms on his chest, and looked down at the earl. "*I* am innocent in this. You want me to ruin my life to save your daughter? I am an honorable man, and if what was printed were true, I would offer for Lady Beatrice's hand. But it is a lie, and I will not offer for her under any circumstances."

Gasps came from the doorway as the countess stood there with her mouth open. Lady Beatrice stood beside her looking nervous as she cried.

The earl stood up and turned to his wife, looking displeased. "Both of you come in and close the door. I don't need the whole household gossiping about this, although I presume all the drawing rooms in London are abuzz already." He indicated the chairs in front of his desk. "Sit. Your Grace, you may take my chair."

"I prefer to stand," Andrew said as he leaned on one corner of the desk, staring daggers at the countess. If she wanted to play with fire, she had to prepare to be burned.

Hartford held up the gossip rag and waved it at his wife. "What did you do?"

"Perhaps I should wait outside while you discuss this," Andrew said.

"No," said the earl. "This involves you. Please stay." He looked between his wife and daughter. "Now. Who is responsible for these lies?"

Mother and daughter looked at each other. Lady Hartford looked determined while Lady Beatrice silently cried. "I came up with a solution to a precarious and scandalous situation, my dear," Lady Hartford said to the earl.

"Explain."

"Around midnight, I came upon our daughter in the gardens with Baron Godfrey, who was taking liberties with Beatrice. And when I saw His Grace pause near our fence, I took matters into my own hands. Someone had to make a good match for our daughter."

All eyes swung to Andrew. "I admit, as I was returning home from a friend's, I heard noises and footsteps in your garden, and I peered over the fence, thinking it was a thief. I saw nothing and left right away."

"When I saw Blackstone near the fence, the scandal wrote itself," Lady Hartford said. "If Beatrice was going to be ruined by anyone, it may as well be His Grace."

"What were you thinking meeting Baron Godfrey in our gardens?" bellowed Hartford at his daughter.

Andrew wanted to disappear from the room. Perhaps he would have snuck out the door if his and Emmeline's future weren't on the line.

"It was all innocent, Papa. He did nothing but hold my hand. Mother is exaggerating as she always does."

"Regardless, two unmarried people meeting at midnight in a dark garden without a proper chaperone is cause for scandal."

"If that is the case, he will offer for me," she said dabbing her eyes with her handkerchief. "I love him, Papa."

"Why has he not approached me for permission to court you?"

"Ask Mama."

Countess Hartford stood, her face red and her voice angry.

"Because I will not have our only child marry a baron. I want her to marry a duke. The Duke of Blackstone, to be precise. That's all I have thought about ever since he returned to London. She deserves to be a duchess."

The earl and Andrew exchanged shocked looks. Andrew's insides coiled up tight. He could not believe what the countess had said. He knew she was hungry to procure an advantageous match for Lady Beatrice, but to be so underhanded? To risk ruining her own daughter to get what she wanted, regardless of what her daughter wanted? The lady had no scruples.

"But Blackstone has never shown any interest in Beatrice," Hartford said, apparently dumbfounded. "And he has outright exclaimed he will not marry her under any circumstances. You risked your daughter's reputation and future for something *you* want. You have gone too far this time. Leave this room and pack your things. I hope you will be happy in the country."

The countess left in a huff, leaving Hartford, Lady Beatrice, and Andrew looking at each other. The tension in the room was palpable.

"Thank you for seeing me, Lord Hartford," Andrew said. "I hope you can straighten out this dilemma."

"Yes. Me as well," the earl replied.

Andrew couldn't get out of there fast enough. Just as he entered the hall, Lady Hartford approached. "Mark my words, Your Grace, you will marry my daughter. I will do whatever it takes," she said with a sneer.

Shaking his head, he slipped out the door and waited a moment before his horse was brought to him. He mounted, his head aching to the point he thought it might explode. He pitied the earl being married to such an unreasonable woman and hoped he was true to his word and sent her away to his country seat.

AFTER ANDREW LEFT, Emmeline continued sitting in her pretty gazebo. It took too much energy and strength to move. When she'd woken up that morning, she'd missed Andrew—last night had transcended anything she'd ever experienced. Making love with him completed her. Made her whole. Being with Andrew seemed the most natural and right thing. If she lost him now . . .

Tears slid down her cheeks, and she didn't bother wiping them away. More would only replace them.

She couldn't fathom a life without him. She'd done it before, but she'd had Aiden to love back then, to make up for the lack. If their relationship unraveled this time—and so wretchedly—she would lose all hope of ever having love in the future—with him or anyone else.

She sat there for a long time—she lost track of how long. When footsteps approached again, she knew who they belonged to. Her heart tripled its beat, and her breath paused inside her lungs.

"I believe it is all straightened out. Lady Hartford is to blame for everything, right down to supplying the gossip rag with the scandal." He sat down beside her and took one of her hands in his. "To say I'm shocked at her behavior doesn't do it justice. She is willing to ruin Lady Beatrice in the hope of getting me to marry her. Who does that to their own child, someone they are supposed to protect and love?" He paused and shuddered. "The earl was livid, and poor Lady Beatrice loves Baron Godfrey, as it turns out. But no lowly baron is good enough for her daughter, according to the countess. I give the earl credit for keeping his temper, although he is banishing his wife to the country. Too bad he didn't do it sooner. I highly doubt she only recently turned into a conniving shrew."

"What happens now?" Emmeline asked in a soft voice. Her mental fatigue was causing physical exhaustion, making speaking tiresome. "I'm afraid to hope it will all go away."

"I believe the earl is contacting the baron. Hopefully, they will marry posthaste and squash the rumors. Nothing ends a scandal quicker than a happy marriage. Hartford must convince the paper that there was an error in identifying the gentleman caught in the garden with his daughter. It shouldn't be hard—it was dark."

"What if it fails?" she asked, her voice trembling.

He turned toward her and cupped her face, his compassionate green eyes meeting hers. "We must have faith. We have done nothing to cause this, and I trust Lord Hartford to solve it." He kissed her, soft and gentle. His tongue crept inside her mouth, tasting her. He went slowly, as though he had all the time in the world. She gripped the front of his coat as her body quivered. His kisses and his touch never failed to make her burn for him.

Breaking the kiss, he rested his forehead on hers. "I'm sorry, but I must go. I must return to Hartford Manor and confirm that all is fixed." He pressed his lips to hers. "I will pick you up for the Tremont ball."

CHAPTER FIFTEEN

Andrew was led into Lord Hartford's study for the second time that day. The earl sat at his desk, a glass of brandy in his hands and a distant look on his tense face.

"Please sit, Your Grace." He stood, poured him a drink, and handed over the glass without asking. Andrew didn't mind. He could use a drink or two. It had been a very long day already.

Taking a sip of an excellent brandy, he examined the shuttered look on the earl's face more closely. The back of his neck tingled. Something was wrong.

"I'm glad you returned." The earl downed his drink. "I have a problem. Baron Godfrey admits to a flirtation with my daughter but doesn't love her, nor is he free to marry her. He has an understanding with Lord Berry that when his daughter comes of age next year, they will marry."

Bringing his glass to his lips, Andrew drained the contents. "What are you going to do?"

The earl closed his eyes and groaned. "Forgive me. I am at my wit's end. I'll call in some favors and hope to have my daughter married by special license within a few days. I don't want to marry her to just anyone, though. I've increased her dowry in hopes of attracting a decent man. I'm waiting on some answers."

"Can I help to persuade someone? Perhaps a second or third

son from an upstanding family who can be attracted by the money?"

"Perhaps." Once again, the earl appeared distant. No doubt, he had many thoughts fighting for purchase inside his brain. Andrew didn't envy him trying to save his daughter from ruin. She deserved happiness in her marriage and future family. But even if she could not find happiness exactly, perhaps she could be content.

"Do you think Mr. James Caldwell would consider marrying Lady Beatrice? Or what about his brother, Baron Latham?"

Andrew tamped down his shock at the suggestion. "Truthfully, neither seems ready to settle down. Caldwell has been courting Lady Chesterfield, although it is probably not serious. As for the baron, he doesn't socialize within the *ton* much. He prefers visiting clubs and gambling halls. What of Lord Hollingsworth? He is actively looking for a wife."

"I sent word to Baron Latham and await hearing back from him." He grabbed the brandy decanter off the sideboard and refilled both their glasses. "He has gambled heavily of late and is in debt. He would be wise to accept my offer. But Hollingsworth? I don't believe he would suit my daughter. I don't believe he likes women."

Andrew couldn't help it; he chuckled. "Trust me, Hollingsworth likes ladies just fine. I know the rumor exists about him, but it was all a misunderstanding. But Baron Latham worries me." He became serious. "How did you learn of his debts?"

"By chance. I overheard a conversation between the brothers at White's the other night. It got heated. James Caldwell raised his voice and swore he would not give the baron another pound toward his gambling debts. I wasn't the only one there who overheard them."

Andrew sat back in his chair, closed his eyes, and wondered how often Caldwell had bailed out his brother. Baron Latham wasn't all that bright, so he could imagine Caldwell coming to his rescue quite often. "Forgive me if I offend you, but if the baron agrees to marry Lady Beatrice, the decision could be something you come to regret. He's not likely to change his ways upon marriage. He will go through Lady Beatrice's dowry quickly."

"I know. I already told myself I wouldn't marry her to him unless I were prepared to be bankrupted, bailing out my son-in-law so my daughter's life isn't ruined. But I don't know what else to do. From what I recall, you changed your ways. Why not the baron?"

He had him there.

"What I'm going to ask of you next," the earl continued, "is not something that is easy to do. As a father I must protect my daughter at all costs. I know this is not your business, but I beg of you to agree to form a temporary, fake engagement with my daughter. It will give me time to find a gentleman for her and alleviate some of the pressure. When the time comes, she will break the engagement, and her reputation will be intact when she marries."

Andrew's pulse soared. "That is much to ask a near stranger."

"I agree. But I'm a desperate man. I understand you hating my wife for what she did, but she only acted for the good of our daughter. I know you don't care about my daughter's ruined reputation, but someday when you have a daughter of your own, you will understand and be glad you helped her."

Andrew was shocked the earl could even partly condone his wife's behavior. Though a part of him understood why he asked this of him. After a long pause, he responded. "If you guarantee the pretend engagement will last no longer than one month, I will agree. But do not expect me to dote on Lady Beatrice. I will spend as little time as possible with her, and never in the company of the countess. Meanwhile, please wait until tomorrow before posting the banns. I need to speak to Mrs. Fitzpatrick."

"I'm sorry to do this to you and Mrs. Fitzpatrick."

How could he return to Emmeline and repeat this after seeing how sad, afraid, and upset she had been only a short time ago? It would upset her to no end. And yet, he must.

Andrew returned to Emmeline's home for the third time that day. This time, he found her sitting with her mother in their private parlor. As soon as the baroness saw him, she excused herself, closing the door behind her as she left.

"Can I pour you tea?" Emmeline looked at him with exhaustion.

Sitting beside her on the settee, he replied, "Yes, please. I fear the brandy I drank with Lord Hartford has gone to my head since I've eaten nothing today."

"Would you like me to ring for something to eat?"

Snagging several biscuits off the tray, he said, "No. These will suffice." Leaning back on the sofa, he ate and drank silently until finished. "There is something I must tell you."

He couldn't put it off as tomorrow was Sunday, and the banns would be posted. "The gentleman Lady Beatrice is in love with is promised to another. To give Hartford more time to find a suitable husband, I have agreed to enter into a false betrothal." She gasped. He reached for her hands and gently squeezed them. "It gives Hartford several weeks to procure a husband for Lady Beatrice. When he does, she will break our betrothal." He waited for Emmeline to say something as his heart pounded inside his chest, trying to escape.

"I would be lying if I said this is acceptable, but I have no claim on you. We are not engaged to be married. You may do as you wish. A part of me understands why you are doing it." She paused and sniffed. "You are a good man. It's too bad there aren't more like you. You will put off your happiness to save a young lady you hardly know, regardless of how much you dislike her mother. You are the epitome of a true gentleman. I only pray this plan doesn't fail and you find yourself married to Lady Beatrice."

"I promise it will not. Not with Hartford agreeing to the plan and Lady Hartford safely ensconced in the country. And if the worst happens and Hartford can't procure a husband for Lady Beatrice, you have my promise I will not marry her."

"If you say so." The numbness in her voice startled him. It

was as if she had given up on them.

Turning to her, he wrapped his arms around her, holding her close, never wanting to let her go. The rapid beat of her heart thumped right along in time with his. They would be together. He would see that nothing failed, even if he had to spend every waking hour of every day hunting down a husband for Lady Beatrice himself. Nothing would come between him and Emmeline. "I love you. I will die without you. So believe me when I say we will get through this." He kissed her. "I must go."

"Andrew," she said as she reached for his hand. "I'm not going to the Tremont Ball tonight. I can't possibly . . ."

He brought her hand to his mouth and pressed his lips to her fingers. "I understand, my dear. I will call upon you tomorrow." The last thing Andrew wanted to do was attend the Tremont Ball himself, but he knew he must.

Since the Waterfords' house party, a dark, ominous cloud had followed Emmeline and him. Would it ever release its hold so they could walk in the sunshine again, hand in hand? He prayed for the day that the rest of the world would no longer intrude on their lives, threatening their love and future—for the sake of Emmeline's and his sanity.

When he arrived home, Lord Hartford's note awaited him, informing him that the engagement would be announced right before the dancing began at the Tremont Ball that night. The idea of it had Andrew leaning over the chamber pot, emptying what little contents his stomach held.

As soon as he received the message from Hartford, he penned off two notes, one to Langford and one to Caldwell, warning about the engagement announcement and explaining it was fake and not to discuss it with anyone. Without their support and understanding, he wouldn't survive until it was concluded. He would talk to them tonight about a potential list of marriageable men for Lady Beatrice—this business needed to be handled quickly. He didn't think he would survive for long without Emmeline. And by the way she'd looked and acted today, she wouldn't survive without him either.

He refused to allow her pain to linger. She was innocent in all this and didn't deserve to have her heart ripped from her chest . . . again. He was also innocent, but for some reason, he felt a strange connection to Lady Beatrice, and he wanted to help her. Someone needed to take the young lady under their care. But a nagging suspicion in the back of his mind told him this dilemma needed to end and fast, or he would lose Emmeline. For ten years, the circumstances of their lives and the decisions they'd made had kept them apart. Well, no more.

After dressing for the ball, he climbed inside his carriage and left. The closer he came to the Marquess and Marchioness of Tremont's home, the tighter his muscles coiled up and the more queasy his stomach became.

The receiving line was dastardly long, and he kept pulling at his cravat as the warmth from the crowd overwhelmed him. He had never been one for attacks of nerves, but he'd swear he was experiencing one now. Finally, it was his turn, and he felt sweat soaking through his clothing.

He bowed. "Marquess, thank you for welcoming me into your home."

"You are most welcome, Your Grace."

"Marchioness Tremont," he said as he bowed over her hand and brought it to his lips. "How lovely you look."

"Silver-tongued as always, Your Grace," she giggled.

Once inside the ballroom, his eyes roamed for Langford and Caldwell. Thankfully, he spied them in a corner toward the back. He strolled toward them but was waylaid by the Earl and Countess of Hartford and Lady Beatrice. *So much for the earl sending the countess off to the country.*

"Your Grace," Hartford said with a nod, relief visible on his face. "I thought perhaps you would leave us in a lurch."

"I gave my word," he said with a frown and a narrow gaze, shocked that the man dared insult him at this point.

"Forgive me," Hartford mumbled. At least he had the decency to apologize for the slight.

"Your Grace." The countess curtsied with a twinkle in her eye and a frightening smile. She must be elated at the turn of events, even though they were false.

No words came from him, nor did he bow or acknowledge her in any way. Instead, he turned to her daughter. "Lady Beatrice," Andrew said, "how beautiful you look this evening. I will be the envy of every gentleman here."

"Your Grace." She curtsied with a weary look in her eyes. "Thank you, but I highly doubt it."

As the four of them stood on the outskirts of the ballroom, every eye scrutinized them openly. Were there no members of the *ton* who hadn't read the scandal sheets that morning? Andrew never favored himself for the stage, but he would perform his part of this farce in a manner worthy of a standing ovation during the upcoming days. To save his mind, he thought in days instead of weeks. Letting this fake engagement go on for weeks was something he refused to allow to happen.

"The orchestra leader is signaling me. I must take the stage for our announcement," Lord Hartford said, looking pleased with himself. Andrew's neck itched. He had a terrible feeling the countess wasn't the only Hartford enjoying this little subterfuge. Could they truly be that delusional, thinking it would become something real? Blast it! Perhaps he needed help in controlling them.

"Ladies and gentlemen," the earl said in a deep, booming voice as the room quieted, "I have wonderful news to share. The Duke of Blackstone and my daughter, Lady Beatrice, are betrothed." Murmurs, loud voices, gasps, and clapping bombard-ed Andrew's ears; he wanted to cover them and run and hide like a young child. Not even when Aiden had told him he and Emmeline were getting married had he felt this devastated. Standing here now, his mind far away and looking on, as though someone else stood in his place, was an odd feeling. He wanted to yell out and explain to the two hundred people in the ballroom that it was false. Instead, he stayed silent, his body trembling and sweating again. He thought there was a very real chance he might fall unconscious for the first time in his life. And wouldn't that be a shock?

"I want to thank the Marquess and Marchioness of Tremont for letting me make this joyous announcement at their lovely ball." He held up a glass of champagne. "Let the dancing begin."

As always, the dancing began with a quadrille, and he begged off, instead escorting Lady Beatrice to Langford, Lilly, and Caldwell as all eyes followed them.

"Congratulations, Blackstone," Lilly said in a clipped voice with an angry look.

He bowed. "Thank you, Countess."

"It's fake," Lady Beatrice whispered, looking pale and embarrassed, so only their close circle could hear. "It will be over soon, and he can return to Mrs. Fitzpatrick. I hate that she was dragged into my mother's delusions. It's not fair to either Blackstone or her."

"Indeed," Lady Langford said. "However, sometimes fake things have a way of becoming real."

"Not this time," Andrew said. He turned his attention to Langford and Caldwell. "Do you know of anyone seeking a bride besides Hollingsworth?"

"No," Langford replied. "But let me mull it over."

"Me as well," Caldwell said. "My brother needs a wife and keeper, but I'm afraid Lady Beatrice won't do." He nodded his head toward her. "You are gracious and kind, and my brother needs a lady capable of leading men into battle against France."

Lady Beatrice laughed, then covered it up. "Forgive me."

"Not necessary—I speak the truth. I wouldn't want to foist him off on someone so innocent and kind as yourself," Caldwell said thoughtfully. "He would make you miserable."

"Please," she begged, "if he'll have me, I will marry him anyway. I refuse to allow this sham of an engagement to go on longer than necessary. At this point, I have resigned myself to a loveless and unhappy marriage, and it's nothing I don't deserve."

"Nonsense, Lady Beatrice," Caldwell said. "None of this is your doing."

"No, it is not," she replied. "Yet here we are."

Listening to Caldwell and Lady Beatrice speak as though they were alone made Andrew think wild things. Despite what he'd said earlier to the earl, the two of them may make the perfect couple after all.

Their conversation was interrupted when the next set began with a waltz, and Andrew knew everyone would expect the newly affianced couple to take to the dance floor. He turned to Lady Beatrice and bowed. "May I have this dance?"

She placed her hand on his forearm, and he escorted her through the crush of bodies onto the dance floor. He led her around the polished floor and noticed how graceful she was. "You dance beautifully," he said.

"Thank you, Your Grace," she said with a blush. "I had the best dancing master in London."

"Indeed. I'm sure he knew if he didn't take you on as his pupil, your mother would, no doubt, ruin him."

She looked affronted. "She is not all that bad, Your Grace. She has my best interests in mind."

"Yes, how well I know. Why is she not on her way to the country by now?"

"My father always forgives her."

Not liking that answer, he made a mental note to watch his back. Could he have welcomed the fox into the hen house with his agreement to a fake engagement? When there was a slowing in the tempo and a reprieve from twirling, he asked, "What did you think when your father told you about the plan?" He studied her face carefully for any sign of deception. By all appearances, she appeared an innocent young lady, but she was her mother's daughter after all.

"Truthfully, I was shocked. First, my heart was broken when I found out about Baron Godfrey and how he deceived me, and then when Papa told me about our engagement and that it was fake." Her eyes looked sad. "That he was looking for a gentleman to marry me off to." Her eyes suddenly turned angry and fierce. "How would you feel, Your Grace, if people toyed with your life and future? If you never had a say in anything?"

"Quite angry, I imagine. Fortunately, I was born a male and am now a duke. However, I understand somewhat, thanks to your mother and what she did to me."

"I'm sorry, my parents go too far this time, pulling you into their schemes. And I'm just a pawn in their chess game, as always, being moved from square to square for their benefit. They get my hopes up, and then, in time, I will be cast aside and thrust onto some other man to do with me as he will. My feelings and emotions are scattered all over. One moment, I want to scream, and the next, cry my heart out."

The way she described her life sounded terrible. At least it appeared he had Lady Beatrice's support in ending the ruse as quickly as possible.

When the last chord played, he escorted Lady Beatrice to her parents, made excuses, and left the ball, seeking the solitude of his study and a bottle of brandy. His mind and feelings were scattered as well, and he needed to mull things over before he exploded.

CHAPTER SIXTEEN

PAIN STABBED HER heart, and Emmeline didn't believe she would ever breathe again without feeling it. Or a raw, sore throat. She'd done more crying today than she had in the six years since she'd buried Aiden. It didn't matter that Andrew told her it was a fake engagement and that it would be over soon, that they could soon get on with their lives. Unending agony in her heart told her otherwise. Until that day came when he was free again, she would live in constant anguish, fear, and panic for their future.

When he'd told her he loved her for the first time today, it almost undid her. She wanted to beg him to run away to Gretna Green with her, and to hell with Lady Beatrice and her scandal. After all, it was her fault ... well, her mother's really. And Andrew had done nothing wrong to get dragged into this because the countess was simply a conniving, scheming, hateful woman. One who could not be trusted. She wanted her daughter to marry the Duke of Blackstone, and Emmeline knew, deep down inside, there was no way she would sit back and let this engagement slip through her fingers, fake or not. With every fiber of her being, Emmeline knew that Andrew was in great danger of indeed marrying Lady Beatrice. He thought he was in control and could handle things, but she worried he was being deceived. Trusting Hartford, even if his intentions were honest, did not factor in his wife and her underhanded ways.

Andrew had never faced a determined Marriage Mart Mama and didn't know how ruthless they could be. Also, who was to say the earl wouldn't fall prey to the scheme himself and finally indulge his wife and help trick Andrew into a real marriage? According to Andrew, Lady Beatrice appeared innocent in all this, but perhaps it was just one more ploy to catch him off-guard. Before he knew what was up or down, he could be married.

Andrew was an intelligent man. However, he had a soft side and the ingrained desire to do all that was right and honorable. No one had taken advantage of that side of him until the Countess of Hartford. Somehow, she had seen inside him to the goodness she could manipulate. As strong as he was, Emmeline's heart and mind worried.

The hour was late, yet she wandered the dark halls of her townhouse carrying a lantern. Dressed in her nightclothes and bare feet, she silently repeated her steps over and over until she found herself back inside her chambers, where she paced the floor for what felt like hours. Exhaustion descended on her, and she crawled beneath the coverlet, finally drifting off into a fitful sleep.

The following morning, Andrew sent a note and a beautiful bouquet of red roses, begging her forgiveness for not paying a visit to her that day. It didn't do much to improve her mood, and the tiredness that crept in from lack of sleep the previous night only made her mood worse. Her day was spent lounging on her chaise longue in her room because she wasn't fit for even her mother's company.

MORNING CAME QUICKLY after another restless night's sleep. It was one of two days that week she would travel into the dangerous rookeries of London to deliver goods. Mitchel was due anytime to pick her up, and her maid was still fussing with her hair.

"Amanda, stop. My hair is fine. I'm only going into St. Giles. No need to have it look worthy of a ballroom."

"Yes, ma'am."

"Forgive me. I'm not myself these past two mornings."

"I would think not with what is going on with the duke."

Standing now, her hair presentable, she faced Amanda and said, "Is there much gossip?"

"Some. Most are feeling bad for you and cross at His Grace."

"I'm going to confide something to you, Amanda, but it must remain within this household. The engagement between Lady Beatrice and His Grace is a ruse. Lady Beatrice will call it off once a husband is found for her to alleviate her ruination."

"That is the best news ever." Amanda hugged her quickly. "I always knew His Grace was a good man."

Before Emmeline hurried down the stairs, she put on a plain black cloak, hat, and gloves and waited in the entryway. When she heard the carriage stop before her house, she bid Harrison good day as he opened the door for her.

"Be safe, miss."

"Always, Harrison. Always," she said as she descended the stairs to the street where Mitchel awaited with a hand out to help her inside the carriage.

"Mrs. Bishop is under the weather, and Flynn has other duties. It's just us today. Duchess Greenville apologizes for the inconvenience."

"Thank you, Mitchel," she said as he raised the stairs and closed the door. When she was settled, she knocked on the roof, and as always, Mitchel started the carriage forward with an easy jolt. Not for the first time, she wondered about Mitchel's and Flynn's lives. She didn't even know their family name and had only recently discovered they were brothers. They were always disguised, their true identities well-guarded, but they were educated, perhaps even titled or second or third sons. Maybe tradesmen or barristers. Maybe one day, she would find out what they had to hide.

Until then, she was thankful for them. It wasn't easy getting volunteers for their cause. Well, they had many volunteers to assemble the baskets and procure donations, but not many were willing to travel into the slums. A handful was all they had. And they had lost Lilly since her marriage. Perhaps in time, Langford would allow her to assist in the deliveries again. If he was so worried about Lilly's safety, he could always escort her, which he'd said he would do at one time. A conversation to be had soon in the future.

The floor and the bench opposite her were covered in goods to be delivered. Since more and more people relied on their donations, instead of giving directly to homes as they used to, they sometimes parked at the corner of a main thoroughfare and a side street, and the needy came to them. When the carriage arrived at their destination, many women with and without children were lined up awaiting their arrival. As Emmeline's eyes landed on them from within the confines of the coach, her heart sank but her resolve lifted, and her problems seemed trifling compared to theirs. Dirty, malnourished, some of their clothing no more than rags, these poor souls born into poverty through no fault of their own with no hope of ever getting out and bettering themselves tore at her insides, and tears pooled in her eyes.

Taking a deep breath, she steeled herself to get through the day. These people needed what she brought.

The door opened to Mitchel with his hand out, and she stepped onto the side of the road. "Stand here. I will hand you the donations," Mitchel said as he reached into the carriage, picking up a basket overflowing with goods and handing it to her. "It's heavy."

"Thank you, Mitchel, for everything," she said as she signaled the first person in line to come forth. She handed her bundle off to a young mother, clutching the hand of a toddler with huge blue eyes staring up at her.

"Thank ye, ma'am."

And so it went on until the last goods were gone, and Emmeline's heart hurt at seeing the several anxious faces who would go away empty-handed this day. "Please come back on Thursday. Come early."

Out of the corner of her eye, she saw a small boy across the street looking at her. His clothing hung off his frame. As she went to step inside the coach, she noticed a loaf of bread had fallen onto the floor. She picked it up. "I'll be right back," she said to Mitchel as she looked up and down the street and crossed to the boy. "Take this. It is all I have left."

As she turned to cross back, a large, black carriage and matching four tore out of nowhere and nearly ran her down. If it weren't for the stranger who knocked her out of the way and to the ground, his unyielding body still covering hers now, she would be injured or worse.

"Emmeline," her rescuer said in a deep, concerned voice she knew all too well. "Are you all right? Does anything hurt?"

"Andrew. Please let me up, I can't breathe."

He climbed off her, held out his hand, and helped her to her feet. Mitchel was at their side, looking worried. "I saw the whole thing. It was no accident. I believe the boy was used to lure you across this street. The carriage driver was waiting for you to run you down."

Gasping, her hands gripped Andrew's waist as they stumbled toward the coach.

⟫⟪

"THANK YOU FOR saving her," Mitchel said with his hand out.

"I'm Blackstone. And you are?" Andrew asked as he shook the other man's hand, his brows raised.

"Mitchel, Your Grace. What brings you to these parts?"

By the way Mitchel looked at him, he already knew why. He would be a terrible driver and watchdog if he didn't know Andrew followed them most of the times Emmeline traveled with them. And it was a good thing he'd cleared his appointments for that day. If not—his insides trembled, and his stomach knotted—who knew if the love of this life would be alive?

"This and that." Andrew opened the carriage door and said, "Please get inside, my dear." He turned to the driver and said, "I'm riding with her."

Mitchel nodded. "I expected as much." The door shut, and when Emmeline was settled beside him on the bench, he knocked on the roof, and they were on their way.

"How badly are you hurt?" he asked, knowing they had slid across the road as she'd landed beneath him. On purpose, of course, so his body could protect her if the coach ran them over, even though he knew it would add to her injuries by landing on top of her.

Her hand went to her temple and came away with a slight trace of blood on her glove.

Panicking, Andrew pushed her hood off and cradled her chin with his thumb and forefinger, gently turning her head from side to side. "You have a scrape on your temple. It's not deep, but it will need to be cleaned and the small pieces of gravel removed. What else hurts?"

"My right hip and elbow. I hit the ground with them before I ended up on my stomach." She swatted his hand away from her face. "What were you doing there?" As she admonished him, he pulled up her skirts and pulled down her pantaloons, ignoring her loud gasp. He inspected her hip, which was scraped and red. Then the elbow, as well. She was lucky, and he shivered at what could have happened if he hadn't been there at precisely the right moment.

"I have been accompanying you nearly every time you do this foolish thing of traveling into unsafe areas of London ever since I found out about your endeavors."

"What?" she said, looking confused.

"How hard did you hit your head?"

"Stop it. I heard what you said. You just shocked me, that's all. How did I not know?"

"I kept hidden. Mitchel and the other man knew I did. What do you know about them? Mitchel seems familiar to me, although I can't quite place him. I haven't gotten close to the other man to see if he also appears familiar."

"I would be lying if I said I hadn't wondered about them myself a time or two. But if they work for the Duchess of Greenville, they can be trusted."

"Yes. I gathered that. She is quite a lady, Her Grace," Andrew said. "She kindly sends me messages with your schedule." He glanced out the window. "I had to make a substantial donation to Amelia House so she would send me the notes. What a shrewd businesswoman. We have arrived at your home. I'll see you in. There is something else I wish to discuss."

Once inside the drawing room, Emmeline rang for tea, and he hoped it would help settle her nerves and his. She was silent when she sat down beside him, and he took that time to face his fear of almost losing her today. Instead of taking his carriage or horse when he followed her into the slums that day, he'd hired a hack to hide his identity more easily. Following her at night on horseback was easy, but he'd feared she might spot him in broad daylight, and he knew she would not take kindly to him following her. She would think he didn't trust her. He did trust her—it was others he didn't trust. Today's incident proved how untrustworthy others could be. The beat of his heart was still elevated. When he'd caught sight of the carriage barreling down the street toward Emmeline, something inside him had snapped. With speed he didn't know he possessed, he had run toward her, diving into her and knocking them both off to the side of the road, where he'd covered her body with his and prayed for the best.

He hadn't expected either of them to survive as they flew through the air and landed on the ground. As he lay over her, holding his breath and waiting for the inevitable pain and death of being trampled by horses and coach, his life with Emmeline flashed before his eyes. Never in all his life had he been so frightened or felt so helpless. When the horses' hooves and carriage wheels never made contact, he'd struggled on unsteady legs and helped Emmeline to stand.

It had taken until now for him to realize his body ached all over. Every muscle had tightened up when he'd crashed into Emmeline, and now that he was relaxed or trying to be, his muscles screamed in protest. The first thing he would do when he arrived home was take a warm bath, which made him remember Emmeline's injuries. "You need to soak in hot water and clean your scrapes."

Her hand flitted to her temple, and she winced. "Yes. I will get Mother to help. She was always good at patching me up when I was little."

Just then, a footman arrived with a tray. Emmeline prepared two teas, Andrew's just as he liked it. "There are biscuits as well if you are hungry."

"Thank you," he said as he accepted his cup of tea.

She sat and sipped hers, then turned to him, her eyes sad. "What did you want to talk to me about?"

"Today was no accident."

She blew on her tea to cool it off. "I know. But who would want to hurt me? Or interfere with the duchess's charity?"

"Perhaps a family didn't receive enough food or medicine and took it out on the next person who made a delivery, which happened to be you." His hands shook, clanking the cup and saucer together, so he placed them on the tray resting on the table. "Someone wanted you dead. Or at least injured. I need to find that street urchin, and bribe him with a coin. Secrets can be bought for a price and I believe he is the key to solving this mystery. And I promise you, someone will pay for what they did to you." His eyes met hers while he waited for those words to sink in.

"If you mean to frighten me, you have succeeded."

"I'm sorry. I'm just worried for your safety. There's a slim chance the whole thing was a case of a runaway carriage. Yet . . .

the carriage headed right for you. There is another possibility, actually many possibilities, but another that's worrying around in my mind is Countess Hartford." He combed his hands through his hair. "I have half a mind to visit Lord Hartford when I leave here and confront him. The man is weak and allows his wife to rule their castle." He exhaled loudly. "I'm expected there later today. I hope I can keep my accusations to myself for now. Meanwhile, I don't want you to leave the house."

"Hmmm."

He raised a brow to her non-committal noise. "Would you rather get run over by a carriage?"

"Of course not."

"If you do go out and someone is trying to hurt you, next time, it might be something even more devious and nefarious, and they may succeed in eliminating you."

"Stop trying to scare me!" she exclaimed.

"Is it working?" He hoped to God it was. Her life was in danger, and he needed to convince her to take it seriously. If anything happened to her . . .

"Yes," she said, as she picked up a biscuit and nibbled on it. "Now go and find who did this."

Pulling her into his arms, he cradled her head to his chest and inhaled her unique fragrance of wildflowers. Their bodies trembled. He honestly didn't know if he could extricate himself from her. Taking several deep breaths, he put some distance between them. Just enough so he could kiss her. Her lips tasted like sweet tea.

"I'm going to hire Bow Street Runners to watch over you to ease both our worries," he said as he forced himself to let her go. He was terrified that if something happened to her he would never get the chance to hold her again.

After he took his leave, he went to Brooks's, hoping Caldwell and Langford would be there, taking an afternoon libation as they used to when all three of them lived in London. Four before Aiden married Emmeline. It had been a daily tradition back then.

Sweeping inside the door, he handed off his hat and overcoat to the doorman. He focused on the room and found them at their favorite place in the back. A grouping of four wingback chairs gathered around a low table in front of the large hearth. Three were occupied.

Along with Caldwell and Langford, Hollingsworth took up the third chair. Before Lilly became involved with Redford, and Langford and Lilly became betrothed, Hollingsworth had proposed to Lilly. It was a wonder Langford and he were still civil to each other.

"Gentlemen," Andrew said as he sat in the vacant chair and signaled a waiter. "Whisky, please."

"What happened to you?" Caldwell asked as he sipped from the drink in his hand. "You are disheveled, and you have holes in your breeches." His eyes widened. "Is that blood?"

So intent had he been on Emmeline, he hadn't noticed his breeches. "Bloody hell, so it is." Knowing he could trust all the men present, he explained that day's events.

"Lilly is never going into the slums again," Langford said firmly.

"Emmeline was targeted. And I think I know by who," Andrew said as he downed the contents of his glass and signaled for a refill. "May as well leave the bottle," he grumbled to the server. He proceeded to explain his theory about the accident to his friends.

"You believe Lady Hartford is conniving enough to plan such a thing?" Hollingsworth asked.

"Who else could it be?" As far as Andrew knew, Emmeline didn't have any enemies.

Caldwell stared into his glass. "Perhaps they target the Ladies' Society of Mayfair and want an end to the charity."

"I can't see a reason for it. The charity does good work. People rely on their donations," Langford said.

"Yes, well," Hollingsworth spoke up, "someone always takes offense at what others do. But I'm with Blackstone. Emmeline has been doing this charity work safely for years. Why would they target the charity now? It's most likely Lady Hartford. On the other hand, murder? That does seem extreme."

"I know," Andrew grumbled. "But there is something not quite right with her."

"What about Lady Bea—" Langford began.

"No," Caldwell interjected. "She is innocent in all of this and doesn't have a cruel bone in her body."

Everyone stared at Caldwell. "You should marry her," Andrew said with renewed hope for his future.

"I can't. I don't possess a title."

"You will soon if your brother doesn't stop living so recklessly," Andrew said.

Caldwell looked inside his glass, lost in thought. "I paid off his creditors and gambling debts again. I swore to him that after this time he was on his own. I can't continue to bail him out. It's not about the money. It's that he'll never learn. Unless someone else beats me to it, I need to beat some sense into him."

"How did he take it?" asked Langford.

"Humorously. He laughed in my face."

"Christ," Andrew groaned. "Do you want me to speak to him? He may listen since I spent nearly three years doing what he is."

"Shit, no." Caldwell leaned forward and rested his empty glass on the table. "I'm off. If you need help, Blackstone, let me know. I'll see you both in the office."

"What are you going to do about Emmeline?" Langford asked. "You can't very well arrive at Lord Hartford's house and accuse his wife of attempted murder."

"Indeed. But don't think I didn't consider it. We need to keep our cards hidden for now. I've already sent word to our Bow Street Runner acquaintance. I want Emmeline guarded, and both Lord and Lady Hartford watched. And with any luck, I can convince Caldwell to marry Lady Beatrice. So what if he doesn't possess a title? Lord Hartford doesn't care. At least he said he didn't. He was, in fact, the one who mentioned Caldwell as a possible husband." He finished his drink and stood. "Give Lilly my best. Langford, Hollingsworth." He nodded and left, retrieving his coat and hat from the doorman.

CHAPTER SEVENTEEN

ONCE ANDREW LEFT, Emmeline, her body sore and her heart weary, went to her chambers. Amanda had a hot lavender-scented bath waiting for her. "Did you send for my mother?"

"Yes, Ma'am. She will be here soon."

Her clothing was removed with her maid's help, and she climbed into the soaking tub with a deep sigh.

"This feels wonderful. Thank you, Amanda. You may go."

"Emmeline." Mother entered her chambers, her voice laced with concern. "Amanda explained you were hurt and to bring medical supplies. What happened?"

"A carriage tried to run me over."

The baroness gasped, her hand going to her heart. "How do you feel? Where are you injured?" She hurried to the side of the tub, her fingers gently touching the scrape on her temple. "This is nasty. It needs cleaning and honey to help it heal."

"That is why I sent for you."

Mother paced the room, looking anxious. "Tell me what happened."

"I had just finished handing out the donation baskets when a boy caught my attention." She frowned as she pictured the scene in her head, then. Now that her mind was calmer, more details were coming back to her. "No, that's not right. I think he called out to me and that's why I noticed him." She finished telling the series of events as her mother continued to pace.

"That sounds deliberate." She turned to her, her eyes wide. "Who would do such a thing?"

"Andrew has several theories, but he believes the most plausible is Lady Hartford. She needs me crippled or dead so he will marry Lady Beatrice."

Her mother gasped. "Surely Andrew is wrong. A countess trying to kill you!"

"Andrew plans on hiring Bow Street Runners to watch them and me. He will not let anything happen to me."

Reaching out with her hand, her mother gently touched her cheek. "I can't bear the thought of losing you." Walking over to the dressing table, she came back with tweezers. "This might hurt, but the gravel needs to be removed." Opening the first aid bag, she removed vinegar and a clean white linen cloth. She soaked it with the liquid and touched it to Emmeline's temple.

"Ouch, that stings."

"Sorry, but it's necessary."

"I know. I scraped my hip and elbow also."

"I'll clean them when you get out of the tub."

After pouring whisky on the tweezers, she pulled out several pieces of gravel. Cleaned the abrasion once more and dabbed it with a salve. "That should heal nicely. Luckily, it wasn't a gash, which would leave a scar."

A short time later, her mother treated her other scrapes, and she dressed in nightclothes. She planned to spend the rest of the day in bed, as exhaustion from today's incident weighed heavily from her shoulders to her toes.

Mother tucked her in. "Rest. I'll send up a dinner tray later."

"Thank you."

Once she was alone, the tears flowed. Both she and Andrew could be dead. Covering her heart with her hands, her entire body shuttered at the frightening memory. How would she ever go outside of her townhouse without looking at every person she saw and thinking they wanted to kill her? And if what Andrew said was true and Lady Hartford hired the driver to run her down, then she could hire someone else to do the job, and next time, they might succeed.

Her tears dried up as anger took the place of her fear. Rage coiled up inside her, wanting to be unleashed. Emmeline wanted to call upon Lady Hartford, rip the hair from her head and scratch her eyes out. These feelings and emotions were foreign to her. Never ever had she wanted to hurt another. Then again, no one had tried to kill her before. Nor had they inadvertently almost killed the man she loved. Of course, she would not retaliate against Lady Hartford. Andrew would be the one to handle that. Or the authorities. But if she really was behind this, she belonged in Newgate with all the other criminals.

Turning on her side, she pulled the coverlet up, covering her head so only her face poked out. It made her feel safe for the moment. Because when she left her house, she was fair game to another attack. Sighing loudly, her eyelids drifted closed. Sleep wanted to take hold of her, and she let it. She had to rest if she intended to be strong and fight for her life and the life she deserved with Andrew.

AFTER ANDREW LEFT Brooks's, he was expected at Hartford Manor for a social call, and he hoped the generous glasses of whisky he'd drunk wouldn't loosen his tongue, making him say things he would later regret. He could not let on that he suspected Lady Hartford of trying to kill Emmeline. Damn, but the last several days had weighed him down both mentally and physically. If only he could go back in time and change the trajectory of his life. Return to the Marquess and Marchioness of Waterford's house party and marry her before she found out about the details regarding Aiden's death. They would have been a reckoning over it when she found out, but he would beg forgiveness after the fact. Then, this ordeal with Lady Beatrice would never have solidified. Lady Hartford would have picked some other poor man to foist her daughter off on.

Standing outside Hartford Manor, tingles crawled up Andrew's spine. He did not want to go inside. Taking a deep breath, he stood tall and prepared himself for what awaited inside this house of deceit.

"The Duke of Blackstone," announced the butler.

After completing formalities, Andrew sat next to Lady Beatrice on a settee as Lady Hartford poured tea.

"How do you like your tea, Your Grace?" Lady Hartford asked.

"Sugar, no cream." Andrew took the china cup and saucer from her hands, and took a sip knowing the countess put cream in his tea, no doubt, intentionally. He fought the urge to gag. "Delicious. Just the way I like it." Never would he give her the satisfaction of thinking her antics bothered him in any way.

"We are attending a dinner party tonight at the Duke and Duchess of Deerfield's. Are you by any chance attending?" asked Lady Hartford.

Hiding his smile behind his cup, he turned it into a frown. "No. I declined weeks ago. I hope you have an enjoyable evening."

"Her Grace is a very dear friend of mine. I could send a note and have you added."

"Please don't bother on my account. Besides, I have other plans for the evening."

"I see," she said, trying to hide her disappointment.

Lady Beatrice said, "Since His Grace is not attending, may I stay home?"

"No, my dear, you must attend. It wouldn't look right if you bowed out on the day without good reason."

Andrew felt as though he had witnessed a private conversation between mother and daughter and arrived in the middle of it. It was obvious they had talked about tonight before now and

Lady Beatrice didn't want to attend. After more small talk, Lady Hartford, acting innocent and pleased with herself, had his blood boiling. Leaving quickly would be in his best interest. "Ladies," he said as he bowed. "As always, a pleasure."

His feet ate up the distance to the exit, down the stairs, and out the front door, where he could finally breathe for the first time without almost choking. The air inside the salon had been fermented with lies, underhandedness, and deceit.

After he arrived home, he sat in his study nursing a glass of brandy when Winters entered with a dinner tray. "Thank you, Winters. I'm expecting Mr. Whitcomb. Send him in when he arrives."

"Yes, Your Grace."

Half an hour later, Winters opened the door, and Mr. Whitcomb entered. "Blackstone," said the Bow Street Runner when he entered and bowed. "Have you information for me?"

"Please sit." He poured the Runner a glass of brandy and handed it over. "No. I was hoping you had something for me."

Mr. Whitcomb cleared his throat as he cradled the glass in his hands. "Nothing out of the ordinary has happened, Your Grace."

"Bloody hell, Whitcomb." He tossed back his drink and put the glass on his desk. "What am I supposed to do in the meantime? I'm not one for patience, and my mind is scrambled. I can't concentrate on anything else."

"For what it's worth, my advice is to keep busy. Go to the docks and your warehouse and work until you're exhausted."

"I just told you . . ."

"Yes. I heard you. But you have always found solace in your business endeavors in the past. Perhaps you will now."

He didn't want to admit that Whitcomb was right. Working had saved him in the past. A past that belonged to another version of him. He was so far removed from the man he'd been then. *Thank God.* "You are right. It's been ages since I burned the midnight oil at the warehouse. And goodness knows I have work piled up. Send word to me there if you find anything out."

"I will. And rest assured, Mrs. Fitzpatrick is safe at home tonight. And if she so much as sneezes, my men will know."

His words were both disturbing and reassuring.

Andrew accompanied Mr. Whitcomb to the hall and bid farewell. "Winters, have the carriage brought around."

"Yes, Your Grace."

As the carriage wheels rolled closer and closer to the docks and the scent of the Thames filled his nostrils, Andrew's insides eased. It reminded him of his years traveling the high seas. It was hard, lonely, and tremendously satisfying work, even though he'd come perilously close to losing his life several times due to storms and pirates. He was proud of what Langford, Caldwell, and he had accomplished. Most peers would never stoop so low as to do menial work. But it had paid off for all three of them, even if their lives were changing, and they would eventually need to hire other good men to run Mayfair Imports and Exports for them. They already had several honest, intelligent, and hardworking retired navy captains who were worthy of their salaries and the percentage of cargo they transported. Their ships were in good hands. Caldwell had recently hired their new warehouse manager who had come highly recommended by Mr. Whitcomb. Mr. Warner was a retired Runner himself and trustworthy.

"Come back at dawn," Andrew said to his driver as he took the lamp from inside the carriage and made his way to the door. He unlocked it and entered the quiet warehouse, his footsteps echoing off the wooden floorboards as he made his way to the offices. Once inside, he lit several lanterns and groaned at the pile of paperwork on his desk. He was in charge of the accounts, and he'd been neglecting the invoices and receipts for over a week. Thankfully, Caldwell came daily to keep up with the day-to-day operations, such as the banking and payroll. It was time to find an honest and worthy accountant to replace him. He would ask his banker, next time they met, if he knew of anyone seeking employment.

He poured himself a brandy and opened the inventory ledger

to find Caldwell had already recorded their latest shipments and confirmed they tallied with the captain's log. Next, he sorted the invoices and wrote checks to be delivered tomorrow, recording them in the accounts payable ledger. Since Caldwell had picked up his slack, there was actually less work than the pile on his desk had led him to believe, and before long he lay on the sofa and closed his eyes, hoping to get several hours of sleep.

His eyes popped open, and he sat up with a start. He must have dozed off because several lanterns had burned out, and the room was cast in dark shadows. And then he heard the banging on the door, which must have awoken him. Extinguishing all but the lantern he arrived with, he went to the door, unbolted it, and opened it to find his driver, Avery, standing there. "Sorry to disturb you, Your Grace, but a message arrived. It's from Mr. Whitcomb."

Shutting and locking the door to the warehouse behind him, Andrew climbed inside the carriage, hanging the lantern on the hook because the sun had yet to rise. His fingers quickly opened the sealed note and scanned its contents while Avery awaited his instructions.

"To Mr. Whitcomb's office, Avery."

"Yes, Your Grace."

Once they'd arrived, Andrew bounded up the stairs into the Bow Street offices and beelined into Whitcomb's small office. Once inside, he found Whitcomb behind his desk, two other Runners present, and a young man holding a soiled plaid cap in his shackled hands.

"I see you received my message, Your Grace," Whitcomb said. "Please have a seat."

"I'll stand."

"We caught this man sneaking in the servants' entrance of Mrs. Fitzpatrick's townhouse with a dagger in his hand."

Every muscle in his body tensed, his heart accelerated, and his now wide-awake mind screamed, "Not again." Not another attempt on Emmeline's life.

"Tobias admits to being hired to kill Mrs. Fitzpatrick but refuses to say by whom."

"Give me ten minutes with him."

"You know I cannot do that, Your Grace. You hired me, and I respect the law. However, a few days in Newgate ought to get him talking."

"No," the man said in protest. "'Tis likely I'll die in a day."

"Tell us who hired you," Andrew demanded as he got close to the man's foul-breathed face, nearly gagging from the stench. Even if he confessed, he belonged in Newgate for his actions.

"I don't know who," he cried out. "A man. Perhaps thirty. Dressed in plain clothes. Never said his name or who sent him."

"Damn," Whitcomb said. "It's what he said when we picked him up. Bring him to Shorty at Newgate."

The young man's protests could be heard as the two Runners dragged him out of the office.

"I believe him. If he knew the identity of the person who hired him, he would have told us. He has a real fear of Newgate. As well he should."

"Thankfully, your people were there. I cannot express my gratitude enough."

"Just doing what you hired me to do. Meanwhile, Lord and Lady Hartford and Lady Beatrice traveled to the Duke and Duchess of Deerfield's and returned quite late. All has been quiet since their return. But that doesn't mean they didn't hire Tobias through a servant or other means."

"I know. Thank you. Keep up the good work."

The sun, or what he could see of it through all the rain clouds, peeked over the horizon as he left Bow Street. As soon as he arrived home he would bathe, dress, break his fast, and visit Emmeline to see with his own eyes that she was safe and unharmed. "Please don't let this be a daily and nightly occurrence," he mumbled to himself.

CHAPTER EIGHTEEN

S INCE EMMELINE HAD slept most of the afternoon into the early evening, she sat up reading during the darkest hours of the night. Her mind was not on the gothic novel, and she'd had to reread several pages. Her mind kept drifting to her near-death experience. The driver, all dressed in black, had his hat low on his head, so his face was hidden, and the sharp snap of the reins drifted to her ears even now along with the clopping of the horse's hooves on the street. She could still feel how her heart had lodged in her throat when she saw the coach barreling out of nowhere and how she'd frozen, her feet unable to move.

Then the feel of a large, unyielding body crashing into her. The scream tearing from her throat as they flew through the air and tumbled to the ground. His heavy weight on top of her as she struggled to breathe. And relief when Andrew's voice called out to her.

Would it ever go away, or would she relive the near miss every day? With her heart pounding, she believed she would keep the memory in her mind until the person or persons responsible were caught and punished.

A commotion downstairs traveled up to her chambers, and her heart froze inside her chest.

Donning her robe, she went down the stairs with a candle in her hand and found Harrison in the foyer, speaking to someone just outside the door.

"Harrison," she said, her voice shaking. "Who is it?"

He closed the door and turned to her. She could see the worry etched on his face even though it was in shadow from the darkness and the candle in his hand. "It was a Runner."

She knew he didn't want to tell her. "Why was he at the door in the middle of the night?"

"They caught someone sneaking in the servants' entrance."

"Yes?"

His body visibly shook. "He had a knife."

A strangled cry escaped her lungs. Her hand reached back for a stair tread, and she sank onto it before her legs gave way. "Are they positive?"

"I'm afraid so," Harrison replied. The worry had not faded from his face, and his voice sounded forced and far away from her ears. "The Runners will keep you safe and solve this quickly. They are the best. Blackstone hired the best."

"Yes. I know. Please secure all the doors. I don't want the servants' door unlocked anytime, day or night. Post a footman inside the door to let the servants in. Double-check all the windows on the first floor. Leave none unlocked."

"I will take care of everything. Try to get some rest, miss."

It took her several minutes before her legs were strong enough to support her trembling body. She struggled with fear as she made her way to her chambers. Then, for the first time she could remember, she locked her door out of fear. Sliding down the door, she sat with her knees up, her arms wrapped around them, and her head rested down. She had no more tears left to shed.

All she wanted to do was marry Andrew and have a family. Was that so much to ask for? Hadn't she done her penance for loving two men by losing Aiden and living through the six lonely years after?

Sometime before dawn, she rose from the floor, stretching to ease her stiff, sore, and cold body. She then moved to the chaise longue, wrapping herself in a blanket. She must have dozed and awoke to knocking on her door.

"Ma'am," her lady's maid said. "Can you let me in?"

Emmeline hurried to the door, unlocked it, and swung it open to find Amanda holding a breakfast tray. "Sorry. I didn't feel safe last night."

Amanda walked over to the night table and placed the tray down. "I understand. Harrison told the household this morning about the intruder."

"I don't want anyone to feel unsafe working or staying here. If you or anyone else wants several days off, I will gladly pay you to stay somewhere else until the person is caught."

"Harrison said as much, but we all agreed we were happy to stay and protect you."

Tears threatened to fall at the loyalty of those in her employ. Not that she was surprised. They had always taken good care of her and her mother, and Lilly for the year she'd lived with them, and before that, Aiden. What would Mother say about this latest unsuccessful attempt on her life?

"The Duke of Blackstone is downstairs in the drawing room. He said to take your time as Harrison brought him a breakfast tray, and he could occupy himself."

"Thank you. Help me dress, please. The green muslin will do fine." After dressing and having her hair combed and tied with a ribbon, she excused Amanda and sat on the edge of the bed. She sipped her now lukewarm hot chocolate and nibbled on a piece of toast, finally giving up because her stomach was too unsettled to eat. Besides, she wanted to go downstairs and see Andrew.

"Andrew," Emmeline said as she entered the drawing room moments later, waving him off as he began to rise. "Sit. I'll join you." Sitting beside him, the breakfast tray untouched before him, except for the coffee held in his hand. The strong aroma took up the room. Coffee was not to her liking, but the smell was divine. "Any news about last night?"

"The young man caught sneaking in your house swears he

doesn't know who hired him. I'm inclined to believe him. Even dragging him off to Newgate didn't get him to give up a name."

"So we know nothing." Her voice broke, but she refused to cry again. It solved nothing.

"Come here." His comforting arms wrapped around her and held her tight. "From this night on, I will spend them with you. Last night was the longest of my life."

"Mine too," he admitted. "But what about keeping up appearances of being betrothed to Lady Beatrice?"

"The hell with that. I truly feel sorry for her, but I won't risk your life for her reputation. You are stuck with me."

She snuggled deeper into his arms. "That sounds wonderful. I love you, Andrew."

"And I you." He cradled her face and kissed her. The desperate kiss revealed not only their fears and the turbulent times they experienced together but also the deep, connected love they shared.

"Forgive me," the baroness said as she entered the room.

Breaking the kiss, they sat back on the settee, holding hands. "Good morning, Mama."

"What is this news I heard this morning about a man trying to sneak into our home with a knife?" she said as she sat in a chair opposite them, her face pale and her eyes fearful. "Dear God, Emmeline, this has got to stop. Do something, Blackstone."

"Mama, it isn't Andrew's fault. Please don't be angry with him."

"But it is his fault." She swung out her hand. "If he hadn't gotten mixed up with Lady Beatrice."

"Forgive me, Baroness, but she was forced on me. And her mother admitted to leaking the information to the scandal sheet. I only agreed to a betrothal, a fake one at that, so the earl could have time to find her a suitable husband. However, after yesterday and last night, I don't care what people think of poor Lady Beatrice. Her mother ruined her, not me. I can't take responsibility for Lady Hartford's actions when they put

Emmeline's life at risk."

"Begging your pardon, Blackstone, for my plain speech. But you must understand this is my only daughter whose life is in danger. Perhaps we should leave the city and rent a house in the country until this is over."

"I would say yes, but I don't think that will solve anything," Andrew said. "We need to get to the bottom of it. Otherwise, both Emmeline and I will see potential villains in everyone we encounter, never feeling safe and relaxed, looking over our shoulders every second of every day. Which is a horrible way to live."

"I agree with Andrew, Mama. I will not run away and sulk in the country."

"I sent a message to Lord Hartford this morning saying the betrothal is off. I will not play the game anymore. If he is wise, he will send word to the press that Lady Beatrice has broken our betrothal. I don't care what excuse they use, I just want it over. With any luck, another scandal will happen, and her scandal will be yesterday's news. Her reputation may be salvaged yet. I offered my help, and threatening Emmeline is how I was repaid. I'm sorry for Lady Beatrice, but I truly believe she will persevere through the scandal and come out on the other side unscathed when her mother's schemes are made public. Gentlemen will feel sorry for her, and she will receive numerous proposals."

"I hope you are right. Meanwhile, promise me you will do everything possible to keep Emmeline safe."

"I will guard her with my life."

"Andrew . . ."

He kissed the top of Emmeline's head. "It's true. I will gladly die keeping you safe."

Emmeline appreciated Andrew's protection, but her heart would never survive if he died. Even now, it beat so fast that she expected it to tire out and cease beating at the mere thought.

"It is a warm, sunny day. We could ride in the park and solidify the end of my engagement with Lady Beatrice."

"I'd like to take Marigold. I haven't ridden her in so long. She must think I've forgotten about her."

"Anything you want, my dear."

Not long after, a groomsman brought Marigold and Andrew's mount to the front entrance. Emmeline swung up into the side saddle with the aid of a mounting block. Andrew mounted and said, "Ready?"

"Yes."

They made their way to Hyde Park with the sun shining down all around them. Emmeline wished she could remove her hat and feel the sun on her face. The warmth could penetrate inside her skin, verifying that she was alive. Perhaps later, in the privacy of her garden, she would tilt her face up to the sun and glory in its warmth.

"What are you thinking?" Andrew asked as he slowed his horse to match Marigold's pace.

"How wonderful the sun would feel on my face."

"It would. Don't look now, but we have attracted an audience."

She tried not to let those in the park, staring and whispering without shame, bother her. She straightened her back and nodded acknowledgment to anyone who met her eyes. Many of the ladies, walking or riding, did, their gazes full of judgment. Those in the carriages were just as forward in their glares.

"No wonder we received more attention than I expected," Andrew said as he indicated riders up ahead.

"Is that Caldwell with Lady Beatrice?"

Andrew burst out laughing. "I knew he was sweet on her. Let's say hello."

"This is quite a shock seeing you two together. And in public, no less," Andrew said with a crooked grin as they rode up.

"I had no idea we would cause such a stir," Caldwell said with a cunning grin.

"You did this on purpose?" Emmeline said, shocked.

"We did." Caldwell glanced at Lady Beatrice, his brown eyes

alight with mischief. "I mentioned the other night that I would help Lady Beatrice in any way she needed me, and to my utter surprise, I received a missive this morning from her asking for my help. Lord Hartford refused to send word to the press about breaking the betrothal. But I believed that if Lady Beatrice accompanied me to the park it would give the gossips something else to spread, including the dissolution of your engagement."

"Please accept my apologies for my parents' behavior of late," Lady Beatrice said, looking pale. "My mother should never have gone to the gossip rag and supplied them false information, and for that I am very sorry."

"I accept your apology even if you did nothing to warrant censure," Emmeline said with Andrew agreeing.

Caldwell glanced at Lady Beatrice and smiled. Emmeline could never remember seeing Caldwell look as besotted as he did now. "I asked Lady Beatrice if I could court her—for real—right before you joined us, and she said yes."

"Congratulations," Andrew said. "I'm very happy for you both. I knew there was a mutual attraction between you two the other night."

Hearing the conversation, Emmeline experienced a sudden lightness in her chest, and for the first time in days, air flowed freely through her lungs.

Lady Beatrice blushed. "Caldwell caught my eye at the first ball of the Season. However, many people told me he would never settle down, so I concentrated on Baron Godfrey. I even believed myself in love with Godfrey. What a fool I was. Then when the scandal happened, I thought my chances with Caldwell had ended."

"Do your parents know?" Andrew queried.

Lady Beatrice squirmed in her saddle. "No, but they will soon, as gossip flies faster than a honey bee. And I don't care what they say. My father will be pleased that I'm courting James, but Mother . . . well, needless to say, my relationship with her has suffered, and I no longer listen to her."

"Speaking of Lord and Lady Hartford," Caldwell said, "I shall accompany you home and speak to your father. He dipped his hat. "Good day, Andrew, Emmeline. Try to stay out of trouble."

Before either Andrew or Emmeline could respond, Caldwell, Lady Beatrice, and her groomsman returned the way they'd come. "Shall we continue?" Andrew asked with a genuine smile—the first she had seen on him in a while.

"Yes. I will enjoy our ride much more now that our lives can return to normal."

He laughed. "Since when were our lives ever normal?"

She laughed along with him. "True. Although what constitutes normal?"

The deeper they traveled into the park, the thinner the crowd became. Suddenly a loud blast rang out as they approached an outcropping of dense shrubs and trees. Marigold froze in place, but to Emmeline's horror, Andrew's horse went up on his hind legs, came down, and took off with Andrew barely holding onto the reins.

She watched, her eyes wide, her heart constricting inside her chest as she urged Marigold forward. Then Storm suddenly stopped, throwing Andrew over his head.

"No, no, no!" Emmeline screamed while jumping off her horse and landing on her knees. She stood, pulled up her skirts, and ran. More screams penetrated her ears. The animal-like sound came from her. "Dear God, please don't take him from me."

Several gentlemen had circled around Andrew before she reached him. She shoved one gentleman aside and dropped to the ground beside him. She kept her eyes on his chest, afraid to see his empty eyes wide open in death. Sobs escaped her.

"Please stay back. He's been shot. I was a surgeon's assistant with the army. Let me help."

"He's . . . he's alive?" Her eyes fell on Andrew properly, lying on his back, his eyes closed and blood spreading on his upper arm. "His neck . . . is not broken?"

"No. The only injury I see is the gunshot wound to his arm and a nasty bump on the back of his head. He is unconscious but very much alive."

Emmeline scooched forward and cradled Andrew's head in her lap. A moan broke from his lips, but his eyes remained shut. It was enough of a sign of life that her fears diminished somewhat, at least for the time being. But she would never be at ease until the person responsible for these actions was caught and punished. Several minutes went by as the surgeon's assistant attended to Andrew, examining his arm and putting pressure on the wound with a handkerchief. "Luckily the bullet went straight through. Did anyone see where the shot came from?"

"Yes," said a man Emmeline didn't recognize. "They were apprehended."

"Who?" she asked without taking her eyes off Andrew's face, praying he would wake up soon.

"Let me through," Caldwell said. "I just heard and came as fast as I could." He dropped down to the ground on the other side of Andrew. "Someone shot him? What the bloody hell is going on?"

"It was awful. His horse took off and threw him," Emmeline said, then hiccupped. "All I could think of was Aiden. That Andrew would die the same way Aiden did. That the men I love were cursed to die tragically." Tears rolled down her cheeks as she gently stroked Andrew's handsome face. A face she wanted to see every day as they grew old together.

"Christ," Caldwell inhaled a shaky breath. "He's fortunate to be alive."

"We need to get His Grace home and call for his physician," the surgeon's assistant said. "You should commandeer the nearest carriage."

Caldwell took off running.

"What is your name?" Emmeline asked.

"Lord Stonebrook. My father is the Duke of Allerton. I'm his second son."

"Thank you from the bottom of my heart, Lord Stonebrook."

He bowed, "I was glad to be helpful. Since I left the army, I've been floundering. Perhaps I should attend medical school."

"You would make a fine doctor," Emmeline said as Caldwell returned with a carriage and they loaded an unconscious Andrew. Gently, they placed him on the floor of the borrowed carriage.

Caldwell held out his hand to her. "You go with him. I'll see to the horses and meet you at Blackstone House."

"Thank you, Caldwell."

She was left alone with Andrew and kept a fresh cloth pressed to his bullet wound. No sooner had they left Hyde Park than it seemed they were in front of Blackstone House. His household must have received word because many worried faces met them on the street, ready to help in any way. His butler told them Doctor Higgins had been sent for and barked out orders as several strong footmen carried Andrew to the duke's chambers. Emmeline, her skirts raised, followed right along. She would not be kept from him.

Once he was on his bed and stripped of his clothing from the waist up, Emmeline faded into the corner. She didn't want to attract undue attention in case someone remembered she was present and thought it was improper for an unmarried lady to be in the same room with a half-dressed unmarried man.

Her eyes were riveted on the doctor who flew in the door during the chaos and proceeded to clean, stitch, and bandage Andrew's upper arm. He placed a small brown vial on the nightstand. Emmeline hated laudanum and hoped Andrew wouldn't need it, that his pain would be tolerable. By now, Caldwell stood beside her, his arm on her shoulder for support.

Doctor Higgins finally turned to them. "Barring infection, his arm should heal nicely. The muscles will be sore and need exercise to regain their previous strength, but I don't foresee any problems. As for the bump on his head and his unconsciousness, we must pray he awakes soon. The longer he's unconscious, the more difficult it will become for him to awaken. Keep him comfortable, and when he awakes, give him the laudanum for pain. I will return tomorrow to check on him and rebandage his arm." He nodded his head. "I will see myself out. Send word if his condition worsens."

After the doctor left, Caldwell had everyone else vacate the room, so the three of them were left alone. Emmeline approached the side of the bed. There was just enough room for her to sit on the edge. Stroking Andrew's sweaty hair back from his handsome, pale face, she swallowed the lump in her throat as tears trickled down her cheeks. "I pray he wakes up soon."

Caldwell stood at the foot of the bed, his face drawn, his eyes worried. "As do I. I can't believe this happened."

"Someone caught them—whoever shot Andrew. I just remembered that. Can you go downstairs and have Winters send word to Mr. Whitcomb that we would like to see him as soon as possible? He must know about it. Also, send a note to Langford."

Alone with Andrew, she gently leaned down, resting her head lightly on his chest, listening to the beat of his heart. It was strong and steady. Too bad it didn't ease her worried mind or the scenarios running through it. He needed to wake up for her to see his bright green eyes and his handsome face smiling at her before the tightness in her chest would ease. Until then, she would not leave his side. She needed to be with him. She would only go for short breaks to care for her personal needs. Otherwise, she would call his chambers her room for the foreseeable future. Or until he awoke and she was convinced he would live.

There was a knock on the door. "Can I come in, or would you rather I wait downstairs for Langford and Mr. Whitcomb?" Caldwell asked, his voice sounding tired.

"No. Please come in and watch over him with me." She went back to sitting on the edge of the bed. "Do you think this has to do with the carriage accident? Was the bullet meant for me?" *Dear God.* Her hand flew to her throat. As much as she wanted to believe the carriage accident had been a fluke, Andrew getting shot made her face reality.

"Honestly, I can't say. But if I went with my gut, I'd say yes." Caldwell frowned as he stared at Andrew.

That is what she thought, too. And there was something else she needed to say since they had the time. "This may not be the proper time to bring this up, but it has been weighing on my mind lately. Andrew once told me that you, Langford, and he had never talked about Aiden's death and how it affected each of you. We know how Andrew reacted and that you and Langford immersed yourself in your business."

"We did." Caldwell nodded.

"I told this to Andrew. Can I confide in you with the strictest confidence?"

"Yes."

"The week before the house party, I miscarried, and Aiden took it hard." She explained the changes in Aiden during the unforgettable week leading up to his death. "I was worried about him. He was not acting himself."

"I'm sorry to hear this. Though it does explain why he seemed down during the gathering and drank to excess. He was in mourning." He paused and inhaled. "This is long overdue. Emmeline, please forgive me for my part in Aiden's death. I am so sorry . . ."—his voice broke—"for many things. But mostly for abandoning you after his death. I should have stayed to support you in your grief. Instead, I took to the seas to drown my grief in silence. I shared the story with Lady Clarice, at the Waterford's house party, and forgive me for doing so. Being together with you and Andrew brought back the memories and it was easier to talk to an acquaintance than to talk to you or Andrew."

Taking one of his hands in hers, she squeezed. "I forgive you, even though there is nothing to forgive. Aiden was dead, but you were very much alive and had your own life to live. I never resented that. Aiden loved you. He wouldn't want you to continue suffering. Forgive yourself so you can move on and marry Lady Beatrice and be happy."

They both wiped the tears from their eyes. "Thank you,

Emmeline. That means the world to me. I loved Aiden. I also know he would want you to forgive yourself for whatever guilt you harbor, marry Andrew, and be happy."

"I believe that. Or at least I'm coming to believe it." She squeezed his hand once more, then removed it.

"It's time we all put the past in the past. We will never forget Aiden. He will always live in each of us. Yet, it is time for those he loved and left behind to find happiness. I envy Langford. He and Lilly seem so in love and happy. Yet I know he struggled after Aiden's death and probably still has his demons. Lilly will ease his, as you and Andrew will ease each other's, and Lady Beatrice will ease mine."

"Why do I feel there is more to the story about you and Lady Beatrice than I know?"

Caldwell blushed. He actually averted his gaze and turned red. "I have had my eye on her since the beginning of the Season. I've never courted anyone, so I didn't know how to begin. Then there was the fact that her mother sought a title for her daughter—the title of duke."

Emmeline had always believed Caldwell was the epitome of a rakehell, one who scattered lady's hearts all over London. Was it all a ruse? Or just her imagination? He'd been away from England most of the time during the past six years, yet the reputation seemed to persist.

"Lady Beatrice is taken with you. Courting her should be easy. Just be yourself."

"And who am I?" he asked. "The second son of a baron. Rich because of my hard work. Nothing was handed to me as it was handed to my wastrel of a brother, yet people respect him more because of his title."

How strange that Caldwell struggled with self-esteem. "You are a member of the peerage. The son of a baron. A kind man and a worthy friend. Hold your head high. You made your wealth by using your brain. You should be proud of yourself. I know I am." She swiped at her tears. She hadn't been prepared for the conversation with Caldwell to turn so emotional. But emotional in a good way.

"Thank you, Emmeline. That means a lot coming from you. And you are right. It is time I believed in myself regarding pursuits other than business."

"I feel as though this has happened before," Langford said as he and Lilly entered Andrew's chambers. "Only it was me in the bed. How is he?"

Lilly stood beside Emmeline, holding her hand as Caldwell explained all that had happened and what the doctor had said.

"Christ," Langford moved to the other side of Andrew's bed and frowned down at him. "Has he stirred at all?"

"Not since we arrived here. I'm worried . . ." She fought down her sobs. She would break down later when she was alone with Andrew.

The four of them silently watched over Andrew. Langford and Lilly held hands, Emmeline sat on the edge of the bed, and Caldwell watched from the foot of the bed. Time ticked on, and Emmeline wanted to grab Andrew by his shoulders, shake him and scream, "Wake up!" But she didn't act on her impulses. Instead, she hugged herself as ice and fear penetrated her heart. She could not lose him. She had just got him back.

Winters knocked and entered the room. "Pardon me, but Mr. Whitcomb is downstairs and wishes to speak with Mr. Caldwell and Lord Langford only." Before he left, he asked, "Any change in His Grace's condition?"

"No," Caldwell answered as the three men exited the room.

"I remember Mr. Whitcomb," Lilly said as she dragged a chair close to the bedside. "I cringe whenever I hear his name mentioned."

"As will I from now on."

"Does he know who did this?"

"They caught someone in the park right after they shot Andrew," Emmeline said. "They tried to kill me twice before. They must have meant to shoot me and missed, hitting Andrew instead." She jumped up and paced the room, her skirts swaying with her quickness as her mind whirred. "The shot can't have been meant for Andrew. If he were dead, he could not marry Lady Beatrice. I don't know how many more times they can attempt to kill me and fail."

"Please calm yourself, Emmeline," Lilly said. "There will be no more attempts. They were caught and will go to jail for a very long time. Attempted murder of a duke will not go over well in court. With any justice, they will be sent to Newgate for the rest of their lives."

Emmeline paused her pacing. "I have always admired your strength and wisdom at your young age, but you have become even stronger since your ordeal with Redford. Henry would be very proud of you."

Sadness flashed on Lilly's face, then disappeared as quickly as it appeared. "I love Edmund with all my heart, but I miss my first husband. Learning from his example and my father's is how I attained such strength and wisdom. They were also two of the kindest men ever to live." She paused and huffed. "Remember when I first met Edmund, and I thought he was an arrogant, heartless beast of a bear?"

"How could I forget?" Emmeline said with a giggle.

"Thank goodness I was wrong."

"Yes, indeed."

When footsteps came down the hallway, Emmeline tensed and hurried back to sit with Andrew, who had yet to do anything. Except his face just twitched. Was that good or bad?

Her eyes went to Caldwell and Langford entering the room. Both looked haggard. The events of the past few days were getting to them. Before they had time to speak, she blurted out, "Well, who was it?"

Langford and Caldwell both frowned and made their way to Andrew's bedside. Langford reached for Lilly's hand. Caldwell stood watch at the end of the bed again, arms crossed over his chest, his body tense.

"As Andrew suspected, Lady Hartford has been behind this. She hired criminals to commit the crimes," Caldwell said.

"Did they say Andrew was their intended target?" Emmeline asked.

"No. They were aiming at you. They sang at the top of their lungs when they realized they'd shot a duke. They hoped for leniency now by giving up the Hartfords. There will be none for them." Caldwell paused and frowned. "Unfortunately, because of their titles, Lord and Lady Hartford are unlikely to suffer any punishment."

"You said Lord and Lady Hartford. Does that mean Lord Hartford was involved?" Emmeline asked, feeling angry and sad at the same time. Poor Lady Beatrice.

"Mr. Whitcomb had an enlightening conversation with Lord and Lady Hartford. Apparently, Lord Hartford couldn't take his wife nagging him anymore, so he hired the thugs. He is remorseful, but Lady Hartford had such a breakdown, he plans to send her to a convent to spend the remainder of her days," Langford said. "As for Lord Hartford, he has agreed to live at his country seat."

"How did you convince him to live at his country estate?" Lilly asked.

"Whitcomb told him that Blackstone was livid and swore he would spend his life making Lord Hartford's a living hell until he was ruined and his family name worthless. Blackstone would keep his actions quiet if he moved from London and never returned. But if he ever stepped foot in London again, the agreement was off. He believed Whitcomb. According to him, he is already packing."

"What about Lady Beatrice?" Emmeline asked.

"Hartford agreed to the marriage proposal between me and Lady Beatrice. I just signed the marriage contract. Whitcomb had Hartford write up the contract while he was there and he brought it with him. Her dowry was increased three times." Caldwell chuckled. "Not that I need the money. I'll be investing it for Lady

Beatrice. All that's left is getting the special license."

"This all seems so fictional. Worthy of a gothic novel." Lilly entered the conversation. "I'm having trouble believing such things occur in the *ton*."

"How can you say that after what Redford planned for you?" Langford growled.

"Indeed. You are right," she replied.

"I'm glad to know the truth finally, and that the attempts on my life will end, but that doesn't solve the problem that Andrew is still unconscious," Emmeline said.

⫸⫷

"FORGIVE ME," ANDREW mumbled. "I heard every word since Caldwell and Langford entered the room." All eyes turned to him in shock. Emmeline reached out and placed her small hand on his cheek, and he turned into it, seeking its warmth. He'd been too shocked to speak as he listened silently to the conversation going around the room. Being betrayed by Lord Hartford stung. The man could make his living on the stage. He'd lied right to his face repeatedly. He was as vile a creature as his wife, and Andrew was glad to know he would never see either of them again.

To know they were so brazen as to try and shoot Emmeline in Hyde Park in broad daylight froze his heart when he thought about it.

"What are you thinking?" Langford broke the silence.

"Everything. How much my head and arm hurt, not to mention the rest of my body. I still had the aches and pains from jumping out of the way of the carriage when it tried to run Emmeline down. And then to be shot and thrown from my horse. It's no wonder I can't move. Christ." He placed his hand over Emmeline's, which still cradled his cheek. "The thought that they shot at Emmeline boils my blood. These three attempts on her life will haunt me."

She smiled at him tentatively. "It is over. No one will ever try to kill me again. Please rest easy knowing this. We must be brave and live our lives carefree. If we don't, Lord and Lady Hartford win."

If his head didn't feel like it would explode at any moment, he would sit up, pull her onto his lap, and kiss her until neither could breathe. But since every hair on his body ached, he didn't think he could do any of that.

The sound of the gunshot and the immediate sting on his upper arm hadn't panicked him. What had frightened him was being thrown from his horse. The whole event had been fast and exceptionally slow at the same time. His mind had flashed to Aiden's accident. Then, his own life flashed through his eyes, and he'd believed the worst would happen. He would die of a broken neck like Aiden. His heart constricted painfully now thinking about it. What would it do to Emmeline, he'd wondered. Would she survive losing someone else she loved? As he'd hit the ground excruciatingly hard, the last thing he saw in his mind was her lovely face with tears in her eyes.

Even though he'd been unconscious, some part of him had known he still lived. He'd heard worried voices, felt tugs on his body, and he'd known he would see her again. Right before he'd woken up, he heard muffled voices and people coming and going. He'd struggled to open his eyelids, but they were heavy and stuck. He'd pictured his arms and tried to move them but to no avail. It was the same with his legs. And then, instantly, every-thing changed. His eyes popped open, and his body twitched, allowing him freedom of movement, even if it was difficult and hurt deep inside his bones.

When he opened his eyes and saw Emmeline's relieved face, tears rolling down her cheeks, his heart broke for the pain he'd caused her, even if he'd had no control over the situation. But now they had both been given a second chance at a life together. And he would spend however long he had loving her, making up for past mistakes, making babies, and worshiping her. Caldwell wasn't the only one needing a special license.

"You are quiet," Emmeline said, gently caressing his hair. "Can I get you anything?"

"Something to drink would be nice." He hadn't noticed until that moment how stuck his tongue was to the roof of his mouth. Parched. He'd never been so thirsty in all his life.

"Here," Caldwell said as he approached the bed with a glass of brandy. "This will ease the pain and help you sleep."

"I don't need to sleep," he mumbled. "I need help sitting up so I don't dribble on myself like a baby."

Caldwell cocked a brow. "For someone who just defied death, you are grouchy."

"Forgive me. It's the pain."

"The doctor left laudanum. Do you want some?" Emmeline asked.

"Hell, no. I'd rather be in pain than floating in a cloud, unable to see or focus." Once Caldwell and Langford had him sitting up, propped on pillows, he downed the entire glass in one swallow. "Another, please." This time, he finished it in three. "I'll beg your forgiveness now for falling asleep. I can't keep my eyes open anymore." He looked at Emmeline. "Will you kiss me?"

Tears pooled in her eyes as she leaned forward and brushed her soft lips against his. If only he could pull her on top of him and kiss her properly. Soon. His eyes closed, his body eased, and he fell into a deep slumber.

CHAPTER NINETEEN

AFTER CALDWELL, LANGFORD, and Lilly left, Andrew awoke briefly. Long enough for Clayton to help him with his personal needs and deliver broth for him to drink, which he did right before his eyes rolled back into his head and he fell back asleep. Emmeline knew sleeping was the best thing for him, to fight infection and allow his body to heal from being bruised and battered.

Winters had personally delivered a missive to her mother explaining everything. He also picked up Amanda and some of her belongings. She didn't plan to leave Andrew's side until he was up and mobile with no sign of infection from the bullet wound. Having Amanda in the house would ease her burden.

Emmeline stripped down to her chemise and climbed beneath the covers, snuggling up against Andrew's good side as a sigh escaped her lips. She still had the scrapes and bruises, but with all that had happened to Andrew, she had forgotten about herself and her injuries. Although now that she was resting comfortably beside the man she loved, little twinges of pain from her tight muscles reminded her she had a body to heal. Exhaustion, both mental and physical, tightened its hold on her. Her head ached from the events of the past days. Today's events were the worst. Exhaustion had seeped inside her bones; only a deep sleep would alleviate it.

Snuggling closer against him, she closed her eyes and let the pull of sleep take over. Her breathing evened out, and her body became weightless as she entered the place of dreams.

BOTH ANDREW'S VALET and her maid entered the chambers the following morning. Emmeline didn't need to open her eyes to know which footsteps belonged to whom. Amanda parted the curtains to a miserable rainy day while Clayton spoke to a third set of footsteps and ordered a fire started in the hearth. Emmeline was grateful—the chill from the night and the morning air had her shivering deeper into the covers and against Andrew's body, hoping to get warm.

Before they left the room, Amanda said, "Your breakfast trays will be up shortly. Is there anything you need now?"

"No, thank you, Amanda."

After Amanda left, Emmeline rolled onto her side and smiled at how young and innocent Andrew looked in sleep. Neither of them was yet thirty, but both had lived full and tragic lives up until now. She prayed their future held calm, tranquility, and happiness.

"Are you going to stare at me all day?"

The teasing in his voice sparked warmth inside her body. "Only if it doesn't bother you."

"Not at all." He slid his uninjured arm around her and hugged her to his chest. "This is much better, don't you think?"

She rested her hand on his bare chest, wrapped a leg across his, and snuggled into his side. "This is even better."

"Yes, it is." He kissed the top of her head, his body relaxing against hers. "Thank God the drama with the Earl and Countess of Hartford is over, and we can get on with our lives. Whitcomb's quick thinking made my life easier. I didn't have to see Lord Hartford and threaten him myself." He kissed the top of her head.

"No more speaking of them. It's over, and we can plan for the future." He kissed the top of her head again. "I love you."

Just as Emmeline went to straddle Andrew's waist, a knock on the door had her lying back down. Two servants entered with breakfast trays, placed one on each bedside table, and left as quietly and quickly as they appeared.

"Do you think those young kitchen maids were scandalized finding you in bed with an unmarried woman and neither of us wearing much clothing?"

Andrew's carefree chuckling was music to her ears. "They better get used to it, because from this day forward, I expect you in my bed every night for the rest of time."

This time, she succeeded in straddling his waist, easing up her chemise so nothing existed between them except his drawers.

Moans escaped his mouth, coming from deep inside his chest. "Are you trying to seduce me?"

Bending forward, she nuzzled his neck. "Yes. Do you have an issue with that?"

"Hell, no," he grunted. "Do that again."

This time, she giggled. She nibbled his neck and continued to do so until his one good arm gripped her chin, guiding her mouth to his, and he kissed her as if he were indeed a dying man and this was the last taste of a woman he would ever experience. Thank goodness it wasn't true. Emmeline kissed him back, letting him know how much she loved him.

With one of Andrew's hands and one of hers, they pushed down his drawers, freeing his erection. Breaking the kiss, she hovered over his waist and took him in her hands, lining his manhood up with her entrance, and lowered, taking him inside. She gasped at the fullness and the feeling of being complete.

Andrew rested his free hand on her waist, and she rested both of hers on his muscular chest. Her hips ground against his, eliciting groans from them both.

"Deeper, faster, harder," Andrew said as his fingers moved to her core, igniting her body. Her hips rose, and she slammed down on Andrew repeatedly, taking him deep inside her. Again and again, she rose and fell. She arched her back. Her body tightened around his member until she collapsed lifelessly on his chest, breathing hard and spent. While in the throes of her release, Andrew's body tightened. He growled and spent his warm seed deep inside her.

Emmeline lifted her hips, removing Andrew from her body, and lay back down on him with a deep and contented sigh. "I think I need a nap." She laughed as she kissed his chest.

"Me too. Although, I can't think of a better way to wake up and welcome in a new day." His hand stroked her hair, causing her head to tingle.

Her fingers combed through his chest hair. "I didn't hurt you, did I?"

"Absolutely not." He chuckled. "I've never felt better."

She kissed him, rolled off the bed, pushed her chemise back down, and said two words she'd never uttered to Andrew before, "Chamber pot?"

"In my bathing chamber, through my dressing room."

Crossing the room, she ducked inside his dressing room full of his clothes and inhaled the familiar scent of sandalwood. Her eyes rested on a blue banyan, and she slipped it over her chemise, rolling up the overly long sleeves. She gripped the collar, inhaling Andrew's pure masculine scent, and smiled. She entered the adjoining tiled room with a large copper tub taking up half the space. From there, she found a clean chamber pot sitting on a shelf. Before she left the room, she washed up at a basin and pitcher resting on a small dresser. Once back in Andrew's bedchamber, she helped him sit up, put his breakfast tray on his lap, climbed in, and did the same with her tray. "I'm afraid everything is cold."

"Not to worry," he said as he sipped his coffee. There was no mistaking the smell wafting her way as she sipped her chocolate. "I see you found my clothes."

"Do you mind?"

"Not at all." He laughed. "Does my heart good to see you in my robe."

"Not to bring up a very private and delicate subject, but your bathing chamber appears to be in the process of being remodeled."

"Yes. My father started it but unfortunately died before it was complete. When finished, it will have a flushing toilet."

She coughed as she inhaled her chocolate down the wrong way. "Really?"

"He wanted to be one of the first in his circle of friends to have one. It should be finished next month. "We can use the London sewer system now for drainage since the ban was lifted." He suddenly roared out laughing.

"What is so amusing?"

"Us, having this conversation. Speaking of taboo subjects between a lady and a gentleman. Most ladies would fan themselves and swoon."

"I am not most ladies. And I must say I look forward to a flushing toilet."

He leaned over and kissed her cheek. "And thank goodness for that. The first comment—not the second. I love everything about you. Even during your first Season, you were never a delicate debutante. You were strong, opinionated, and not afraid to let it be known. Just like you are now." He kissed her again. "Please don't ever change. I love you just as you are. Please get this damn tray off my lap."

Emmeline removed both trays and went into Andrew's welcoming arm. "I imagine the doctor will be here soon."

"If he gets here soon, he can wait," he said as he encouraged her onto his lap and kissed her until she gave him what he wanted.

SINCE ANDREW HAD woken up with Emmeline beside him, his body had desired her. He hadn't expected to make love with her twice, and yet he could make it three quickly enough, except that she was dozing curled up against his side, making little breathy sounds, causing him to smile. When she'd inquired if he was in pain, he had lied. His head throbbed, and every muscle in his body ached and felt stiff, never mind the deep, burning pain from the bullet wound. Making love eased the pain for a short time, but it was back now with a vengeance. Even so, he would never regret the pleasure they'd both given and received. He grinned again. Lying back and watching her do all the work was an aphrodisiac. Imagining her face flushed pink, her eyes peeking through heavy lids, her breasts bouncing as she rode him, had him hard again.

He loved her so much and feared she might slip through his fingers again, that she might find another man more worthy of her, no matter how much she professed to love him. But there was nothing like the present to take the future into his hands. He extricated himself from her, which was difficult with one working arm. Not that he couldn't use his arm; it just hurt like bloody hell. Once on unsteady legs, he went to the bell pull and rang for Clayton, then leaned against the wall, afraid he wouldn't make it back to the bed without collapsing into a heap on the floor. And what a sight he would be wearing nothing but his undergarments.

"Your Grace," Clayton said, his eyes widening when he opened the door and saw him. "What are you doing up? Let me help you back to bed."

"No. Can you get me to the bathing chamber? I want to wash up and put on clean clothes. Trousers and a shirt will do nicely. Also, please open the safe in my study and bring Emmeline's engagement ring. The key is hidden underneath the second drawer."

"Yes, Your Grace."

After Andrew was presentable again and feeling clean and rejuvenated, he sat on an overstuffed chair before the hearth and waited for Emmeline to awaken. It wasn't long before she did. Fortunately, Clayton had already slipped him the black velvet ring box, which currently rested on the small table beside his chair.

"Andrew, what are you doing up?" Emmeline's voice was soft and sleepy, causing his heart to pound inside his chest.

"Why don't you join me?"

"Let me ring for Amanda. I want to dress."

Half an hour later, Emmeline sat on the matching chair on the other side of the small table. She was wearing a lovely blue day dress that accentuated her eye color.

He grinned at her. "You're too far away."

"I feel this is a safe distance," she said with a twinkle in her lovely eyes. "Otherwise, we may find ourselves back in bed. It's almost noon, and I imagine Doctor Higgins will be here soon."

"You said that hours ago."

"Yes, well, I mean it now. Also, I suspect my mother, Langford, Caldwell, and Lilly will visit soon."

He stood a little unsteadily but was determined to do this properly. "In that case . . ." He plucked the ring off the table, dropped carefully to one knee, and held out the box, grinning when she gasped and smiled. "Emmeline, I first knew I loved you when I was a young earl of nineteen. I never stopped loving you for ten years. I'm twenty-nine and a duke now, and my love for you has only deepened. You are a part of me. My body, my heart, and my soul. My entire world . . ." His voice cracked as his emotions got the better of him as he lay himself bare to her. "Emmeline, will you do me the greatest honor and marry me and become my duchess?" He forced his injured arm to work to open the box to show her the emerald and diamond ring he had commissioned just for her.

"Yes, Andrew. I will marry you," she said as tears slid down her cheeks. She slipped off the chair and knelt in front of him. "I first knew I loved you when I was a young debutante making my come out at eighteen. Even though I married Aiden, whom I loved, I never stopped caring for you. I'm embarrassed to say I dreamed about you often during those years. Now, at twenty-eight and no longer an innocent young lady, I love you more than I ever thought possible. My heart, my body, and my soul belong to you. I look forward to growing old with you and being surrounded by our children, grandchildren, and great-grandchildren."

Tears trickled from his eyes as he placed the ring on the love of his life's finger. "I almost used a sapphire for your eyes, but I thought since you love the color of my eyes, I would get an emerald." More tears slid down his cheeks. "That way, when we are apart, you can look at the stone that resembles my eyes and know I'm with you . . . always." He wrapped his good arm around her waist, pulling her toward him. He kissed her with everything he had. One moment, they were clinging to each other, kissing deeply. Next, Andrew lost his balance and fell backward, with Emmeline landing on top of him. Andrew ignored the searing pain in his arm and continued kissing her. When they broke apart, they gasped for air and laughed uncontrollably. They laughed so hard they didn't hear the knock on the door.

⋙✦⋘

"WHAT IS SO funny? Where are you, Emmeline?" her mother queried.

"Mama," she whispered as she pushed herself off Andrew, stood, and held out her hand. "Let me help you."

"Thank you. It's difficult to get up off the floor with one arm."

Before she turned to greet her mother, Emmeline smoothed down her clothing and combed her fingers through her long, unbound hair. When she glanced at Andrew, her eyes widened at his obvious erection. "Don't turn around yet," she murmured as she pointed to Andrew's trousers, feeling her face heat up.

"Oh . . ." He blushed and adjusted his trousers. "I wonder who the idiot was who thought designing tight breeches and trousers for men was a good idea."

She swallowed down a laugh as she forced her feet to move across the room and kiss her mother's cheek. "Mama, I am so glad you're here. Andrew and I have wonderful news. We are betrothed!"

By now, Andrew had joined them. "Baroness." He bowed. "Forgive me for not asking your permission."

Mother curtsied, "You are forgiven, Your Grace." She wiped tears from her eyes. "I am thrilled for you both."

Andrew leaned down and kissed her mother's cheek. "Please call me Andrew. We are family now."

"Call me Vivian."

"Done," he replied. "Let's go downstairs to the drawing room and toast this happy occasion."

Andrew leaned on Emmeline for support as they descended the elegant staircase and went down the hall into the deep blue drawing room. Emmeline's heart thrummed excitedly, and she could not stop smiling. She wanted to pinch herself in case she was dreaming. Because her dream had just become real.

The housekeeper, Mrs. Hanson, came in with a luncheon tray and champagne. The servants had heard the good news. "On behalf of the household," Mrs. Hanson said as she curtsied, "we are overjoyed at the news of your betrothal, Your Grace, to Mrs. Fitzpatrick. Congratulations."

"Thank you, Mrs. Hanson," they said together.

No sooner had the housekeeper left than Doctor Higgins arrived. "Your Grace, shall we retire to your chambers so I may examine you?"

"Let us stay right here," he replied to the doctor. "Vivian, would you give us a moment?" Andrew asked of his soon-to-be mother-in-law.

"I'll take Mama to the library."

Andrew held out his hand to her. "Please stay with me."

"I'll see her there and return."

Moments later, Emmeline returned to find her fiancé's shirt removed, baring his muscular chest, well-defined shoulders, and abdomen. Her eyes moved to his upper arm. She gasped and frowned at the blood soaking through his bandage.

"Your Grace," the doctor said as he unwound the bloody bandage. "This may hurt a bit. I'm surprised to see blood, but that's not all I'm shocked to see. Although I'm very pleased, I'm just surprised you are awake and looking no worse for wear after yesterday's accident. Besides your arm, does anything else hurt?"

"To be honest, my head hurts like a bugger, and my body feels as though I was thrown from a horse, which I was. And my arm . . . well, it aches." He chuckled, met Emmeline's eyes, and winked. "Other than that, I'm wonderful. I proposed to this lovely lady today, and she said yes."

Hearing the last of Andrew's words caused her cheeks to heat up.

"Felicitations to you both."

Emmeline moved to Andrew's side and winced at the wound on his arm but kept silent.

Mrs. Hanson entered the room, wheeling a cart. "Here is the hot water, soap, and towels you requested, Doctor Higgins."

The doctor washed his hands with soap and water and turned his attention back to Andrew. "You tore the stitches. I need to redo them." He used two fingers and poked around the wound. Andrew sucked in his breath loudly but remained still. "It's soft around the wound, which is good. We don't want it to be hard. The tissue around the wound is red but not overly angry." He prepared his needle and thread, using hot water, and then re-stitched his wound closed. Emmeline cringed every time Andrew inhaled deeply. When the doctor finished, he patted dry, smeared salve, and rebandaged his arm with clean linens.

"I'm going to look at your head now," the doctor said as he moved his fingers over the back of Andrew's head. "The swelling has gone down considerably. You should be headache-free in a few days. Meanwhile, please rest your arm. If you keep tearing the stitches, infection will likely set in, which we don't want." He packed up his belongings in his black medical bag. "If anything worsens, send for me immediately. If you see blood from your wound, send for me. Keep it dry. If I don't hear from you, I'll return in two days to re-bandage it." He lowered his head. "Good day, Your Grace, Mrs. Fitzpatrick."

After he left, Emmeline sank on the settee beside Andrew, her cheeks still warm. "No more sex until your arm is healed."

Laughter was his reply.

He was still chuckling when Langford, Caldwell, and Lilly entered the room, along with her mother.

"Was Winters not at the door?" Andrew asked as his friends entered.

Caldwell and Langford laughed while Lilly looked apologetic. "He and the household appear to be celebrating some happy occasion," Langford said with a grin. "Does anyone have any news to share?"

Emmeline stood and blurted out, "We are betrothed!"

Lilly clapped her hands and practically jumped up and down in her excitement. "Emmeline, I am so happy for you," she said as she rushed forward and hugged her. "Oh dear, I'm crying again. I've been so emotional lately." Langford rushed forward and handed his wife his handkerchief.

Her mother and Emmeline exchanged knowing looks, but remained silent, each knowing what the other was suspicious of. Lilly would know soon enough if she was expecting, and Emmeline was so happy to think it might be so. This was what her cousin Henry had wanted for the young wife he left behind: a marriage and a family created from love. And now she and Andrew would have that as well.

Wishes, dreams, true love, and second chances really did exist!

EPILOGUE

"HOLD ON TIGHT," Andrew said to his two-year-old son, who clung to his back as he galloped around pretending to be a horse.

"Papa, Papa," yelled Aiden. "Faster. Go faster."

"You want faster?" Andrew bellowed. "I'll give you faster."

Emmeline smiled at their antics as she sat on a blanket beneath a large English Oak on the lawn at Blackstone Hall, holding their four-month-old son, Alexander. They'd left London for Andrew's country seat when Aiden arrived, but they traveled to London often for Parliament and to visit friends. Her mother preferred London to the country and kept her abreast of the gossip. Not that she believed everything she heard. Although there had been a little snippet regarding Hollingsworth recently that she thought Andrew might find amusing.

"Papa, again." Sprawled on the grass on his stomach was her husband. Aiden was straddling his back and pulling on Andrew's linen shirt, no doubt choking him.

"Give me a minute to rest."

He pulled his shirt again, and Andrew made gagging sounds. "No rest, Papa. Horsey ride! Get up, old horsey, get up." More tugging and gagging.

Giggles burst from Emmeline at hearing their son call his papa old. As she expected, he rose, and Aiden got his way as

Andrew galloped around, making horse noises again. Her heart burst at how blessed they had been since their nuptials. Two healthy sons and many friends they loved. Most of whom would arrive later that day for a fortnight of entertainment.

Many times, like today, when she sat watching Andrew and Aiden play, she remembered back to when she first met Andrew's and Aiden's namesake, Mr. Aiden Fitzpatrick, her first husband and her present husband's onetime best friend. When she'd met Andrew, he was the Earl of Quincy, and now their son, Aiden, was the Earl of Quincy. Twinges of sadness still visited her from time to time when remembering Aiden Fitzpatrick, and she knew Andrew experienced them also. But they both believed he would be happy for them for the life they'd forged together. They'd honored their love for him by naming their firstborn after him: Aiden Patrick Hampton.

"Andrew," she called out, waving her hand, "It's time for the boys' nap." She handed little Alex off to his nurse while Aiden's nanny approached him and took his small hand in hers.

When they were alone, Andrew collapsed on the blanket and groaned. "I need a nap."

Yet, somehow, he rolled over, facing her with a mischievous twinkle in his beautiful green eyes, and leaned in for a kiss.

She leaned away. "I thought you needed a nap?"

"Not anymore," he said, wrapping his arms around her, pulling her close, and kissing her deeply. "Have I told you today how much I adore you? How much I love you?"

"I believe you did this morning when you woke me up." She pushed his shoulders so he lay flat on the blanket. Raising her skirts, she straddled him, coming down with a sigh. "Now I have you where I want you. You had your fun in the wee hours of the morning. Now it's my turn."

Laughter, deep and throaty, wrapped around her heart. "I am yours to take at will."

This man, her husband, the Duke of Blackstone, was incredibly precious to her. She was so fortunate that he chose her and that he loved her. Every day, she woke up with a smile on her face and a heart overflowing with love for her family.

She leaned down and whispered in her love's ear. "I love you with all my heart and soul and everything else I have."

THE END

About the Author

Christine Donovan is an International Bestselling Author who writes romance that touches the heart, soothes the soul and feeds the mind. In addition to writing historical romance set in the Regency era, she also writes contemporary romance.

When she landed her first job at sixteen as a cashier at a supermarket, the first thing she did each week on payday was stop at the local bookstore and buy the latest historical romance. It was a dream of hers back then to become a romance author.

She lives on the Southeast Coast of Massachusetts with her husband. She has four grown sons, two granddaughters, two cats, and a black lab named Luna. In her spare time, she can be found at the beach, reading, painting, or gardening. She loves to tackle DIY projects.

Website: authorchristinedonovan.com
Newletter: www.authorchristinedonovan.com/newsletter
Amazon: amazon.com/Christine-Donovan/e/B00APR743Y
Facebook: authorchristinedonovan
Instagram: christinedonovan6